Terminal Event

Ali Spooner

Terminal Event

Ali Spooner

An Affinity Romance

Affinity
eBook Press
NZ
2015

Terminal Event

© by Ali Spooner 2015

Affinity E-Book Press NZ LTD
Canterbury, New Zealand

1st Edition

ISBN: 978-1-927328-82-8

Editor: Ruth Stanley
Proof Editor: Alexis Smith
Cover Design: Irish Dragon Designs

Acknowledgments

I would like to thank my readers, for supporting me and providing feedback on my stories. Thanks to Affinity for continuing to believe, and Irish for the fantastic cover art.

Dedication

To Rhonda, thanks for all you do.

Table of Contents

Also by Ali Spooner

Love's Playlist

Cowgirl Up

Twisted Lives

The Epitaph

Bailey's Run

Sugarland

Bayou Justice

Chapter One

"One Mississippi, two Mississippi, three Mississippi, four Mississippi," I whispered, and then shuddered when the familiar crash of thunder boomed in the distance. The hairs on my arms stood at attention as the midsummer electrical storm continued to approach. I felt a cold trickle of sweat trace down my spine as it dropped to the waistband of my jeans and disappeared. Another blinding flash lit the front yard, and I continued to count. "One Mississippi, two Mississippi, three Mississippi," and boom, the sound rattled the windows in my bedroom as I sat huddled on my bed, my arms wrapped protectively around my knees. There were no sirens going off in town to announce the presence of tornado storm cells in the area, but that could also change rapidly as the summer heat dimmed minutely after nightfall in north Georgia.

I was born out of wedlock to a single mother, Shelby Rainwater, a full-blooded Cherokee woman. She named me Tallulah, after nearby Tallulah Falls. She had fallen for the blue-eyed, silver-tongued salesman who had repeatedly shown interest in her at the diner on his numerous trips through our little town. One night of steamy passion in the backseat of his car had left her smitten, until he never stopped in the diner again, and nine months later, she became a mother at barely nineteen.

In addition to being a bastard child, I was born with one blue eye and one brown eye. I remember mothers pulling their children behind them for protection as my mama and I walked past on the sidewalk, hearing the faint whisperings of "Demon Eyes," as we passed.

So, even at the ripe old age of four, I remember being "different." Mama would glare at the other women for their absurd behavior and clutch my hand a little tighter as we raced to our destination. She explained to me later, when I was almost ten, that my eyes would hold a special gift for me. Native American beliefs told of children born with eyes of different colors having a special gift of sight, but she could not tell me exactly what the gift would entail.

As a young child, I can remember closing my left eye, the brown one, and being able to see the world differently through my right eye, the blue one, which I later began to think of as my smart eye. At first, I thought my vision was just blurry, but as I aged, I learned to focus the vision in that eye and the objects that appeared as misty shadows began to take human shape. I never shared this fact with anyone other than Mama, as the town already feared me for my Demon Eyes. They would certainly ship me off to the nearest loony bin, if they knew what my smart eye could see.

"Your gift is emerging," was all Mama would say when I told her of the visions I had.

I yearned for more knowledge, but Mama, not having the gift, could not give me more information, further frustrating me. Even my own mama did not possess the knowledge to guide me toward my special gift. I grew up feeling odd, and so different from others.

And, I grew up alone.

I had one friend growing up. Her name was Amy Groves, and we were inseparable from kindergarten until the end of our sixth grade year when her grandmother in Michigan took ill, and her family had to move to care for her. The loss of my only true friend left me devastated the summer of my twelfth year, the season that my life really changed.

Chapter Two

June of 1982 was exceptionally hot. Amy had been gone for almost three weeks, and I spent my days wandering aimlessly, alone and depressed. Most of my classmates were playing Little League baseball or off at summer camps, and had little interest in me regardless. While Mama worked days at the diner, I would ride my bike around town and gather empty soda bottles to return for a refund. I would take my money and buy an RC cola and a moon pie, or sometimes I'd get a bag of peanuts to pour into the long neck of the cold glass bottle. The salty snack mixed with the cola was my favorite.

Fortune had shone down on me already, and I had amassed a three-dollar profit. I was excited to have some pocket change as Mama had promised we would take a trip to the beach for a long weekend before school started.

She would have given me spare change to buy my midday snack, but I took pride in finding bottles that I could exchange for refunds. It gave me something to occupy my time, and filled my days without Amy with some sense of adventure. So, each day we settled into a summer routine. Mama would wake me, and see that I had a hearty breakfast in me, before she left for her shift at the diner. Afterward I would clean up the kitchen then head off on my bike for my daily adventure. I would search my little town for the glass bottles that I would stack in the basket on my bike. I'd take them to the local store to exchange before meeting Mama at the diner at three to walk home together.

Home was a small bare lot with a singlewide trailer. There was nothing luxurious about it, but it was comfortable, met our needs, besides, it was finally paid for. I remember the night Mama brought home two steaks for us to grill. We rarely had beef, much less a steak, and when I asked her if I had missed a holiday, Mama laughed.

"No, Tally," she had said. "We are celebrating something much better than a holiday."

"What Mama?"

Shelby pulled out the small book that held coupons from the bank for her monthly payments for the mortgage. She showed me the empty book. "We have finally paid off the mortgage, and this place is now officially ours," she said. "Will you help me celebrate?"

I didn't really understand the complete significance of the event, but when she tore the coupon book in two and handed me half, I couldn't help but return her smile. "One, two, three," she counted, and then dropped her half into the flame that was burning in our small charcoal grill. I dropped my half into the flames and hugged her close as the paper turned black, and then disappeared completely. "I know it's not fancy, but this place is finally ours," Shelby had said with great pride.

"I love our home," I told her and she smiled, a tear trickling down her cheek.

"I do too," she said. "Will you come inside and help me make a salad while the coals are getting ready?"

"Yes ma'am," I answered and followed my mama into our home.

I remember that night as one of my happiest memories with Mama. It was a few short weeks later that I gave her the scare of her life.

†

It happened on a Thursday. The local weather report was rampant with news of a hurricane in the Gulf of Mexico that promised devastating damage to the Gulf Coast. The weatherman announced that landfall would occur later in the morning, and he projected the storm would veer off to the northeast at a rapid pace. If we were lucky, we'd only receive intense rainstorms. Hopefully, being over land for several hours would kill the winds or at least diminish them to tropical storm force. Still, there would be plenty of excitement with the coming of the storm.

I had experienced a boon of good fortune that morning. I'd already emptied one basket of bottles for a refund, and was on my way back to the grocery store with a second when the weather began to change. The air that had been stagnant all morning with sweltering humidity suddenly began to move. It was by no means a cool breeze, but if you stretched your imagination just a bit you could smell the salt air in the wind. Dark, heavy clouds, pregnant with rain rolled in quickly on the winds, and the sky darkened as I decided against trying to beat the weather to the grocery store and pedaled for the diner. The rain was holding off, but would soon arrive with a vengeance as the skies opened up to purge. I could hear the angry rumbling of thunder in the distance as my feet worked the pedals of my bike furiously. The last thing I wanted today was to be soaked by the rain.

I was a little more than a mile away from the diner when the first raindrops began to fall, pelting my skin with their cold touch. For a brief moment, I debated stopping off at one of the downtown businesses to take shelter from the approaching storm, then decided to pedal on. The people at the diner were used to me by now and always treated me with kindness, unlike most of the shop owners on Main Street who seemed uncomfortable the moment I walked in their door.

I sorely regretted my decision as the lightning suddenly grew close, but I could now see the diner and I pedaled with all my might. Trees were swaying wildly along the street, the raindrops grew larger. I was only a few hundred yards from reaching my destination when a blinding flash filled my eyes. I felt an intense pain in my left arm and smelled something burning. I sensed myself falling to the ground in slow motion.

Mama had been pacing the front window, watching for me, and saw the whole event or else I would never have known what truly happened to me that day. The last thing I remembered was her screaming my name just as my body hit the ground. My eyes focused on the green and yellow Sun Drop bottle that had fallen unbroken from my basket. It was spinning slowly in front of my eyes, and I could feel the smile form on my lips, happy the bottle hadn't broken right before my world went blank.

I felt like I was floating on a cloud through the darkness. I could not see anything through the dense blackness and there was no sound to hear. My body felt relaxed as I pretended to lie back and nap while I floated through the darkness on my magic cloud.

What seemed like a few minutes passed before a high-pitched noise filled my ears. The volunteer fire department was on the move, but I had no idea they were coming for me. They were the town's first responders. It would be several minutes before an ambulance from a neighboring town could arrive in cases of extreme emergency. I could hear my mama's anxious voice as the firemen moved her back so they could begin attending to me. Laura, the owner of the diner, talked to her softly, trying to calm her down. My heart ached for my distraught mama, but when I tried to open my mouth to speak no sound would emerge.

I relaxed back into the darkness.

I was aware of my body moving, but had no idea what was going on around me. Voices were garbled, and every time I opened my eyes my surroundings were blurred.

The next thing I remembered was hearing the thumping, muffled sound that I recognized as helicopter rotors, and then felt a slight bump as the flying machine touched down on a hard surface. The anxious voices grew louder and I felt my body lifted and rushed across a short distance in the bright sunlight. Then I entered into a dark place. A long hall that felt like a tunnel. I saw large dim lights passing overhead as the gurney I lay on was wheeled into a room.

"Tally, can you hear me?" I heard a voice calling. I didn't recognize the voice, but at least I could understand the words. My ears vibrated as the sound of the voice reached me. Gentle hands placed small adhesive patches on my body while wires and machines were set to monitor my vital signs. I could hear the beeping of a heart monitor, and the pulse matched the rhythm in my ears, slow and strong. I sighed, when I felt my chest rising with each breath I took.

A nurse lifted my eyelids, and I heard her gasp when she realized my eyes were of two different colors. If I had been alert, I might have issued a laugh at her response. The nurse moved away as a deep voice boomed through the room.

"Your daughter is a very lucky girl," I heard someone say. "The rubber wheels kept her from electrocution, but her body took quite a shock. And the burn on her arm will leave a scar she will always carry with her."

"Why won't she wake?" I heard Mama ask.

"Her body is trying to get back into a normal rhythm after the shock," Deep Voice explained. "I plan to give her a sedative to help her rest tonight, and if her vitals remain strong, she can go home in the morning."

I didn't need to open my eyes to see my mama's tears. I could hear them in her voice. "Will she really be all right?"

"Yes, she will," he answered. "A nurse will be in to dress the burn on her arm, and administer the sedative while we get a room assigned for her. I will check on her again before I end my shift tonight," he promised and left the room, leaving Mama and I alone.

Even though I struggled, I could not will my eyes to open or my mouth to form words that would have given her comfort. I was able to squeeze her hand as she settled into a chair beside my bed and took my right hand in hers.

I felt a cold sensation on my burnt left arm as a nurse returned to clean the wound. She hummed as her hands moved gently to spread a warm cream over my damaged skin. Then, I felt a sharp pain, like a bee sting in my arm, and my body drifted high, back into the fluffy clouds.

I dreamed.

Up high above the earth there seemed to be a hundred people floating in the clouds. My first thought was they must be angels watching over the people below, but then I realized that these people were not happy, so they couldn't be angels. They appeared sad and lost, which made my heart ache in a strange way that I didn't understand. I could hear their muffled whispers, but in my drug-induced stupor, I could not make out any of their words.

Suddenly, through a beam of light, another figure began to appear. This one was smaller, unlike the adults I had seen, and my eyes attempted to focus. Finally, after what seemed like hours, a young girl, who appeared close to my age, stood beside me on my cloud, smiling at me. Her brilliant red hair fell like a halo around her pale face, and I knew she had to be a beautiful angel. Her green eyes glittered intensely as she reached out and touched my wounded arm.

Everything will be all right, I heard in my head, even though I did not see her lips move.

I lifted my head and tried to ask her name, but found my voice still lost somewhere in my dreams.

We will meet again soon, I heard in my head as she slowly floated out of my vision.

I felt a smile grow on my face as the blackness closed around me again.

When my eyes opened again Mama was sitting beside my hospital bed, still holding my hand as her head rested on the mattress. The tension had disappeared from her face, and I remember thinking if ever there was an angelic face on this earth, I was looking at it now. I removed my hand from hers, and let my fingers slide down the trail of tears that had stained her face.

Mama stirred beneath my touch, and when her eyes opened she smiled to see me awake. I opened my mouth, and croaked out a weak, "Hello, Mama, I'm thirsty."

Shelby jumped from her seat and walked to a small table to pour me some ice water. She placed a bent straw in the cup and returned to the bed to raise it to my lips. "Go slow," she warned.

The cool water felt heavenly as it trickled down my parched throat. When I had enough, I nodded my head.

"Is that better?"

"Much, thanks Mama." I still sounded a bit croaky, but she was relieved to hear my voice.

"You gave me quite a scare. How are you feeling?"

"My arm hurts a bit, and my eyes feel funny."

"Feel funny how?"

"I don't know how to explain it. They feel more sensitive," I said, grasping for a word that described how my eyes felt.

The door to the room opened and a tall young man walked in, greeting Mama with a cheery "Good evening." I recognized Deep Voice from the emergency room.

"I'm glad to see you're awake. I'm Dr. Hill," he said as he bent over my bed and touched my arm. "How are you feeling?"

"My arm hurts a little, and my eyes feel strange."

"I will get some more pain medication for your arm. Would you mind if I take a look at your eyes?"

"No sir."

He reached for his breast pocket to pull out a penlight. He clicked the end, turning the light toward his face to ensure it was operating correctly, and then leaned down across the bed. When he shone the bright light in my left eye, I cried out in pain.

"I'm sorry," he said, flipping the beam of light toward the ceiling before turning the penlight off and slipping it back in his pocket. "I didn't mean to hurt you."

"I know."

He lifted his right hand with two fingers raised. "How many fingers am I showing?"

"Two," I answered with a slight laugh.

"Okay, I want you to follow the path of my fingers with your eyes. Don't move your head, just your eyes," he instructed.

I followed the movement side to side, then up and down. He seemed satisfied that my vision was fine. He turned to point at the door. "What does that sign above the door say?"

"Exit," I answered.

"What color is it?"

"Blue." I heard my mama gasp in surprise.

He pulled a pen from his pocket and held it in front of my eyes. "What color is this?"

"Green," I answered with a frown growing on my face.

The doctor sighed and sat down on the edge of my bed. He spoke directly to me instead of my mama, which gave me some comfort. "Your sight seems fine, but the flash of brightness from the lightning has affected your vision. Your eyes are extremely sensitive to light, which is not unusual," he explained. "Were you color-blind before the accident?"

"No, not that I know," I said, and looked at Mama for assurance.

She shook her head in response.

"Maybe this will also be a temporary thing. The sign you say is blue is actually red, and my pen is blue. Hopefully as your body heals from the shock you will regain color vision again."

"I will be okay then?"

"No headaches or other pain?" he asked.

"No sir, just my arm."

"You will be just fine. I recommend you wear a pair of dark sunglasses until your eyes readjust to brightness. Don't sweat the color blindness. I really think it will disappear in a few days."

He turned to my mama then. "If it doesn't, I would recommend a follow-up with an eye doctor, and if she has any other pain, don't hesitate to bring her back. I will leave an order for discharge in the morning, and ask the nurse to bring her a pain pill." He smiled, and nodded to her before leaving the room.

"Thank you, Doctor," I said.

"You're very welcome. Sleep well."

"I need to go make a phone call," Mama said. "Will you be okay for a few minutes?"

"Yes, Mama," I said and rolled my eyes at her with a grin.

"I'm going to call Laura to ask her for a ride home tomorrow."

Until that moment, I had forgotten she had ridden in the ambulance with me and we had no way to get home.

Minutes after she left, a young black-haired nurse came in carrying a small pill cup. "Here is your pain medicine," she explained as she poured me a fresh cup of ice water. I took the small white pill she handed me and placed the cup of water on the small bedside table. "How are you feeling? Are you hungry?"

"I'm feeling okay. Yes, I'm hungry."

"Why don't I have a sandwich sent up from the kitchen for you and your mom? Do you like turkey?"

"Yes ma'am, turkey would be great."

"Let me go and get it ordered then. Do you know how to call me if you need me?"

I pointed to the call button hanging from the side rails of the bed.

She smiled and said, "Call if you need anything."

I nodded. Alone in the room I looked at the large bandage on my arm and grimaced at the memory of the smell of my burning flesh. I pushed the memory from my thoughts and closed my eyes to wait for Mama to return.

I had almost drifted off to sleep when I heard my door open and saw Mama, followed by a small woman carrying a tray.

"I brought some sandwiches and sodas for you ladies," the kind woman said as she placed the tray on the table. "If there is anything else you need, just have the nurse call."

"Thank you," Mama said.

Mama lifted the cover from the tray to find two turkey sandwiches, two bags of chips, and two cans of RC Cola.

"I'm starved," I said as I picked up a half a sandwich and took a bite.

"Laura will be here at eight in the morning, and will take us home as soon as you are discharged."

"It'll be good to be home," I said as I opened a bag of chips.

"I will take a few days off to watch over you."

"There's no need for that, Mama," I said. "I promise I will take it easy and call the diner if I need you." I knew how tight money was for us and that she couldn't afford to take time off work to look after me.

She cocked her head to look at me. "Okay, but after tomorrow. I want to be sure you are going to take it easy."

"I have a few new library books I can read."

"That's a very good idea."

"Is my bike okay?"

"Yes, Laura has it locked in the storeroom," she said. "She even kept your bottles for you."

I smiled at that thought, remembering I had a second basket full of returnable bottles.

"The heavy rains from the storm have finally arrived," she said as I turned my head to the sound of drops striking the window.

I finished the sandwich and chips just as the pain pill was starting to take effect. My eyes grew heavy and I stifled a yawn. "Will you sleep with me tonight?" I asked as I scooted over in the bed.

"Sure," she answered and kicked her shoes off before climbing onto the bed with me. I felt her arm slide around my shoulders as my eyes closed for the night.

†

I heard the distant rumble of thunder and felt my body shiver as I began to float up into the clouds. The now familiar faces of the people in the clouds welcomed my return. As I lounged against my soft cloud, I watched a young woman approach. She was beautiful with long, dark hair and sad, dark eyes. She sat beside me on the cloud and surprised me when she spoke.

"Hello Tally," she said.

"How do you know my name?"

"Because you were sent here to help me, help all of us," she said.

"To help you? Help you how?"

"We are all stuck here, and need your help to leave," she replied.

"How am I supposed to help?"

"You will know one day soon."

"Why are there so many of you here?"

"We were all killed before our time, and we won't know peace until justice is found for us on earth."

"How can you do that?"

"You will help us when the time is right," she assured me.

"But how," I implored?

"I cannot say. But you will know how, when you are ready," she said. She stood and faded into the darkness, leaving me frustrated with so many questions and no answers for any of them.

The faces smiled at me as I drifted deeper into the night to dream no more.

Chapter Three

The clatter of food trays woke me the next morning, and I opened my eyes to find my mama sitting beside my bed. The rain still pelted the windows, and the weak daylight hurt my eyes. I squinted at her and whispered, "Good morning."

"Does the light hurt your eyes?"

"Yes, Mama, it does."

"A nurse dropped these by for you this morning," she said as she handed me a pair of light sunglasses, generally used after surgery. "If this danged rain lets up when we get home, I will go to the drugstore and get you a good pair," she promised as I slid the glasses on.

"Is that better?"

"Much. Thanks, Mama."

"Here are your clothes if you want to go ahead and get dressed. After you have breakfast, and the nurse changes your bandage, we can be on our way. Laura should be here soon."

"That sounds really good."

When my tray arrived, Mama took the cup of coffee, and spread the jelly across my toast. I was nearly finished eating when a knock came to the door and Laura stepped inside.

"Good morning. How do you feel Tally?"

"I'm good thank you."

"I appreciate you coming to take us home," Mama said.

"No problem. With this weather, most everyone is staying home so I closed the diner for the day."

"Is it still bad out?"

"Not near as bad as it was last night. The television weatherman says it is supposed to clear late this afternoon."

"That's great news. May I ask one more favor?"

"Sure, anything you need," Laura answered.

"I need to stop by the drugstore and pick up some sunglasses for Tally."

"No problem. It's right on the way. I need to pick up some aspirin anyhow."

"As soon as the nurse changes the dressing and brings up a wheelchair, we'll be ready to go," Mama said.

"A wheelchair," I asked, confused. "I can walk."

"Hospital rules," the nurse said as she entered the room pushing a wheelchair. "Let's get that dressing changed and you can be on your way."

Laura, Mama, and I watched as the nurse gently cut away the bandage from my arm. As the bandage dropped away, an angry red patch of skin almost six inches long came to view. "Does it hurt this morning?"

"Not too bad," I answered, smiling at the nurse.

She cleaned the wound and then spread a soothing cream across it. "This should help reduce the scarring, but you'll have a scar."

"That can't be helped."

My answer seemed to surprise the nurse. She smiled, then replaced the cap on the tube of cream and handed it to Mama. "You can take the rest of this with you too."

"Thanks," she said and added it to the bag the hospital had given her containing supplies to change the dressing and a bottle of medication for me.

The nurse placed a fresh bandage over my arm, and then wound soft gauze around it to add some padding. "This will be good for two days. Just be sure to keep it dry and you will be fine."

"Can I shower or take a bath?"

"Sure. A bath would probably be easier. Just place some plastic wrap around it to keep the bandages dry."

I stood up and slipped into the wheelchair. The nurse pushed me out of the room followed closely by my mama and Laura.

When we reached the lobby, Laura turned to Mama, "You wait here, Shelby, and let me go get the car." She opened her umbrella and dashed out into the rain.

†

Within the hour, we had made it home and Mama had me settled onto the couch, wearing some cool new shades. After Laura left, she pulled the blinds tight to eliminate as much outdoor light as possible from the room, and I was able to remove the shades and open my eyes without pain. Mama placed fluffy pillows around me on the couch and brought me a book to read while she worked around the house.

The rain fell briskly on the tin of the roof, quickly lulling me to sleep. I remembered Mama removing the book from my hands and pulling a sheet up over my body as I slept.

The strong winds gently rocked the trailer from time to time as I slept. I was jarred awake by a loud clap of thunder, which sounded just above the roof of the trailer. I sat up with a start and called for my mama.

"It's okay, Tally," she called from the kitchen where she was preparing lunch. "It's just the storm passing through." She came into the living room and placed egg salad sandwiches on the coffee table. "Do you want some sweet pickles and an RC?"

"Yes, please."

A bolt of lightning lit the front yard with a brilliant flash. I felt my body shudder with the electricity in the air. My mind went numb as the faces from the clouds flashed across my vision. I shook my head, hoping to clear the images, but the faces remained even though I was certain I was awake.

Mama returned to the room, her hands full of drinks and a bowl of pickles, to find me staring out the front window. "Tally, are you okay?"

I could hear my mama's voice, but my vocal chords would not respond. She set the items on the table and moved closer to me. Placing her hand on my shoulder she repeated her question. "Tally, are you okay?"

The physical contact of her hand broke the trance I was in. I tore my eyes away from the window to look into her worried eyes. "Yes, I am, Mama," I finally managed to answer. "I think I zoned out for a minute."

"Well, you have been through a lot in the last twenty-four hours."

"I think I'll take a pain pill and go lie in my bed after we eat, if that's okay with you."

"That's fine, baby. Are you sure you're okay?"

I could see the worry on her face as she frowned at me. "Yeah, my arm is starting to ache, and this weather is making me tired."

I could tell from the look in my mama's eye that she knew there was more to my odd behavior. She also knew me well enough that when I was ready to talk about what was bothering me, I would be the one to make the approach. I knew she was worried that when the time came, she would not have the answers I would be looking for. She handed me an RC and opened one for herself. "I thought I'd take a nap too after lunch. I'll crash on the couch so I'll hear if you call out."

I nodded, comforted knowing she would still be close. Our home was small, with our bedrooms on opposite ends of the trailer, but there was no doubt she could hear me calling from the couch right outside my door.

"Do you know what you would like for supper?"

"Do you have the ingredients for spaghetti?"

"I do believe so," Mama answered.

"That sounds good to me," I said as I kissed her on the cheek before going to my room. I pulled back the sheets on my bed and my eyes squinted as I looked toward the window. I walked over and closed the blinds, shutting out the muted sunlight. Off in the distance I saw bright flashes of lightning once again growing more frequent. I crawled into bed and wrapped a pillow around my head to shut out the sounds of the approaching storm.

My body buzzed with the electricity of the storm. The ache behind my eyes continued to grow as I squeezed them shut against the dreams that were sure to come. I prayed sleep would capture me soon.

The faces in my dreams appeared in clouds and floated in front of my eyes. Their voices had still not formed in my mind, but the low rumble of their moans rang in my ears. My body was exhausted and I knew if I concentrated on the faces I would get no rest. In my mind I cried out, "Leave me be, so I can get some rest." I was surprised as one by one each of the faces faded into the darkness and I was able to slip into a dreamless sleep.

†

For the next eight years, I learned how to communicate with the faces in the clouds. As foretold years earlier by the young woman in my hospital room vision, I began to understand how I could help them. It did not surprise me that she was the first shadow person I would help, as she was the first, and most frequent, to communicate with me in my dreams. As I grew older, she was able to share with me the events that surrounded her death.

Her name was Lisa Evans and she was nineteen when murdered in Bogalusa, Louisiana, on a hot and humid summer night. She was home for the summer from her first year in college. She had walked to a nearby store for a cool drink to gain some relief from the heat. It was a walk she had made hundreds of times and she had no reason to fear the darkness of the night. At the store she reveled in the conditioned cool air for several minutes while she made her selection of drinks.

"It's a mighty hot one out there tonight," the clerk had commented to her as she placed her money on the counter to pay for her purchase.

"That it is. I think we're in for a long, hot summer," she had replied.

"Good for da gators, but hell on earth for humans," he said as he handed her the change.

She grinned and nodded as she took the change and slipped it into the pocket of her shorts. "Thanks," Lisa said and left the store.

The full moon loomed huge against the dark sky as a hot breeze blew gently through the trees. She had made notice of the white van parked along the side of the street earlier, but did not hesitate in her stroll. Nothing happened in her sleepy little town she thought. However, a chill, and gooseflesh, rose on her skin as she approached the van.

The sharp squeal of a hinge froze her in her tracks. She looked toward the van. There was no interior light, so she could not see anything inside the van, but she was certain the driver's door had just opened.

Wordlessly, but with amazing speed, someone grabbed her and placed a vile-smelling rag against her face. Her body went limp as she fell into a pair of strong arms that easily placed her in the back of the van. As Lisa's story unfolded in my dreams I watched in horror as the driver quietly slipped back behind the wheel and slowly drove out of town.

I was thankful Lisa spared me the brutal details of the treatment she had received over the next two days, before her captor became tired of her and ended her life.

I was crying in my dream as Lisa told me how she could remember the strong hands that choked the breath from her body. I watched tears trail down her cheeks as she painfully recalled how her body was dumped at a local water tower, to be found two days later by a county worker.

Lisa reached over to my face and wiped the tears away. "Don't cry for me," she said. "What's done is done."

"You didn't deserve to have that happen to you," I said between sniffles.

"None of us did," she calmly answered. "I wasn't his only victim. There have been, and will be, others."

"You mean he hasn't been caught yet?"

"Not even close. I think the new girl over there is one of his victims, but she won't quit crying long enough for me to talk to her," Lisa said, motioning at a young girl of barely sixteen.

"What can you tell me about him?" I asked.

"I was drugged most of the time, so I can't tell much. I do remember he had cold blue eyes, and I remember thinking he would have been handsome if not for the scar that traveled down the left side of his face."

"Do you have any idea how old he was?"

"He was young when he killed me. I would say he's probably in his forties by now," Lisa said. "I do know he was from the Bayou and had a distinctive Cajun accent."

That probably described half of the men in the state, I thought to myself. "Is there anything else you can remember?"

Lisa's body shuddered. "He reeked of stale cigarettes and the space between his knuckles and fingers of his right hand were tattooed."

"What did the tattoo say?"

"DEATH," Lisa said. "I remember seeing the lettering right before I blacked out."

"Are you the one?" a fragile voice asked from the dark.

"The one what?" I asked of the young girl who had approached.

"The one who can help us?" she replied.

"I can only try," I answered.

"I need you to find me and take me home, so I can move on," she said through a veil of tears.

"How am I supposed to do that?"

"Please call my mama in Birmingham and tell her to give you my charm bracelet. Through that I can draw you to where I am, if you will listen for me."

"Your mama will probably call the police on me thinking I'm crazy," I said.

"No, she won't if you tell her Beanie sends you. She's called me that since I was a little girl."

"What's your mother's name?"

"Hope Carter," the girl said. "Her number's in the book."

"Do you know who killed you?"

Fresh tears welled up in her eyes. "He was a bad, bad man, with a horrible scar on his face," she said before bursting into tears again. "He hurt me bad then dropped me in a quarry, but I don't know for sure where."

Lisa and I shared a look. We suspected the young girl had been a victim of the same man who had killed Lisa.

Maybe, just maybe, there would be some evidence left that could help the authorities begin to track him down.

"I will do what I can, Beanie," I promised the girl who had faded back into the darkness.

"You are ready now for your first assignment, Tally," Lisa said. "Help Beanie go home." She faded away as my body started to wake from a deep sleep.

I'm twenty now and it's time for me to accept the responsibility given to me, to use my gift for good. Yeah, I can do this.

Chapter Four

I awoke that morning to a brilliant fall sunrise. I showered and dressed then found Mama in the kitchen cooking breakfast.

"Good morning, Tally. Did you sleep well?"

"Good morning, Mama. Yes, I did, and you?"

"Like a rock as usual."

I poured a cup of coffee and leaned against the counter. "Can I borrow your car for a few days?"

"You know you can, sweetheart. Where are you going?"

"I have something to do in Alabama," I answered.

"Have your visions returned?"

I never kept much from my mama, but we didn't often speak of what the visions brought me. "Yes, they have, and I think it's time for me to start doing something about them."

"Do you want me to go with you?"

"Thanks, but this is something I have to do for myself."

"At least take my cell phone, and call to let me know what's going on."

"I will, I promise."

"Do you need some money?"

"No, I have some saved up, but thanks." I am good with computers and occasionally did some data entry for a local firm, when I wasn't busy with my online studies. I hoped one day to have a degree in business management.

"Well, take my credit card in case you have an emergency," she said as she handed me a card from her wallet. "When do you plan to leave?"

"There's no time like the present," I said.

"Okay, smarty-pants, go pack your bag while I finish breakfast. At least you can eat a good meal before you go."

"Thanks Mama," I said and kissed her cheek before leaving the kitchen to go pack a small bag.

When I returned to the kitchen she had made a huge breakfast. I was already preoccupied about the mission I was about to undertake and could only pick at my food.

"I had a feeling you wouldn't be able to eat," she said, "so I packed up a bag to send with you."

"You're the best, Mama."

"Don't I know it," she said with a wink. "Call me when you get settled in tonight." She handed me the keys and her cell phone. "The car charger is in the console," she added as she walked me to the door.

I slipped on my shades and opened the door. Even through the dark lenses, I squinted in the bright sunlight. The doctor had been right about the color blindness fading, but the sensitivity to light had never improved. The pain forced me to wear sunglasses during most of the daylight hours.

"I love you, Tally."

"Love you too, Mama. See you soon."

"Be careful out there."

"I will."

I walked over to the car and dropped my bag in the backseat. Placing the bag of food on the passenger seat, I climbed in behind the wheel and closed the door. Mama watched as I buckled my seat belt and backed the car out of the drive.

†

I had driven to Birmingham before so I knew which back roads to take to bypass the snarl of Atlanta traffic. As I drove, I contemplated how I would contact Mrs. Carter without coming across as a raving lunatic. I didn't know how long Beanie had been gone, but I was certain the pain would still be fresh, especially since they had not located a body and she would still have hope that her daughter would return home alive.

The miles passed quickly, and all too soon I was entering the city limits of Birmingham. I stopped at a gas station to refuel and spotted a phone booth that looked like it still housed a phone book. I filled the car and paid the attendant. Then I pulled the car next to the phone booth and stepped inside. My hands shook as I opened the book in search of Beanie's mother's address and phone number.

It took a few turns to make it to the correct page, and when I found the page, I scribbled down the address and phone number before fishing coins out of my pocket. I took a deep breath and dropped the coins in the machine. After six unanswered rings, I hung up. I checked the time. It was one in the afternoon, so possibly her mother was still at a Sunday church service or busy with some other task.

I walked back inside, bought a city map from the attendant, and asked for directions to the nearest library. The young man pulled out a yellow highlighter pen and traced the route I would need to take to get to the library. I thanked him and bought a Sun Drop before leaving the store to walk back to my car.

With the map spread across the steering wheel, I dipped my hand into the bag of food Mama had prepared and pulled out a bacon biscuit. I looked at my notepad at the address I had scribbled and searched the map for the location. As luck would have it, the address for Beanie's mom didn't look too far from the library. If my luck held out, the library would be open for the afternoon. If not, I would try to find a cheap hotel room to rest in until I could get in touch with Mrs. Carter.

The library was small, but surprisingly enough, it was open on a Sunday afternoon. Not surprisingly, the building was nearly vacant as I made my way to the media room that would house the local newspapers and microfilm sections. I started with the current newspaper and immediately realized I didn't know what Beanie's real name was. As it turned out, it wasn't necessary; I saw the headline 'No New Leads in Missing Girl Case' at the bottom of the front page

The article described how sixteen-year-old Loren Carter had failed to return home after cheerleader practice the previous Tuesday. The article implied the police had no leads, and were pleading with anyone who had any information to contact them immediately. I looked at the small photograph attached to the article, which confirmed that Loren was the Beanie in my dreams. The bright cheerful face that had smiled for the camera was now the tear-streaked face of a child who desperately wanted to go home. My heart ached for her loss as I read through the article again.

I searched the microfilm reels from the week but failed to find any other information that would assist me in finding Beanie. Fighting discouragement, I replaced the film and walked back to the car. I found another phone and tried her mother's number again. Still no answer. I hadn't thought of what I would do if I couldn't locate Beanie's mother.

I wanted to locate the address before the sun started to set. I didn't want to have to try to find it after dark for the first time. I rechecked the directions and left the library. Twenty minutes later, I parked in front of a nice brick house with an immaculate lawn and bright fall flowers. I could just imagine Beanie and her mother working together to plant the flowers in the beds. I climbed out of the car, walked up the front porch to the door, and pressed the bell. There was no answer. Giving up I turned to leave but spied a white swing hanging at the far end of the porch. My feet moved automatically to it, and I took a seat at one end and began swinging slowly back and forth.

Closing my eyes I tried to bring up the vision of Beanie. I had tried before to conjure up the faces in the shadows at will, but had never succeeded, and now was no different. I had the gift of sight, but I didn't have control over when or where I would see the visions. Somehow, I would have to learn to control the visions if I was going to act upon them. That was just another problem I would have to solve if, and when, I was able to help Beanie come to rest.

The gentle rocking of the swing had lulled me to sleep and I failed to hear a car pull into the drive. It was only when I heard the click of heels on the wooden front porch that I came alert and jumped to attention. My sudden movement startled a woman and she stopped in her tracks to stare at me.

"May I help you?" she asked confidently.

"Are you Mrs. Carter?"

"Yes, I am, and who are you?"

"My name is Tallulah Rainwater, but people call me Tally."

"So why are you sitting on my porch, young lady?"

"I was hoping I could talk with you for a few minutes."

The woman looked me up and down, and I could sense she doubted we had little in common to talk about. Her behavior and the coldness I felt from the woman surprised me. I hadn't imagined Beanie's mom would be like this.

"What do you have to talk with me about? If you are looking for a donation or something, I don't have the time for this right now," she added curtly.

"No ma'am, I don't want money, I want to talk to you about Beanie."

The woman's face blanched white, and for a moment, I thought her knees would buckle. "What do you know about my daughter?"

"Would you please come to sit with me so we can talk? This is going to be a difficult conversation."

The woman approached on shaking legs, and took a seat at the end of the swing opposite me.

I took a deep breath and started to speak. "You will probably think I'm crazy, but please hear me out, Mrs. Carter."

"Okay young lady, you have my attention, but please take those glasses off so I can see you."

"I'm sorry, ma'am, but I can't. I had an accident when I was young and my eyes are very sensitive to light."

"I'm sorry to hear that. Would you rather go inside out of the sun?"

"Not until you hear what I have to say. Then if you choose to invite me inside, I will accept."

"Okay, go on then. Tell me what you want and how you know my daughter."

After another deep breath, I turned toward Mrs. Carter. "Ever since I can remember I have had visions."

"What kind of visions?"

"At first they were just blurry shapes, but after my accident they became faces in the shadows in my mind, and now they or at least some of them come to me in full body forms."

"I'm in no mood for jokes," she said angrily.

"I'm not joking, Mrs. Carter. Your daughter Loren has contacted me through a vision."

"That's a cruel joke," she said her hand flying to her neck. "My daughter has been missing for the last five days," she said, her anger rising.

"I know this is hard, Mrs. Carter, but your daughter has been murdered."

Mrs. Carter fainted and fell off the swing. I leapt to my feet, and knelt down to her taking her head in my lap, gently patting her cheeks. "Mrs. Carter, please wake up," I repeated until her eyes began to flutter open, and I breathed more easily. "Mrs. Carter, please wake up."

"How…how do you know this?"

"Because she came to me last night in my vision and asked me to help her come home to you. She told me that if I called her Beanie you would know I'm telling the truth, that you had called her that since she was a little girl."

She blanched white again and I feared she would faint once more as she took in my words. "Not many people know of that nickname."

"She knows she's gone, and there is nothing I can do to change that, but she wants to come home to you so she can move on, and she can rest in peace."

"Do you know where she is, and are you sure she is dead?"

"I don't know exactly where, but yes she told me she was murdered by a stranger. She said to get her charm bracelet from you and she will help me find her. She says she is in a quarry someplace."

"Dear God. Shelby County has several quarries."

"I feel certain that Beanie can lead us to her, if I hold on to the bracelet," I said.

"Please come inside, Tally. I need to call my brother, Joe. He's a policeman and can help us."

I became a little nervous at the mention of the police, but followed the woman inside the lovely home. She showed me into a small sitting room, then disappeared to make her phone call. I scanned the photographs around the room, seeing the progression of Beanie's life from infant to teenager pass in front of my eyes.

"Joe will be here in five minutes," Mrs. Carter said as she reentered the room.

"Do you think I'm crazy?"

"I admit, the thought did cross my mind, but no stranger would ever know the nickname Beanie. It breaks my heart to know that she may be dead, but it gives me a small measure of comfort to know where she is, if that makes any sense."

"It does make sense. I can tell you she is as okay as she can be in death, but she won't move on until you can bring her home."

"Still, it's hard to believe."

"I'm sorry, I couldn't think of any other way to tell you," I said.

"No, I appreciate everything you are doing. It's just as a parent you never expect to bury your only child."

The front door burst open and the largest man I have ever seen came rushing through.

"What is this nonsense, Hope?" he demanded to know.

"Now Joe, settle down," Mrs. Carter said. "Come sit down for a minute and hear this young woman's story," she pleaded.

Joe shook his head, but settled into a large recliner across from me. "I hope she hasn't tried to get any money out of you," he grumbled.

"Joe, will you calm down and quit being rude," his sister scolded. "This is Tally Rainwater, and no, she hasn't asked for any money for her help."

"You know I don't believe in psychics, or whatever they call themselves these days."

"Sir, I don't call myself anything, but I do have visions that I believe are from people who are trapped and need assistance to go to their final rest. Beanie has come to me and asked for my help."

When I mentioned the name Beanie, his head whipped toward his sister. "No, I didn't tell her about Loren's nickname. She knew from the visit she received from Loren."

"So, what do you think you can do that the police haven't already done?" he asked defensively.

"Beanie told me she knows where her body is and how she thinks I can find it using her bracelet so she can come home," I stated as calmly as I could.

"This is ludicrous! he said. "We don't even know if she is still alive."

"I can assure you, sir, that she is not. She told me she was killed by a stranger with a long scar on his face."

Joe sat in stunned silence.

"Other than a wild goose chase, what do we have to lose?" Mrs. Carter asked. "Your people have not been able to track her down." She immediately regretted her words when she saw her brother's face flinch.

"We are doing everything we can, Hope."

"I know. I'm sorry. I didn't mean for it to come out that way."

"So how are you supposed to find her," he asked.

"She told me her body is in a quarry, and that if her mother can give me her charm bracelet, I should be able to use it so she can pull me toward her."

"I still think this is ludicrous, Hope, but I will drive you if you want to give it a try."

"Let me go find the bracelet then," she said and left the room.

Joe glared at me. "I swear if this is some sort of scam, I will put you under the jail," he warned.

"I am only trying to help, sir. The only thing I want is to see Beanie get the peace she deserves."

"Did she say anything else at all about the man?"

"She didn't know him, but said he has cold, evil blue eyes and a long scar down his face. I also believe it's possible that he has tattoos on the fingers of his right hand that spell DEATH."

"Have you seen this man in your vision?"

33

"No, sir, but I believe she is not his only victim. I think he has killed before in a small town called Bogalusa."

"Louisiana?"

"Yes, sir. I have been contacted by a young woman who was killed years ago, but her description of the man is eerily similar."

He raised his hand to rub his chin. "So this could be a serial killer on the loose?" He looked up at me with damp eyes. "If this is true, and he has crossed state lines, this would make it a federal offense, and the FBI should be involved."

"I don't know about that, sir, I just want to find her."

Hope returned to the room and handed me a beautiful charm bracelet. "She has been adding to that since she was a little girl. It's rare that she would have not worn it the day she disappeared. She hardly left home without it on her wrist."

I took the cold metal bracelet into my hands and closed my eyes. The bracelet began to grow warm in my palms, and I felt a vibration run through my body. In the darkness, I could feel the shapes of the faces beginning to form and watched as Loren appeared out of the shimmering light. She reached for me and I felt the tips of her fingers brush my cheek, then I saw a road sign flash before my eyes. It had the number 25 on it. *Thank you for coming. I knew I could depend on you.*

How do I find you? I asked her in my vision.

I am somewhere off Highway 25, in an abandoned quarry. Keep the bracelet in your hand and I'll try to lead you as close as possible. Tell Uncle Joe I said to peace out, and maybe he will have more faith in you.

I will try that, I said and opened my eyes. I looked at Joe. "She said to tell you to 'peace out,' whatever that means."

A tear slid down the big man's cheek. "Beanie used to always tell me that when I got stressed out over a case I was working on," he explained as he wiped the tear away. "What else did she tell you?"

"She said to keep the bracelet in my hand as we drive on Highway 25, and she'll try to bring us close."

"That's down in Shelby County. There are several old quarries in the area. Come on, I'll drive since I know the area pretty well."

We drove south for thirty minutes until we reached Highway 25. Joe turned onto the small two-lane road. The sun was beginning to sink toward the horizon as we reached the first of three quarries Joe said he knew of in the area. The site, converted into a scuba diving school, failed to offer any feeling that Loren was there. "This isn't the place," I said as I turned back to the car.

We drove back to the paved road, and when Joe turned left to go further south, I felt the bracelet start to turn warm again in my hand. I leaned back against the headrest and listened for Loren to contact me. I felt a wave of nausea pass through my body and was about to ask Joe to pull over when it finally passed. "Turn left up ahead."

Joe pulled onto a small side road, secured with an iron bar across the lane. The padlock looked new and shiny. "Can you get us in there?"

Joe smiled. "It won't take but just a minute." He turned off the car and unlocked the trunk, pulling out a pair of bolt cutters. He walked to the gate and snipped through the padlock like he was cutting butter. He set the destroyed lock on the post and returned the bolt cutters to his trunk. "Piece of cake," he said as he started the car, and pulled onto an overgrown trail. "It doesn't look like anyone has been down this path in a while."

"It feels cold," I said. "I think this is the place."

Joe shook his head. It was still almost ninety degrees outside.

Loren showed me the layout of the quarry in a vision and said she was near the waterwheel. I could see a faint outline of a rusted waterwheel off in the distance. "The quarry should be just off to the right and over a long hill," I instructed him.

When the path ahead split, Joe took the fork to the right, and just ahead, we could see a hill rising in front of us.

I felt a jolt of energy run through me when we crested the hill and felt Loren's presence strongly. Don't let Mama find me, Loren pleaded. Tell Uncle Joe where I am, but keep Mama in the car please, Tally. I don't want her to see me like this, please.

"Stop the car here please, sir," I said. I turned around in the seat to face Mrs. Carter. "Beanie wants you to stay in the car, please."

Mrs. Carter nodded her head in agreement. Her tears began to flow. I looked at Joe and then followed him out of the car to the crest of the hill.

"This is it. Beanie says her body is over by the waterwheel," I told him. "If you don't mind, I'll wait here."

Joe nodded his head solemnly and turned to walk away. I watched as he cautiously approached the area I had pointed out, searching for any sign of clues. It seemed like forever before he reached the waterwheel and collapsed to his knees in the tall grass.

Still clutching Beanie's bracelet I watched him find a length of rope tethered to the brace of the waterwheel. I knew Joe needed to go no further than the water's edge to find that a body was visible from the shore. The body was facedown in the clear, cold water of the quarry. In my vision, I could see her long hair floating just beneath the surface.

I was thankful Mrs. Carter could not see him as he stood and walked to the edge of the woods where he purged the contents of his stomach until his body shook with dry heaves. When he again took to his feet, he carefully returned to the waterwheel and reached for the rope. Tally watched as he worked with great restraint to keep from jerking on the rope, possibly damaging the body. He gently retracted the rope until the body floated closer to the surface. The bruised, swollen face of his niece appeared; her eyes were open, locked in terror from the moment of her death. Joe reluctantly released the rope, moved up the back of the quarry, and, with shaking hands, opened his phone.

He made the call to the local authorities before slowly walking back to the car to await their arrival. He nodded his head at me and from the look on his face; I knew he found Beanie. "I'm sorry I doubted you, young lady," he said as he reached out to shake my hand. "Thank you for bringing her home."

"I am sorry for your loss, but now she can find peace," I said as I smiled softly at him.

"Do you think you can find your way back to Hope's?" he asked.

"Yes sir, with her help I'm sure I can."

"Take my car and get her home. She doesn't need to be here to see what is about to happen."

"How will you get home?"

"The sheriff here is a fishing buddy of mine. I'm sure he will want to ask you a few questions, so once her body is removed I will have him take me to Hope's."

"I'll take her home and wait for you there then," I said. "Do you need a few minutes to talk with your sister?"

"Yes, I need to let her know what is going on. Give us a minute please, Tally."

I walked to the crest of the hill and looked down toward the waterwheel. There was a soft glow over the area where Loren's body was located that shimmered for a few minutes and then disappeared. I was watching the water surface closely to see if it would return when Joe approached and placed his large paw of a hand on my shoulder.

"She is ready to go now. The local authorities will be here soon. Please take her home."

"Yes sir," I said and walked to the driver's side of the car then climbed in. My heart went out to Mrs. Carter, but for once, I was at a loss for words. I adjusted the seat for my shorter legs, and reached to turn the key in the ignition. I didn't realize I still held the bracelet in my hand until I felt it cool against my skin. I looked at it, and then smiled as I reached out to Mrs. Carter to place the bracelet in her hand. "She's at peace now."

"Thank you," Mrs. Carter said as tears slid down her face. Her fingers wrapped around the bracelet, and she rested her head against the headrest as I drove away from the quarry. I had just turned onto Highway 25 when I heard sirens blaring in the distance. A few minutes later, a sheriff's cruiser flew by us followed shortly after by a van from the county medical examiner's office.

Chapter Five

The sunlight was almost gone when I pulled the large vehicle into Mrs. Carter's driveway. Our drive had been silent as she began the grieving process for her daughter. As we walked toward the front door, I asked, "Do you need some time alone?"

"I'm afraid I will be having plenty of that in the future," she answered. "Please come in, and I'll make some iced tea."

I followed her into the house to the kitchen. I took a seat at the small breakfast table at her beckoning.

"Are you hungry?"

"No ma'am, I'm fine."

"I'm afraid we are in for a long night. Do you have plans to stay in town?"

"I was hoping to start for home, but I think I will get a motel room and start out early tomorrow morning instead."

"Nonsense, young lady, you will stay right here tonight in my guest room. It's the least I can do for you after what you have done for my family."

I opened my mouth to protest and was immediately cut off. "No need to argue. I know your mother would approve of you staying here versus some seedy motel."

"Yes ma'am, she would, and I thank you for the offer," I said. "If you don't mind, I'm going to step outside and give her a call. I forgot to call her when I arrived and I don't want to worry her. I'll be right back."

She nodded and I walked outside to give my mama a call.

"Hello sweetheart. I hope everything's gone well. I got worried when I didn't hear from you."

"I'm sorry I forgot to call." I hesitated for a moment then blurted out, "I found her, Mama." Tears threatened to break my voice.

"I knew you could do it. Are you okay?"

"Yes ma'am, I can't believe I could actually find her. I'll be staying at Mrs. Carter's tonight, and I'll come home tomorrow."

"I'm very proud of you, Tally. You've done a wonderful thing for the family."

"Thanks Mama," I said. "I love you, and I'll see you sometime tomorrow."

"I love you too, Tally. Be safe, but hurry home."

"Goodnight." I ended the call and walked back into the kitchen.

Mrs. Carter was standing at the kitchen sink, looking out the window, and I knew she had been crying. She raised her hands to wipe her tears and then brought two glasses of iced tea to the table, sitting down across from me, still clutching the bracelet. She opened her hand and looked at me. "Can you still reach her with this?"

"No ma'am. Beanie is gone, but rest assured she knows how much you love her."

"I still can't believe this is happening," she said as she stared across the room. "Do these visions occur often to you?"

"I have seen the faces in the dark since I was a little girl, but the images have grown more vivid as I've gotten older."

"Have you helped others find peace?"

"Beanie is the first. Until she came to me, I really didn't know what my visions meant or what I was supposed to do with them. But now, with her help, I know."

"You have been given quite a gift."

"I just hope I can do what is necessary to help them."

"You mentioned that Beanie wasn't the first woman killed by this man. How do you know?"

"I don't know for certain, but the first person to come to me was killed by someone who sounds too similar to the man Beanie described, to be a coincidence," I explained.

"Do you think you will be able to lead the authorities to him?"

"I will certainly try my best, and give them all the information that I can, but Joe's initial reaction to my skills seems to be pretty typical of law enforcement. Psychics or people with "gifts" aren't usually looked upon kindly by police."

"Well, I know you certainly made a believer of Joe today."

Darkness had fallen completely outside and I reached up to take my sunglasses off.

Mrs. Carter gasped when she saw my eyes. "I'm sorry, I didn't mean to be rude."

I chuckled softly. "I am very used to that reaction, Mrs. Carter. People's reactions no longer make me uncomfortable."

"Does the uniqueness of your eyes have anything to do with your gift?" she asked.

"I think so. When I was twelve I was struck by lightning, and since then the visions have come more clearly to me."

"Oh my goodness," she declared.

"It was just a glancing blow," I said, lifting the sleeve of my shirt to show her the scar on my arm. "The flash did make my eyes extremely sensitive to light, so I have to wear sunglasses to prevent getting headaches."

"You are a very interesting young woman, Tally. You and Beanie could have easily been good friends," she said, breaking out in tears again.

"She seemed like a great young woman," I said as I walked to the counter to retrieve a Kleenex for her.

"Beanie always thought she had the world by the horns, and there was nothing she couldn't accomplish," she said.

We spent several more minutes in comfortable silence before she wiped the last tears from her cheeks. "I assume Joe and the sheriff will be here soon to talk with us. Would you help me make some sandwiches for everyone?"

"I would love to," I said with a warm smile.

Shortly after we finished preparing the sandwiches, Joe entered the house followed by a very tall man he introduced as Bill Thorne, the Sheriff of Shelby County. Another gentleman arrived a few minutes later. Introduced as Tommy Smythe, a homicide detective with Jefferson County, he nodded and took a seat. Once settled around the small kitchen table, Hope brought out a platter of sandwiches, and glasses of iced tea.

"Thank you, ma'am," both the sheriff and detective said.

"I know this is a terribly troubling time for you right now, Mrs. Carter, but we need to get all the information we can about your daughter," Bill said.

"I understand," Hope answered.

Bill turned his bright blue eyes to me. "Joe here tells me you have quite a talent, young lady."

I was impressed that he didn't flinch or drop his gaze when I looked him in the eyes. "I don't know about talent, but I answered a call from a distressed young woman." I went on to explain my vision of Beanie and Lisa, and how similar I thought the two murders appeared.

"That's a very interesting theory," Tommy said. "Any other information you can give us about this man?"

I shared with them everything I could remember from my conversations with both women, and they took detailed notes as I spoke.

"It certainly seems there may be a connection, and I may have enough information now to ask the Feds for assistance," Bill stated to both Joe and Hope. Then he turned back to me. "There is a press conference scheduled in an hour. I want to assure you that your identity won't be released, but I would like to know how to contact you if we have further questions."

I gave both men my address and phone number, and took a business card from each of them in case I learned more information that may be of value to them. I had no idea what would happen next with Beanie moving on, but maybe Lisa would be able to provide more information.

When Joe finally stood up to leave with the other men, it was nearly ten. "I can't thank you enough for what you have done for our family," he said to me. "Is there anything I can do for you? Do you need a room or gas money?"

"She is staying here with me tonight, Joe. I will feed her good before she heads for home in the morning," Hope said.

"Very good, is there anything I can do for you?"

"I guess I will need to begin making funeral arrangements," Hope said with a deep sigh.

Joe flinched. "Go ahead and make a contact, but I don't know when her body will be released. It may take a few more days before all the evidence is collected."

"Do they have to do an autopsy?"

"Yes, it's state law due to her being murdered, but I promise you the medical examiner will make this a top priority."

"My poor little girl," Hope said, tears filling her eyes.

I reached over to take her hand. "She was very happy to be moving on, so I don't think she will mind a few more days before her body is put to rest," I said, not knowing what else I could say to provide comfort to the sweet woman.

The smile Joe gave me issued all the thanks he could muster as he had no clue how to comfort his sister either. "I'm only a phone call away," he said and left the house.

"I don't know about you, Tally, but I am exhausted. Let's get you set up in the guest room and get some sleep."

"I'll go get my bag and be right back," I said.

"Lock the door behind you when you come in, and come on up the stairs. I'll get some towels ready for you."

"Yes ma'am," I called from the front door.

When I climbed the steps, Hope was standing outside a bedroom door clutching a set of towels as she stared into the room. I approached slowly and looked into the room. It was obvious that this had been Beanie's room.

"I can't believe she's gone."

I hugged Hope and whispered in her ear. "She will never be gone from your heart."

"I know that's true," she said as she hugged me back.

Later, after I had showered and settled into the comfortable bed in the guest room, I lay awake listening to the sounds of the night. My mind and body were totally exhausted from the day's events, but I had trouble drifting off to sleep. A soft wind came up, bringing a gentle rain, and I was finally lulled to sleep. I was glad the faces did not appear in the darkness of sleep, and my body rested for the night.

The next morning I awoke to the smell of bacon. I dressed and packed my small bag for the journey home before walking down the stairs to the kitchen. I slipped on my sunglasses, protecting my eyes from the sunlight flowing through the kitchen windows. "Good morning."

"Good morning. I hope you slept well."

"Yes ma'am, I did, thank you." It was obvious from the dark circles beneath her eyes that Hope had not slept much. Given the shock she had received the previous day that was to be expected.

"Is there anything I can help with?"

"You can drop the toast, and pour us some juice," Hope said.

"Yes ma'am," I said and went to work.

"How long will it take you to drive home?"

"About four hours depending on traffic."

"That is not too awful bad. Will you at least take some money for gas?"

"That I can do," I said and saw relief cross her face.

"Thank you," she said as she placed two plates of food on the table. "Let me get the toast and we'll be good to go."

After breakfast, Hope walked me to the door and slipped sixty dollars in my hand. "I hope if you come through this way again you will stop in for a visit."

"I would like that," I said as I hugged her good-bye.

Hope stood on the porch watching as I walked to my car. She waved and watched until my car disappeared from view just like my mama had done, and probably as she had done many times with Beanie. My heart filled with sorrow for her loss, but also with joy for Beanie finding the peace she deserved.

I quickly found my way back to the interstate and headed for home. Rain clouds were forming off to the south, and I silently prayed that I would make it home before the storm broke. I had learned that whenever an electrical storm was near, I almost certainly would have a vision. I did not want to be driving down the interstate at high speeds if that was going to happen. My body always began to vibrate with the buzz of electricity before it happened, but I would prefer to be someplace sheltered from the storm.

Twenty minutes later, a flash of lightning in the distance got my attention, so I pulled off the next exit to wait out the approaching storm. I located a rest area, and parked in an open spot, just as raindrops began to pelt the windshield. I reclined the seat to wait for the vision that was sure to come.

✝

At the FBI office in northern Virginia, an agent knocked on a door and walked into the office of Blair Cooper. "Hey Spooky, you need to take a look at this report," the young man said as he walked toward her desk.

"Forbes, how many times do I have to tell you to NOT call me that?" she declared.

"I'm sorry, Blair, the name just fits you so well, and your father will always be Coop, so what else is there to call you?" he asked jokingly.

"Blair would do fine for starters, or Special Agent Cooper would work too," she said with a stern look of her deep green eyes.

"Okay, Blair, like I said, I think you might want to take a look at this report we just received from Alabama," he said as he handed her several pages of paper.

There was never any doubt in her mind that she would follow in her father's footsteps and join the FBI after college. After all, Thomas Cooper was a legend with the Bureau. He had retired two years ago, but she'd had the good fortune of working missing persons with him for three years and he had taught her more than any instructor at the academy could. He would never admit to using the services of a psychic to any of his co-workers, but on numerous occasions tips and leads on some of his cases came about after a conversation with an elderly woman in Rhode Island.

She had blundered one day in front of several other agents by suggesting the use of a local psychic. Blair was instantly ridiculed by her cohorts and given the nickname "Spooky" for her belief in their talents. Never mind the fact that she was able to break the case that had stymied them for weeks and brought a traumatized, but alive, victim home. She had received a call from her father's contact that had led to the break, but unfortunately, the woman died in a car crash a year later, so "Spooky" had to rely on plain old investigative techniques.

She ignored the continued jabbering of the young agent and immersed herself in the report. The Joint Task Force of Jefferson and Shelby County, Alabama, was requesting the FBI's assistance in a case they believed was a serial killer who had crossed state lines, making it a federal crime. She skimmed down the report until she read the witness statement of one Tally Rainwater, from north Georgia, who claimed to have visions of the dead girl, which had led investigators to discover her missing body. This psychic also claimed the same man who killed this young woman had killed another woman years ago in Bogalusa, Louisiana.

She entered Tally's name into the system and the report came back clean. Apparently, this young woman had never been in any trouble, nor had she been involved in any other cases. Intrigued by the woman's story, she read over the information she could find on the psychic. Maybe she should take a trip down south to interview this young lady. An idea began to form in her head. She would do some legwork on missing persons and other cold murder cases of women that might be similar in nature. Then she would put together a profile of faces. Maybe, just maybe, one of them would be one of the faces in the shadows she claimed to see.

It could all be a hoax, but it could also be the beginning of a psychic career for a very talented young woman. She would start some research, and then run the idea up the ladder to see if she could get approval to travel to Georgia.

As she began her search in the database, she was alarmed at the number of potential victims the computer began to generate. She trimmed her search parameters down to the last ten years and limited the age range of victims to between fifteen and twenty-five years old. She released a sigh of relief when the numbers were reduced by two-thirds. Still, twenty possible victims would be a lot to investigate. She decided to start with the woman in Bogalusa, which would give her the opportunity to open the door with Ms. Rainwater. Her printer lurched to life and began printing off reports and profiles.

Spooky Cooper was on a mission, she thought to herself as she watched a ream of paper quickly disappear. She brushed her unruly red hair away from her face as she delved into the reports.

Chapter Six

Electricity crackled through the air as the hairs on my arms rose to attention and I felt the familiar vibrations running through my body. The darkness began to form behind my eyes, and faces started to appear in the shadows.

Lisa was the first to appear. "You did fine by Loren," she said. "She was happy to finally move on, even though it hurt to see her mother's sadness."

"I'm happy she was able to find her peace."

"Me too, and I want to let you know you are on the right track. The man who killed her is the same one who killed me."

"What can I do to help catch him?"

"I don't know the answer to that just yet, but I have started to talk with others here to find out if there are more of us that he murdered. I have found two so far."

"Can they provide any other information?"

"They are just finding their voice in this world, so be patient," Lisa said. "There is another on your side who will come to your aid soon that can help catch him. That much I do know."

"Who," I asked, curious to know more.

"I don't know for sure, but I get a name "Spooky.""

"Spooky?" I asked even more curious. "I wonder what that's all about."

"I think you will find out soon enough," Lisa said.

A clap of thunder just above my car made me jump in fear. When I closed my eyes again, something strange was happening. I felt like I was looking through someone else's eyes, and it was a very evil person.

A young girl in her late teens was cowering in a corner. A halo of golden curls surrounded her tear-streaked face. The look in her bright blue eyes was pure terror, as the person approached her. *Please don't hurt me anymore mister*, the young girl pleaded as she drew her legs up under her.

The man swung out with a board and struck the girl on the left arm. I could almost feel the breaking of the bones. *Shut up you little bitch*, he growled.

Stop it, you bastard! I screamed in my mind, and his arm froze in midstrike. The man looked around the room, searching for the source of the voice he had heard so clearly.

Don't hurt her anymore, I yelled at him.

He realized the voice was coming from within his head. *Go to hell*, he said, and continued beating the defenseless girl. I saw a strike to the top of her head and my own forehead rang with pain.

The vision went blank. I lurched up in my seat, a fine patina of sweat coated my skin and my heart pounded in my chest. The windshield wipers worked furiously against the glass and I concentrated on their motion until I could get my body under control. The rain still came down in buckets, but it appeared the lightning had passed through quickly. I felt filthy, tainted from being in the vile man's head, and needed to wash myself clean of his presence. I stepped out of the car and walked to the middle of the vacant parking lot. I lifted my arms into the air and let the cool, cleansing rainwater pour down my body. I was soaked and chilled to the bone before I felt clean again. The storm was almost finished as I climbed behind the wheel and started the engine. I turned the heat on full blast and pulled back onto the interstate.

Twenty minutes later, I felt the chill leave my body like a soft breeze, and I turned on to the small county road that would lead me on the final leg home.

My clothes were still soaking wet as I pulled into our yard and climbed from the car. Mama heard my approach and met me on the front porch, wrapping me in her warm arms.

"Oh Tally, I'm so glad to have you home," she said as she stroked down my wet hair. "I was so worried something bad would happen to you."

"It's good to be home too. The last two days have been exhausting," I murmured, breathing into her neck.

"Come inside, get out of those wet clothes, and get yourself warmed up. I'll fix us something to eat," she said.

I lifted my face to hers, watching as my mama's eyes grew wide. "What is this?" she asked, touching my hair softly with her fingertips.

"What are you talking about?"

"This white streak in your hair."

"What white streak in my hair? My hair is black just like it always has been."

"Come look," she said and took me by the hand to a mirror so I could see my reflection.

I gasped in surprise as I looked at my face. Above my left eye was a patch of hair that had turned pure white. When I realized it was the same area as where the killer had struck the young woman in my vision my knees went weak. Mama caught me under the arms before I fell to the ground and guided me to a chair.

When she was certain I was safely in the chair, she said, "Let me get a towel and a blanket, then I we'll get you out of these wet clothes." She left the room, returning with supplies moments later and began helping me out of my wet clothes. Exhaustion suddenly overtook my body and the last I remembered was a warm blanket wrapping around me as she stretched me out on the couch.

My body shivered with the bone-deep chill as I rapidly descended into the darkness. I squeezed my eyes closed praying that my next vision was not through his eyes, showing the evil he was doing to the terrified young woman. I was relieved when Lisa emerged from the shadows and placed a calming hand on my cheek.

You saw him didn't you?

I didn't exactly see him, but I saw through his eyes.

That cannot be good. That means you linked with him somehow. You will have to find him or his vileness will drive you crazy.

How can I do that?

You will have to discipline yourself, take advantage of every opportunity you have to ride within him to gain information of who and where he is, Lisa said.

I hate even the thought of being back in his mind. It's such an evil place.

But now that it is started, you must see it done.

Can I seek him out, or is he in control?

I cannot answer that for you. I have no idea what your limitations are. Try to contact him and see if it works, but Tally you must be prepared for what you might see, she warned. Let your body rest and be nourished before you try. His spirit is strong, and his negative energy will drain you quickly if you aren't prepared.

I will try my best. I'll rest and then eat a hearty meal when I wake.

Stay strong, Tally, Lisa said and faded back into the darkness. I slept for three hours before I began to stir.

When I woke, Mama was sitting in the recliner next to me watching over her baby girl. "There you are," she whispered when my eyes finally opened. "I was starting to worry."

"I'm okay. I just had an exhausting trip. I needed that nap and now some food."

"I have a roast, vegetables, and hot biscuits waiting on you. Do you want to take a quick shower?"

"That's not a bad idea."

That night I ate as I hadn't eaten in ages. Mama smiled at the voraciousness of my appetite. "I'm glad to see you appreciate my cooking," she said as she passed the bowl of vegetables to me.

"There is nothing in this world like your home cooking, Mama."

"I hate I didn't make a dessert now."

"This will be plenty."

After we had cleaned up the kitchen, we sat at the table. "Do you want to tell me about your experience?"

"The trip to Birmingham went better than I expected. I was able to accomplish my task and help a family receive some closure."

"I hope they appreciated your efforts and treated you kindly."

"Oh yes, they treated me well." I wanted to tell her about the vision I had on my return home. "There's something else I need to share with you, Mama."

"Go ahead, honey."

"I got caught in a bad storm on the way back this morning. That wasn't the worst, though."

She waited patiently for me to continue. I chose my words carefully.

"I think I am involved in something that is very bad. There is an evil man who is killing young women, and somehow I think I have become psychically linked with him."

"What do you mean by that?"

"Well, I knew enough to pull over prior to the thunderstorm arriving, and when I did I had a vision, but this one was totally different."

"How was it different?"

I really hadn't shared much about my visions with my mama, and she had always allowed me to keep them private, never pried to find out information.

"Usually I see faces in the shadows of my mind, although some spirits come in full-body form. The vision I had of this murderer was through his eyes, and it was horrible. He was torturing another young woman, beating her with a board."

"That could explain your new hair coloring, I guess," she said.

"Yes, I'm afraid so. Right before I blanked out of the vision, he struck the woman on the head, in the same spot that has turned white on me."

"This all sounds very dangerous for you."

"I've got to find a way to stop him," I said. "I started this and I can't stop now, even if I wanted to."

"Do you think he knows about you?"

"He knows that I have been in his head, and he's none too happy with it, but he's going to have to deal with it."

"I really don't like the sound of this. Is there no way you can get out of his head?"

"I don't think so. Not until he is caught and punished."

"You don't think there is any way he can find out where you live do you?"

"I certainly hope not, Mama. He is a bad, bad man."

"Oh Tally, what are we going to do?"

"I'm going to do everything I can to help the authorities catch him," I said. My pronouncement didn't seem to bring Mama much comfort.

She got up from the table and locked the front door. Then she walked around to check all of the windows. "Do you think we need to buy a gun?"

I couldn't help but chuckle at her response. "I would be afraid we would end up shooting ourselves with it, Mama, but if it will make you sleep better then go for it."

"I think I'll talk it over with Laura and get her advice; she will know what to do," she said.

"That's a good idea," I said, yawning. "If you don't mind, I think I'm going to head off to bed early. I'm still tired."

"Okay, honey, sleep well."

"I love you, Mama."

"I love you too, Tally."

"Goodnight then."

"Goodnight."

I walked into my bathroom and looked at the reflection staring back at me from the mirror. The patch of white hair was certainly going to take some getting used to I thought as I brushed my teeth. I also hoped I wouldn't have too many more occasions that would cause physical trauma to my body as I followed the path my gift was taking me.

When I finally crawled into bed, I lay and listened to the peaceful sound of the night surrounding me. The soft whirring of the ceiling fan blew a cool breeze against my skin as I listened to the chorus of crickets through the partially opened window. The comforting sounds of home helped me relax as I felt my body sink into the bed. In the distance, I heard the old barn owl hooting, and I began to drift off to sleep.

My body shuddered with revulsion and I felt a wave of nausea pass through me as my mind searched through the darkness, looking for the evil man. I arrived in his mind with a bone-jarring jolt, and I opened my eyes to see through his. He was on the move. He was driving a vehicle and it was dark where he was. I tried to steady my eyes out of the window to see if I could catch a road sign or some other marker to determine where he was located. I was quiet as a church mouse, unwilling to let him know I was riding along with him in the dark of the night. I had no idea if he could sense my presence, but he began rubbing his head like someone with a migraine. It pleased me to no end to think I was causing him at least a bit of discomfort.

I saw the glow of a green road sign up ahead and strained my focus to read it: Picayune 10 miles. So, at least I knew he was in Mississippi. Was he just traveling or was this where his latest victim was?

The killer answered my question when he slowed down and turned onto a small trail that led into the woods. He pulled up next to a large barn-type building and turned the vehicle off. The moon was shining brightly in the sky and the ground had patches of white. I immediately thought of snow, but knew there was no chance of snow this time of year. Upon closer inspection, I saw bits of cotton floating in the air. This must be part of a cotton farm, I surmised. I was even more surprised when he stopped at the door and looked back at his vehicle. He was no longer in a white van. He now drove a red pickup truck with a camper shell attached to the back. I couldn't tell for sure, but it looked like a Ford.

Turning back to the door, he used a key to remove a padlock. The door creaked and squealed as he slid it open. The sound was terrifying in the dark. He flipped a switch to operate a flashlight, illuminating the wide-open space. There in the corner was the young woman, still chained, battered, bruised, and bloody. At first, I wasn't even sure it was the same person. I caught a glimpse of her face, swollen almost beyond recognition, when she looked up at him and begged, "Please just kill me. I can't take any more of this."

"You will take anything I give you," he growled and dropped a bag of cold fast food in front of her. He turned away to sit on a small stool several feet away. At first, her stubbornness prevented her from taking the food, but within minutes her survival instinct kicked in. She ripped open the grease-stained bag and began wolfing down the food. He glared at her with an evil grin. "See. What did I tell you?" he taunted her.

I so wanted to hurt this man. But aside from screaming in his head, I had no clue about what I could do and I wasn't keen on him knowing I was riding along with him. He allowed her to consume the meager meal under his watchful eye. He left the flashlight shining on her and stepped into the darkness to retrieve an object from a duffel bag. My eyes caught the flash of sharp steel that gleamed in the dim light as he pulled out a cane knife.

Oh dear Lord, he's going to cut her, I thought. My anger rose like bile in my throat, and I screamed out at him without thinking. "She's just a little girl, you bastard."

He stopped dead in his tracks and grabbed the sides of his head with both hands. "I see you are back, bitch. You are just in time to watch, since you like it so much," he snarled as his feet lurched toward the cowering young woman.

"Who are you talking to?" the young woman asked, praying someone had come to rescue her.

"No one," he growled. "Wish granted," he said. With one swift movement of the sharp knife, he sliced open her throat like a ripe melon.

Arterial spray coated the walls surrounding the young woman before I could squeeze my eyes shut against the horror. My body shot up straight in my bed and my eyes flew open. Dear God, I had just witnessed a murder. My body was on the verge of going into shock. I knew I had to do something, but what could I do? I had already failed the young blond girl. My bag was sitting in the corner of my bedroom and the moonlight was shining on it eerily.

A flash of Joe's business card crossed my mind's eye, and I climbed from the bed. I still had Mama's cell phone in the bag. I dug the two items out in the dark and crept quietly out of the house. On the front porch I sat on the wooden swing. The air was cool from the storm as I looked at the business card I held in my hand. If Joe didn't already think I was dangerously insane, surely he would after I called him to say I had just witnessed a murder in Mississippi. Joe was the only person I could think of to call for help. With his law enforcement connections, maybe he could do something if only I could make him believe me.

A flash of green heat lightning in the distance caught my eye, and with a sigh I flipped open the phone and dialed Joe's number.

Three rings went unanswered. I looked down at my wrist to find it was two in the morning. I cringed as I heard Joe pick up on the fourth ring. "Hello," he growled.

"Joe, I'm sorry for calling so late. This is Tally Rainwater, and I didn't know who else to call."

I could hear Joe moving to sit up in bed and clicking on a light. "What's wrong? Are you all right?" he asked with genuine concern.

"Yes, I'm as okay as I can be, but *you* may think I'm completely crazy."

"Why Tally, what's happened?"

"He just killed another girl," I blurted out.

"He who?" Joe asked, confused.

"The man that killed Beanie," I said.

Silence crackled across the phone line for several long seconds.

"Explain to me how you know this."

"I can't explain how or why, but somehow I have become linked to him. Now when I have visions, I sometimes see through his eyes and can feel his thoughts."

"That is crazy," he exclaimed and then went silent.

I was afraid he would think exactly that.

"I'm sorry, Tally," he said in the long silence that followed his exclamation. "That wasn't the best choice of words I could have used. I didn't mean to imply you're crazy, it's just this linkage theory is...is just incredulous."

"Trust me, it's not a pleasant experience."

"I can't begin to imagine. Tell me what you saw."

"I know that he is in or near Picayune, Mississippi, and he has killed a young blond girl in her midteens. I saw him driving. He turned off the road just after passing a road sign that read Picayune, 10 miles."

"Are you certain of that?" Joe asked.

"Yes, very much so, Joe, I read it very clearly. I also know he's driving a red pickup truck with a camper shell on the back. I think it's a Ford. He also killed her inside some type of barn. There were fragments of cotton on the ground that looked like snow."

"That's a prime area for cotton farms," Joe said. "How did he kill her?"

I shuddered with the memory. "He cut her throat with a cane knife," I said.

"How do you know it was a cane knife and not a machete?" he asked.

"Mama and I drove through Louisiana one summer when they were harvesting cane, and the workers in the field were using the same straight-bladed knife to cut the cane."

I could hear him scribbling notes as we talked.

"Joe, there is one more thing," I said, my voice cracking with emotion.

"What?"

"He knows about me," I said.

"What do you mean? Does he know your name or who you are?"

"Not that I am aware of, but he knows I'm in his head, and he can hear me."

More silence. Then Joe spoke again.

"I need you to come back here Tally," he said.

"Why?"

"Before I left the office tonight a fax came across that reported a young girl in Picayune who had been abducted two days ago."

My mind went blank. I held my breath and remained silent. I did not expect confirmation this fast.

"Tally, are you there?"

"Yes, yes, Joe, I'm sorry, it's all such a shock."

"I will send a state trooper for you. Will you come?"

"Do I have any choice?"

"Of course you do, but I would feel a lot better if I knew you were safe until this bastard gets caught."

"Do you think I'm in danger?"

"If he finds out who you are, you can bet he will come after you. I don't mean to scare you, but this killer we are dealing with is an evil man. I know you know that."

"Yes I do. Let me wake my mama and let her know what is going on, and I'll pack a bag."

"Is there someone she can stay with until all this is done?" he asked.

Until then I hadn't contemplated that he might come into our home; that both Mama and I would be in danger. Joe sensed my fear through the silence.

"I think she is still safe, but a bit of caution never hurts," he warned.

"Yes, yes I will take care of that."

I gave Joe the address. "I will have an Alabama State Trooper there within two hours, so be ready."

"I will Joe. Thanks for believing me," I said.

"You are a very special young woman," he said. "I would have never believed what you are capable of if I hadn't seen what you had done with Beanie."

"Thank you, Joe."

"I will see you soon, Tally."

"Good-bye," I said and closed the phone.

I saw the light come on in my mama's room. I took a few deep breaths and walked back into the house. I went down to her room and knocked on her door.

"What's wrong, Tally?" she asked when I entered her room. "You are white as a sheet."

"He killed her, Mama," I said, my voice quivering with emotion. "I saw him do it."

"Oh Tally," she cried and wrapped me in her arms.

I told her what I been forced to witness.

"I'm sorry you saw that, baby."

"I called Joe in Alabama, and he is sending a car for me. He wants me there to help them catch him. He also wants you to go stay with someone for a while. Can you stay with Laura?"

"I'm sure I can. Are we in danger?"

"Not as long as he doesn't know who I am, Mama, but I don't want to take any unnecessary chances."

"Oh my baby girl, please be careful. I know you feel like you have to do this, but please be careful."

"I will, Mama. I'm pretty sure Joe will keep me under close surveillance while I'm there."

"Keep my cell phone, and let me know what is going on. Let's go get you packed up."

I hugged her tight. "I love you, Mama."

"I love you too, Tally."

†

Joe hung up the phone and went to find his phone book. His first call was to the East Alabama State Trooper's Headquarters. The sergeant he spoke to promised he would have Tally in Birmingham before the sun was up.

61

He had to call the office to get one of the detectives to pull the fax they had received earlier in the day to get the next number he needed. Two calls later, he woke the detective on the case to tell him an incredible story. He ended the conversation with a promise to have Tally in Picayune before the day's end.

Chapter Seven

Blair reported to the Office of the Director early the next morning. "Good morning, Blair. I've looked over your proposal," Director Rick Jordan said. "I think you might be onto something here."

"So, I have approval to go to Georgia?" she asked with excitement.

"No, not Georgia. I have you booked on the next flight to Jackson, Mississippi."

"Why Jackson?"

"There has been another murder and this psychic saw it happen."

"What?"

"There was a young woman abducted in Picayune, Mississippi, and this woman claims she saw it happen through the killer's eyes."

"This just gets weirder and weirder."

"Three other agents will meet you in Picayune, but this is your case to lead. Bring him in," the director said as he handed her a plane ticket.

Every agent kept a ready bag in his locker, and she rushed to get hers as she asked the secretary to schedule a car to take her to the airport. She retrieved her bag and checked her weapon, adding several extra clips to her bag while she waited for the car to come around.

†

I hugged Mama one last time and walked out of our home. "Call me tonight," Mama said from the porch as I slipped into the front seat of the state trooper's car.

"Settle back and try to get some rest, ma'am," the young trooper said. "I don't know what is going on, but for you to be summoned like this it must be important. I will have you in Birmingham before you know it."

"Thanks, I think I will," I said as I reclined the seat and stretched out. There was absolutely no interest in retelling the horrific events I had experienced tonight. I had a feeling I would be reciting the events many times in the hours to come, so a break from the trooper's curiosity was very much welcomed.

Relief washed through me as my mind drifted off to sleep. No faces in the shadows appeared. My restless spirits must have sensed I needed rest after the turmoil of the night and I slept deeply with no dreams.

†

Joe was working on his second pot of coffee when he got word from the front desk that Tally had arrived. "I wish we had time to welcome you properly, but we need to grab some breakfast and hit the road again," he said when she walked in.

"That's okay, sir, the sooner we get started the better," I said.

"Will you do a favor and just call me Joe, like everyone else?"

I smiled and nodded my head.

64

"Do you want a cup of coffee?"

"I think I'll wait until we stop for breakfast. I hear station coffee can be lethal," I teased.

"That's probably a wise decision," he said with a grin. "Let me grab my bag and we'll be on our way."

†

Blair settled into her first-class seat with a glass of orange juice and opened her file. If this was the same killer, he was cycling much faster than anyone had expected. He was less than a week between victims, which led her to believe he had been killing for longer than anyone had expected. The latest addition to her file was the young woman from Picayune. Brianna Bishop was seventeen. She was abducted leaving the mall two nights ago from her part-time job at a retail store. Her purse and cell phone found on the top of her car alerted security to the event.

Such a waste of a young life, she thought as she read through the initial report. When she turned the page, she saw the addendum to the report from early this morning. Apparently Tally, the psychic, had witnessed the murder of the young woman in one of her visions and provided police with good detail. She read further into the report and thought the information would be enough to help the authorities find her body, if the killer hadn't taken the time to conceal it from detection.

Blair doubted he would take the time since his victim was already in a discreet location. He did not appear to be the type of killer that wanted media exposure to get his jollies. He killed for the pure pleasure of the kill. He would make for some interesting psychology once captured. She had no doubt they would track him down, but doubted they would take him alive. Suicide by cop seemed to be popular with this type of serial. She also knew that he was a hunter, and finding him could prove difficult.

†

Joe and I had stopped at Waffle House for breakfast. When we finished eating and got back into the car, he said, "We're making excellent time and I think we should be in Picayune by lunch. Have you remembered anything else?"

"Nothing I haven't already shared with you," I said. "Have you ever had a killer like this?"

"A serial killer, no, this is my first exposure. We've had several multiple murders, but those have generally been domestic, a spouse killing his family or a botched burglary. I've never been involved with a stranger preying on innocent young women."

"I bet you have seen a lot of horrific things in your career."

"More than I care to admit sometimes, but that's the life of law enforcement," he said. "We see terrible things and very little positive. It can wear on the human psyche after a while."

I let the discussion digest as we traveled down the interstate.

I felt his eyes on me as he drove.

"I meant to ask you earlier, what happened to your hair?"

My hand instinctively went to the white patch. "When I was driving home yesterday, I pulled over during a thunderstorm. That is when I first realized I was a rider in the man's brain. He was torturing a young girl, beating her with a board," I said as the memory flashed in front of my eyes. I felt myself flinch. "The last blow I saw struck her in the head, and when I was able to break free of his mind my hair had turned white in that same spot. I didn't realize it had happened until I made it home."

"There was a storm at your place last night too, wasn't there?"

"Yes, there was. My gift seems to be most active during times of turbulent weather."

"The forecast for tonight is for storms in the late afternoon or early evening," he said.

"What would help you most if I can make contact with him?"

"A name and address would be great," Joe said with a smirk.

"If only it could be that easy."

"I think you have done a great job so far of being observant of his surroundings. Keep trying to discover his location. If you could get more information on his appearance, and possible age, that would be a help."

Joe reached into a pocket and pulled out a small notepad and ink pen. "Write down everything that you know so far to keep it fresh, and when you make contact again add to your notes. I've found that really helps me to piece cases together."

I began making notes and was surprised to find I had filled several pages of the notepad. Joe was right—the more I wrote, the more information I remembered.

"The FBI will be joining us in Picayune," he said. "They can be assholes sometimes, but don't allow them to make you doubt your abilities, Tally. You have a true and accurate gift."

"Thanks Joe. In an odd way, it's kind of a relief to finally know what I am supposed to do with my gift. I just hope there will be some positive outcomes from it, and they won't all end horribly."

"Well, if we can capture this man that will be very positive. There's no telling how many lives you will have saved, Tally. These types of killers don't quit killing until they are dead or captured."

I noticed the landscape had begun to change. The small towns grew farther apart and fields filled with crops as far as the eye could see.

"Soybeans, it looks like," Joe said, noticing my attention. "They grow a lot of cotton and soybeans in this area. We are getting close, and should be there soon."

†

Blair dropped a pair of shades over her eyes as she stepped out of the airport terminal into the bright sun. She still had quite a drive ahead of her, so she located her rental and hit the road. She replayed the facts of the case in her head as she drove to help pass the time and to ingrain the information into her brain. She was very interested in meeting Tally Rainwater and hoped the young woman was as talented as she appeared. In just a few short days, she had provided more information on the killer than trained law enforcement officers had gathered in a much longer time.

At a stoplight, she pulled open the file folder and removed a photograph of Tally. Two different colored eyes stared back at her. She felt her body shudder with a chill running down her spine. Startled by her reaction, Blair remained curious as to why she reacted so strangely. She had certainly seen some bizarre things over her years at the Bureau, but something about what the woman's strange eyes could see made her uneasy.

†

Joe's directional instinct took him directly to the police station.

"Is Detective Johnson in the house?" he asked after introducing himself to the desk sergeant.

"No sir, he is out at a crime scene, but he left a message to send you to the scene as soon as you got here. Here's a map to the location."

"Thank you, son," he said, taking the paper from the young man. Joe had a bad feeling growling in his gut. He suspected they had located the body of the missing girl.

Joe drove out to the location. When he turned off the road and the barn came in sight, Tally gasped.

"Are you okay?"

"Yes, I'm just surprised at how accurate the vision was. It's exactly as I saw it through his eyes."

"Why don't you stay here, and let me go in first," he suggested.

I appreciated the fact Joe was trying to spare me the gruesome details, but couldn't resist reminding him that I witnessed the death. "Okay, Joe, but remember I already know what happened."

"Crime scenes can be pretty gory. I also need to see if Johnson would mind if you take a look at the crime scene."

"I'll wait right here," I promised.

"Thanks Tally."

Joe walked inside the barn and conversations stopped as people turned to look at him. "Joe Bryant from Birmingham PD," he said.

A short stocky man approached him and held out his hand. "Dan Johnson," he said. "Thanks for coming."

"It's personal," Joe said. "This bastard killed my only niece."

"I'm sorry to hear that," Johnson said.

"I brought Tally Rainwater with me."

"Do you really believe in her abilities?" Johnson asked.

"She located my niece, and she obviously gave you enough information to find this young lady," Joe said.

"Yeah, we found her about two hours ago. It took some convincing to persuade my chief to follow her leads, but he finally agreed."

Joe looked past him and saw a white sheet covering what he assumed was the body. "How bad is it?"

"She didn't die easy," Johnson said. "It's obvious she took quite a lot of abuse before she died."

"How far along are you on processing the scene?"

"We've got a good start, but we're waiting on the ME to pronounce and view before she can be removed. She won't stay preserved well for long in this heat, so we covered her."

"That was a good idea," Joe said. "Are there any personal belongings that have already been processed?"

"She had minimal clothing and jewelry. A watch, necklace, and her high school class ring. Why?"

"Tally seems to get energy from the victim's items that feed her visions. I would like for her to try to see if she can pick up anything else, if you don't mind."

Johnson waved over one of the techs. "Bring us the ring," he said. "Do you want to take this out to her?"

"Actually, I would like for her to see the scene if possible."

"I don't know if that would be a good idea. I mean, look at this place, man, there's blood everywhere," Johnson said.

"She witnessed the murder remember," Joe said. "She's a really courageous young woman who has helped out greatly so far."

A young man in a dark suit walked over to where they were talking. "I'm Special Agent Thomas," he said, introducing himself to Joe. "Did the psychic agree to come with you?"

"Joe Bryant, and yes, Ms. Rainwater is in my car. We were just discussing allowing her to view the scene."

"At this point, what can it hurt?"

"Let me go talk with her for a minute," Joe said and left the barn carrying the ring.

✝

I opened the door and stepped out of the car when I saw Joe emerge from the barn. The humidity draped over my body like a shroud as the heat welcomed me.

"Are you really sure you want to see this? The body is covered, but it's still a gruesome scene."

"Yes. Joe, do you think they will allow just you, and me to go in for a few minutes?"

"I'm pretty sure the local detective will insist on remaining inside to ensure the scene is not compromised."

"I just don't think I will be able to concentrate with all those people in there."

"I'll see what I can do. I brought this for you to take a look at," he said as he handed me the ring. "I'll be right back."

I studied the ring as he disappeared inside the barn. A small green stone was set in the center, and the ring still hummed with energy as it rested in the palm of my hand. My concentration was broken when the door swung open and men started walking out to their vehicles.

I looked up to see more than one set of eyes watching me as I leaned back against the car.

Joe stepped outside and waved me forward. He stopped me at the door. "Are you sure you're ready for this?"

I nodded my head and followed him inside the barn. Bright lights set up to aid in the discovery process made my eyes ache. "Will you turn some of the lights off?"

"Sure I will. Tally, this is Detective Johnson."

I held out my hand and he took it in his large paw. "Nice to meet you, sir," I said.

"Likewise, and thanks for coming down to offer your assistance," he said. "You have been right on target so far."

"Thanks," I said, feeling immediate relief when Joe shut down some of the lights. I stepped further into the barn and the smell of blood and death filled the air. I covered my nose with my hand with hopes of blocking some of the smell, to no avail. I saw the white tarp covering what I supposed was the body and the vision returned of the young woman cowering in the corner, her wrists secured to a support beam.

"Did you find a stool?" I asked after a brief inspection. "He sat on a small three-legged stool and verbally taunted her."

Joe looked at Detective Johnson, who shook his head. "I will have the barn searched again when we are done here."

I held the ring tightly in my palm as I approached the tarp. The warmth continued to grow as I felt the faint buzzing in my head. "The stool is still here somewhere," I said. "I can feel it."

I stopped outside the dark ring of blood that had soaked into the dirt and squatted close to the ground. The smell of blood was strong. A draft gently moved the tarp to reveal her right hand. "He took something from her, didn't he?"

"We think so, but we cannot confirm with the family yet," Johnson said.

I could see the young woman as she had been before she died. "She wore a thin gold band on her right thumb," I said. "Did you find it?"

Johnson looked down to the list of personal possessions, collected and inventoried, but there was no gold band listed.

"Did her watch stop at 12:55?" I asked.

Johnson turned the watch toward him inside the plastic evidence bag. His jaw dropped when he looked at the face. The time was precise.

"She's missing an earring too, a diamond stud from her left ear."

Johnson turned deathly white. He had noted the missing stud during his initial inspection. "How do you know all this?"

"I can see her. Her spirit is still with us yet," I said. "You need to find the stool. He left part of himself on it."

"What do you mean?" Joe asked.

"I don't know, but I feel it is very important to find it."

Suddenly out of the dark shadows, I could hear his wicked laugh ringing in my ears. I threw my hands up to cover them, trying to block the sound. I got up onto my feet and rushed from the barn with Joe and Johnson right behind me.

"Tally, are you okay?" Joe asked.

"I could hear him laughing, and I couldn't take any more of it," I said.

"I can understand that," Joe said.

I reached out to hand the ring back to Detective Johnson. "She's gone from here now."

He took the ring and stared at me in disbelief. I was beginning to get used to the look. I turned and started walking toward Joe's car. I heard a distinctive female voice calling my name. I didn't remember seeing another female on the scene, so I turned toward the voice. It was my turn to stare in disbelief as I looked into the face of the little red haired, green-eyed girl from my childhood dreams, and then promptly fainted.

Chapter Eight

Joe lurched forward to catch Tally before she hit the ground. With Johnson's help, he placed her across his backseat. "Anybody got some bottled water?" he called out. He looked at the red-haired woman. "Who the hell are you?"

"I am Special Agent in Charge Blair Cooper," she said, "and you?"

"Detective Joe Bryant, Birmingham PD. Johnson here's the local," Joe said, nodding toward the shorter man.

"Is this Ms. Rainwater?" she asked.

"Yes it is," Joe said as Blair watched him trying to revive the young woman. Someone handed him a cold bottle of water. He drenched a handkerchief with it and caressed Tally's face. Her eyes began to flutter. Her shades had fallen off when she fainted, and when her eyes cracked open a sharp pain raced to her brain, causing her to cry out.

"My glasses please," Tally said weakly as her hand protectively covered her eyes. "What happened?"

"You took one look at the FBI agent here and did a swan dive," Joe teased.

Tally's cheeks felt flushed. "Sorry, I guess I got too warm in there."

"No problem," the agent said with a warm tone to her voice. "I think my car is the coolest. Why don't you come with me to cool down?"

Tally nodded her head and was walking toward the dark SUV when one of the techs came bolting out the barn door.

"Detective, you need to see this," he said. Joe and Johnson both turned and walked back into the barn.

†

Blair, torn between speaking with me and discovering what new evidence had been found, climbed inside the SUV and waited for the officer to help me inside. She cranked the vehicle and turned the air-conditioning to full blast. "It shouldn't be but just a minute or two before it cools off a bit more."

"Thanks, I feel better already," I said as the cool air blew into my face, tendrils of loose hair swirling around my head.

She handed me the bottle of water and I took a deep drink.

"That's good," I said as I lifted the cool bottle to my heated cheek. "The humidity is horrible this time of year."

"It's not much better in DC this year. We generally don't have heat like this, but it's been a brutally hot summer."

She had pulled her shades off when we sat inside her car and her green eyes shone like gemstones as she looked at me.

"They call you Spooky, don't they?"

Her head snapped backward. Her shock was apparent on her face when I asked the question.

"How would you even know to ask that?" she asked. "There are very few people at the Bureau who dare call me that," she warned.

"I'm sorry. I didn't mean to offend you."

"I'm not offended, but I am astounded by you. Yes, some call me Spooky, but I much prefer Blair or SA Cooper."

"Blair it is then," I said. "You may call me Tally."

"Fair enough," she answered. "Tell me though, how did you know?"

I smiled softly. "That's a conversation for a later time. Right now, I believe we have detectives and a murder victim to tend to."

"Have you cooled down enough?" she asked.

"Yes, I think I am fine now. Thanks."

"Are you okay to go back inside? I really need to get a look before they move the body."

"Very well," I said as I exited the car and followed the woman back to the barn door.

†

Joe and Johnson were talking with the techs. Johnson had asked the techs to search for the stool and one of them had uncovered it in a back stall, tossed on a small pile of raw cotton fibers. The tech was smiling.

"There's a bloody palm print, and I think at least a partial fingerprint, from what I can see," he said.

"Bag it carefully and let's get it processed as quickly as possible," Johnson ordered.

While the three male federal agents surveyed the crime scene around the body, I leaned against one of the support beams just inside the door and pulled out the notepad Joe had given me earlier and wrote down several words.

Blair turned her head briefly to look back at me and saw me furiously scribbling notes on the notepad. She turned and walked over to the corner where the body rested, hidden beneath a tarp.

The men from the coroner's office were prepared to transfer the victim to a body bag for transport to the morgue, but they knew she would want to see the body first. Blair stopped next to a young man and nodded. He reached down in slow motion and gently pulled the tarp off her body. "She took one hell of a beating," he whispered softly. "The killing blow of a cane knife nearly took her head off completely."

"Did we find the murder weapon?"

"Not yet."

"How do you know he used a cane knife?"

The young agent nodded his head toward me. "She saw it and described a cane knife to perfection."

Feeling her eyes on me I looked up to find Blair staring at me curiously. Then she looked back at the body.

Blair shook her head. The damage to the young woman's body was heinous, as if he took great pride in ruining the perfection of her young body. What could drive a total stranger to that level of hate, she wondered. Unfortunately, she knew there were many answers.

"Are you going to need much more time here?" Johnson asked.

She turned toward the door and saw the men from the coroner's office fidgeting. "Are the natives getting restless?"

"Yeah, something like that," he answered.

"Do you have accommodations for a war room for a combined task force?"

"It's not extremely high-tech, but we've got some space," Johnson asked.

"I don't see that we can do much more here, so why don't we go get set up at your place," she said.

"You'll get no complaints from me," Joe said as he took out a handkerchief and wiped the sweat dripping down his face.

"Y'all follow me then," Johnson said.

Blair gathered her troops, and they all loaded up in their vehicles and began a convoy back toward town.

†

Joe turned the air-conditioning on full blast and dropped the car into Drive before asking, "Are you doing okay, Tally?"

"Yeah, I am, Joe. Sorry for fainting on you earlier."

"You have nothing to apologize for, Tally. Was it really the heat?"

"No Joe, it wasn't. My body went into overload when Agent Cooper showed up."

"Why? I didn't think she was all that bad, even for a Fed," he teased.

"She's not bad," I answered.

"What was it then?"

"I was shocked to see her again."

"What do you mean again?"

"I've seen her before Joe, when I was twelve years old."

"What?"

"She came to me in a vision not long after my accident. I knew one day we would be meeting face-to-face. I just didn't expect it to be now."

"You never cease to amaze me, Tally," he said with a grin while shaking his head in disbelief.

"She might think me completely off my rocker if I tell her," I said.

"Give her a chance to form her own opinion on that. I would think someone with a nickname of Spooky would have a fairly open mind."

"Good point," I said and took a long drink from the bottle of water. "How do you know about her nickname?"

"I've studied their case files before. Blair and her father, Thomas, are known for working with psychics to help them solve crimes," he explained. "And, by the way, you are officially on retainer of the City of Birmingham. Your meals and accommodations are being paid for, and you will receive a small daily stipend for your help, so let me know if there is anything you need."

"Wow, thanks Joe. I really didn't expect all that."

"It is the least we can do for all your help." His mind seemed to shift gears as he drove. "I hope we can get an ID off those prints."

"I hope so too. It would be a very lucky break."

"I know you probably have never been a part of a task force before so let me explain a bit to you. Once we get the room set up and all the players arrive, it will be chaotic at times." He smiled warmly. "Whenever you get that much testosterone in a room it can get heated, but mostly they will be bouncing ideas and theories across the team, trying to make sense of what this man is doing. Hopefully we can learn enough about him to put an end to this nightmare soon."

"Is there anything special I need to do?"

"Just listen and observe. If you think you have information that might be helpful, speak up, no matter how loud it gets. I think one of the first tasks we should complete is to get you to address the team on what you have learned so far." Joe looked over at me. "I am out of my jurisdiction here, but that would be my first move."

"Who will be in charge then?"

"The Feds take over from here, now that he has crossed state lines. Johnson and I, and anyone else local, are just extras from this point on," he explained. "There will be crime scene photos plastered on work boards, and some of them could be disturbing to you, so don't feel like you have to look. I'm sure what you have already seen through your visions is disturbing enough."

I didn't respond other than to simply nod my head. I knew deep in my heart, I had to look to find the others in my visions.

When we arrived at the station, I followed Joe inside and we joined a growing crowd walking to a large empty room. The agents that had met them at the crime scene were already pinning photos up on the boards, writing identifying information and data beside each one.

Joe ushered me to a chair at a safe distance from all the activity. "I'm getting some coffee. May I bring you some?"

"If you think I can drink it, yes," I said and shot Joe a grin. For a moment, I contemplated removing the dark shades from my eyes but decided against it. The lights were bright enough to cause pain, and I didn't want to freak anyone out before we even got to know each other. So I sat back in my chair and flipped open my notepad. I wrote several letters down to form a word I didn't recognize. I wasn't even sure if it was a word, for that matter, but I did know the letters meant something to the killer. I reviewed my other notes as the rest of the task force assembled in the room.

Once everyone settled, Blair stood at the end of the table and introduced herself and then asked the other members to introduce themselves. When it was my turn, I introduced myself, and then stumbled when I had no clue as what to call myself. Thankfully, Joe piped up to call me a "Consultant." The others seemed satisfied and the introductions continued.

"Thank you all for coming," she said. "We have a lot of work to do here, and I expect everyone will work together until we can bring this subject in."

There was low grumblings around the table. Blair smiled a wicked smile at the almost all male task force. "I know how uneasy it is for you when the Feds come in your territory, but this is a case that will take more than one unit to solve. We know now he isn't a local, and he won't just quit killing. We have reviewed open cases in the tri-state area and, based on some similarities, he may have twenty or more kills under his belt. We also know he has been killing for years, so even twenty may be a low estimate."

A low whistle filled the room. "Why are we just now learning about him if he's been around that long?" Johnson asked.

"Because something traumatic in his life has occurred in the last few years and his kill cycle has dramatically increased. Instead of killing months or even years apart, he's now killing more regularly."

"What's it going to take to catch this son of a bitch?" a deep, southern voice asked.

All heads in the room turned toward the largest, darkest man Tally had ever seen. He was leaning against the doorframe, nearly filling the entire doorway.

"Who are you, sir?" Blair asked.

"My name is Toma. Charles Toma and I am a detective with Bogalusa PD. I have been following the wires on this man and I think I have a case that was one of his earliest victims."

"Lisa Evans," I said. All heads in the room turned toward me.

"Yes, that's right," he said. "How do you know?"

"This here little lady's a psychic," one of the Picayune men said with a snicker. "She knows it all."

Johnson jumped to his feet and literally pulled the man out of his seat. "Get out of here now," he said with a stern voice.

"I'm sorry, boss. I was just fooling," the young man said, trying to apologize for his juvenile behavior.

"Out now, and don't come back to this room," Johnson said, pointing to the door.

Toma moved aside as the young man sulked out the door. "Is there anyone else in here that doesn't take this business seriously?" His glare met every man in the room, not a whisper spoken.

Johnson turned to me and said, "I'm sorry for his ignorance Ms. Rainwater. I appreciate everything you have done so far."

"Thank you, Detective," I said and gave him my warmest smile of appreciation.

"Detective Toma, it appears we have an empty slot in our task force if you would care to join us," Blair said.

"Don't mind if I do, ma'am," he said and took the empty spot at the table, placing a large folder on the table.

"Tally, this seems like as good a time as any for you to brief everyone on your skills and what you have learned so far," Blair said.

I stood, and after introducing myself to Detective Toma, I began to tell the story of my gift, and how it had evolved to the point of 'linking' with the killer. Having their full attention, I started from the beginning.

Chapter Nine

Jimmy Dwayne Walker was physically and mentally exhausted as he left the barn and climbed wearily into his red pickup truck. It was time to go home and rest for a bit. Recharge the old batteries so to speak. He climbed behind the wheel and decided he would drive away from Picayune and across the state line before he would pull over for a few hours' sleep. He could not risk falling asleep at the wheel and coming up on the law enforcement radar. He was moving stealthily through the night. They had no clue where he was, and he intended to keep it that way. He took a final look into the rearview mirror at the barn and smiled a contented smile before turning right onto the paved road to start his journey home.

Two hours later his head snapped up when the blaring of a car horn startled him. His head had begun to nod as he drove. Up on his right he saw a sign advertising a rest stop one mile ahead. That was a good place to get a few hours' sleep. He would hide in plain sight, he thought with a wicked grin, and hit the road again when the sun began to rise.

He pulled into a remote corner of the rest stop between two semi-trucks and used the darkness to conceal him as he changed into fresh clothes, wrapping the soiled clothing in a plastic bag to be disposed of later. No longer covered in the stench of death, he stretched out across his front seat. It wasn't the most comfortable position to be in, but it would have to do for now. Tonight he would be back in his own comfortable bed and could sleep for days, if only his mind would let him. For now, he would gladly take the few short hours his body desperately needed. He closed his eyes, praying that sleep would come, and the dreams would stay away.

Twenty years ago he had been an up-and-coming businessman, rising quickly in the company, when he had an accident while on a road trip. He was traveling home late one evening, determined to get home to start his weekend, when the company car he was driving was run off a bridge by a road-weary truck driver. He made it to the hospital despite coding several times on the Life Flight to New Orleans, where they were able to stabilize him enough to perform surgery to relieve the pressure on his injured brain.

After the surgery, JD fell into a coma, his mind floating in a world of dreams. He was transferred to a nursing center specializing in comatose care. When he suddenly woke three years later, he could remember fragments of the vivid dreams, but had no clue who he was or how he had gotten in that shape. When the nursing center notified his mother he had awakened, she began almost daily visits. Three more months of intensive rehab allowed him to walk and function independently. Released, JD returned home.

Hell was more like it. He suffered from intense migraines and body aches so severe, he sometimes wished he had died in the crash. To make matters worse, his mother didn't hesitate to remind him how miserable his life had become and how worthless he was as a man. His rage ignited and grew with every insult she shouted at him.

The world had seemed to pass Jimmy Dwayne by while he was asleep. The three years felt more like twenty. He found himself unemployable and desperate to escape living under his mother's thumb. His grandfather had owned a small hunting cabin, more of a shack really, that he had left to his mother. With her blessing, JD moved out to the bayou, out of her sight. He had always enjoyed being outdoors, and he quickly relearned how to hunt and fish. The bayou held a plethora of game and he rapidly learned to survive on the bounty Mother Nature had to offer. His skills allowed him to fish for gators, shrimp, and crawfish for extra cash. Cajun foods were spreading like wildfire throughout the south and he found himself in the middle of a small gold mine. Gator hides, teeth, heads, and claws were selling for a small fortune in Birmingham, and he had several buyers throughout Mississippi and Alabama that would buy all the shrimp, crawfish, and gator meat he could deliver.

He had found his new niche in life and spent his time deep in the bayou, except for his trips out to sell his goods. JD rarely saw his mother, which seemed just as well to her. On occasion, he would drop by just to see if she was still alive. It was always a disappointment to find her healthy and spry month after unending month.

JD's prize possession was his pickup truck. He had bought it with a bonus check he'd received just before his accident, and he had breathed a sigh of relief when he returned home to find it stored away in his mother's garage, the original two hundred miles still registered on the odometer. It was his lifeline to the outside world. His cabin was several miles into the bayou by boat, but after a few poachers disappeared without any trace, no one bothered JD's truck when he left it parked on the nearest dry land. He had established a reputation for being downright ornery and a little bit "touched in the head," so people steered clear of JD.

A bit "touched in the head" turned out to be an understatement. JD was more than touched. The debilitating headaches and aches would make him howl in pain at times, and he never found the right cocktail of medications to make them fully go away. When the voices began he tried to ignore them, and for months that seemed to work, but each time they began the voices had grown stronger and more insistent. It took every ounce of effort for him to deal with his buyers without screaming his head off when they tried to renegotiate his prices.

Then the visions started, and the voices began taunting him, twisting his pained mind into excruciating knots until he went out to kill something, anything to ease the voices in his head. At first, killing the creatures of the swamp satisfied his needs, but that soon changed. He began seeing images of beautiful young women, and the voices made vile suggestions to him as the evil grew within him.

In the beginning, these dark images only came to him when he was deep in the swamp, but the voices grew impatient with his inaction and he began hearing them as he delivered his goods. He would see a young woman in the car next to him or in one of the stores or restaurants he visited, and his mind would be flooded with deviant images until his body grew hard with desire.

For a short time, he was able to fight off the images, but on one trip through Bogalusa, he saw a beautiful woman walking down a dark street. Driven to possess her, he took her captive. When he tired of taking pleasure from her, he killed the young woman.

The first had seemed so easy, but for weeks he felt like someone was watching him. He knew at any minute the cops would be crashing through his door, coming to drag him off to jail. When that didn't happen after several months, the voices grew even louder. So he began to hunt.

✝

After I finished my update, the detectives from the three known crime scenes gave their reports. There was little information Detective Toma provided that was helpful in the current phase of the investigation, but it did help to provide some background on possibly the killer's first victim. When the group took a break, I made my way over to him and introduced myself directly to him.

"Lisa Evans was the first lost soul to speak to me in my visions, and she has provided information to me that have helped us connect the murders," I told him. "She seems like such a beautiful person."

"She was much more than beautiful," he said. "I went to high school with her, and her future held so much promise," he said with a sigh. "I truly don't understand why the evil people of this world can walk around freely, yet the truly beautiful, kind and innocent fall victims to the likes of this bastard."

"I don't understand it either," I said. "I see more and more faces in the shadows every day, and I know eventually I'll have to find some way for them to find peace."

"I don't envy you that job," he said.

"It's only just begun," I said as Blair called the group back together.

She took complete control of the group, made assignments to the members of the task force as they scribbled notes, and began making phone calls and reviewing faxes. A tip line had already been set up, and tips were coming in by the handfuls. Many, however, would likely turn out to be bogus or prank calls.

†

JD bolted upright in his seat and wiped the sleep from his eyes. It took several minutes before he realized where he was. He looked down at the fresh clothes he was wearing, vaguely remembering turning into a rest stop to change into clean clothes just hours earlier. He looked through the back

87

window of the truck inside the camper shell and saw the small pile of clothing he had tossed in the back. The clothes were bloodstained; however, the odor of seafood that reeked inside the camper disguised the smell of blood. He had always found that people took a wide path from his vehicle once they had gotten a good whiff of the smell. It was more effective than an alarm system to deter prying eyes.

The sun was just starting to rise as he left his truck to use the restroom before hitting the road. With a bit of luck he would make it back to Houma before lunch, be tucked safely away in his little hamlet before the night would fall. He splashed cold water on his face and stared into the mirror at an image he barely recognized. The once handsome face, ruined by a long scar caused by a shard of glass, had carved back his cheek as his head thrust through the windshield. Hard, cold eyes stared back at him from the reflection, and the voice in his head said, "You are a bad, bad man."

"Damn straight," JD said and walked back to his truck.

✝

Not given any particular assignment, I wandered through the room listening to bits and pieces of conversations. When I tired of the useless eavesdropping, I found my seat and notepad and closed my eyes to focus on the killer. I ignored the buzzing in the room and searched through the darkness until I felt the stifling heat generated by his anger, and then I landed in his mind. I could feel him shake his head, as if to shake off a chill, and then my eyes focused through his.

The sunlight was bright and stung my eyes as he focused on an object ahead on the side of the road.

"My, my, what do we have here?" I heard him ask.

88

Just ahead, there was a car disabled on the side of the road and a woman struggling in her attempts to get a spare tire out of her trunk.

I heard the ticking noise of the blinker as he turned it on, and started to slow the truck as he pulled over to the emergency lane.

Dear God, please don't let him be hunting, I silently prayed. I could feel a smile stretching across his face as he pulled up behind the car and turned the truck off.

The woman was in her late thirties and had the extra padding a woman sometimes put on after birthing several children, but was still very attractive. He stepped out of the truck and slowly approached the car.

"Having a bit of trouble are you, miss?"

The woman jumped and squealed in surprise. "I'm sorry, but I didn't hear you pull up. I guess I was focused on getting this tire out of the trunk."

"No ma'am, I'm sorry for scaring you. May I offer my help?"

"That would be very kind of you," she said.

"What's a pretty little thing like you doing all alone on this road anyhow?" he asked.

"Oh, I'm not alone. My mother and my two kids are asleep in the car. We are on our way back to New Orleans."

I felt his eyes dart to the interior of the car. He could vaguely make out the woman's head against the passenger seat but the children were invisible from this angle in the backseat.

"Let me take care of that for you and you can get back on the road," he said, brushing her aside from the trunk.

"Thank you so very much. I hated to stop, but I know its several miles until the next exit."

"My pleasure to help you out, ma'am," he said. He quickly jacked up the car and took off the damaged tire. "Not too sure this one can be fixed," he said as he leaned it against the car. "This spare should get you home though," he said as he began replacing the lugs.

In just a few minutes, he had the tire in place and the blown tire stored safely in the trunk. He gave her a warm smile. He was still facing the back of the car so I quickly jotted down B14-ZAG32, white Toyota on my notepad.

"Can I offer you some money?"

"No ma'am, there's no need for that."

"Are you sure? I'm certain it would have cost me a small fortune to get roadside service out here."

"I'm positive. Stop later today and buy those babies some ice cream," he said.

"They will enjoy that. Thank you again."

"Have a good day, ma'am," he said and turned to walk back to the truck.

He climbed back into the truck and sat behind the wheel, watching as she waved and pulled back onto the road. "She wasn't my type anyhow," he said and reached down to start the truck.

As he accelerated onto the highway, I zoomed back out of his head. "Holy shit," I said, louder than I intended.

Blair heard me, and walked over to me with Joe on her heels. "What is it?"

"He is on the move again. Somewhere on an interstate I think. He stopped to help a woman with a flat tire, and I think if she had been alone, she would have been his next victim, even though she was older and not like his other victims."

"Can you describe the woman, and her vehicle?" she asked.

"I can do better than that," I said and held up my notepad with the tag number and description of the car.

Blair scribbled down the tag number and tore it off her pad. She handed the note to Joe.

"I'm all over it," he said without her saying a word. He raced off to a vacant computer terminal.

She turned back to me and smiled. "That was a great job and could be a very important break in the case if we can locate the woman."

"Thanks."

"Can you always access him like that?"

"Not always. Sometimes it feels like he has me blocked out, but other times I can sneak in without him noticing."

"Amazing," Blair said and walked over to a buzzing group of detectives.

Chapter Ten

It was nearly eight before they took another break. Joe had been successful in tracking down the owner information on the tag number I was able to provide and had contacted New Orleans PD to send a unit out to the address, but the woman had not yet made it home. Blair asked Johnson to send one of his detectives to New Orleans to interview the woman once she arrived home.

"Why don't we call it a day, grab some dinner and check into our hotels," she suggested. "Everyone has had a long day and I'm sure we will have many more before this is through. Let's plan to meet back at seven tomorrow morning."

The group slowly dispersed leaving Joe and me in the room with Blair. "I took the liberty to book rooms for you two."

"I knew there was something I was forgetting," Joe said. "Thanks."

"You are welcome. Do you have any plans for dinner?"

Joe looked at me and I shrugged. "No, I don't reckon we do."

"I think it's time Uncle Sam bought you two some dinner then," she said. "Let's check into our rooms, and once we are settled we can go find something to eat. Follow me and I'll show you where we are staying."

When we stepped outside the sun was fading quickly. I could feel static electricity building in the air and knew we would be getting a storm. I hoped we would make it to the hotel before the storm arrived.

Our rooms were side by side, located on the top floor of the hotel. The large window was wide enough for a window seat and I sat for a moment, looking out over the city as the lights began to interrupt the dark night and bring the city to life. I tore myself away from the view, unpacked my bag, and put away my clean clothing. Just as I finished, someone knocked on my door.

I opened the door to find Joe and Blair. "I don't know about you two, but I'm starving," he said.

"You should be since we haven't eaten since breakfast," I reminded him.

"Damn, that seems like days ago," he teased.

"Did you see that steak house on the ride here?" Blair asked.

"I never miss a steak house," Joe said.

"Let's give it a try then," she suggested.

"Sounds great to me," I said.

†

Thunder rumbled in the distance as we left the restaurant and I could smell the approaching thunderstorm on the warm breeze.

"Looks like we better make a run for it," Joe said.

We had barely pulled into the parking lot of the hotel when the first large drops began to fall, and we all made a mad dash for the safety of the elevator. Joe entered his room with a quiet good night and a promise to meet us at six for breakfast, leaving Blair and I standing in front of my door.

"I was wondering if you could take a look at something for me tonight, if it's not too much trouble," she said.

"Sure thing, but can I have time for a quick shower first? I feel like I haven't bathed in days."

Blair chuckled. "That's no problem, just knock on our adjoining door when you're ready and I'll bring the file in."

"Thanks," I said and used the key to slip inside my room. I could hear the rain pelting against the glass window, but the lightning had not yet moved in, so I rushed to the bathroom to take a quick shower.

†

Blair also took advantage of the time to shower and dress in a pair of sleep pants and a T-shirt. She had pulled out her file and was sitting at a small desk looking through the photos when she heard a light knock at her door. She gathered her file, walked to the door, then entered Tally's room.

"I was hoping you could take a look at some photos and tell me if any of these women are your shadow faces. I really think a good portion of them could be victims of this same killer, based on their profiles."

"Sure," I said, taking the file from her and walking to the small desk. There was only one chair, so she took a seat at the end of my bed and waited. I opened the file to find a large stack of photographs and began arranging them on the desktop. "There are so many," I said as I studied each of the faces. Blair was right. Quite a few of the images staring back at me had grown familiar to me over the years. I sorted the ones I recognized and placed the others back in the folder. I carefully reviewed each one, memorizing the names as I read over their profiles. So many young lives ended way too soon.

My fingertips moved softly over the outline of the twelve faces staring back at me, silent tears streaming down my face.

Blair watched as Tally studied each of the photographs, the tears flowing down her cheeks. She could not begin to fathom the emotional conflict the young woman must endure to share her gift with the world. Blair had faced ridicule for her use of psychics to solve murders, but had never given thought to the pain and trauma they must feel. She continued to watch as Tally's fingers gently traced the faces in the photos and felt her fondness growing for the young woman.

Tally looked up to find Blair anxiously watching her. Wiping the tears from her face, she said, "I know these twelve."

Blair walked over to look at the assortment of photos arranged by the dates reported missing and studied them closely. "Just based on this, I would say he went from killing almost a year apart to now barely a week. That is assuming there are no other victims unaccounted for.

"Thank you," Blair said. "This helps quite a bit. Do you mind helping me with one more task?"

"Not at all," Tally said.

"I'll be right back." She left the room and returned moments later with a red magic marker and a road map of the southern states. "I want to plot out the locations of these women on the map to see if they will show us anything," she explained. She opened the map and spread it across the bed. "Look at each profile and tell me the location and the date please."

✝

I read off each of the names and locations of the twelve women to her, as she circled the towns and wrote down the dates. I think I surprised her by adding names, and dates for Lisa, Beanie, and the latest victim, Brianna.

"There," Blair said when she entered the last date. She became quiet for several minutes as she studied the map. I stood up with the photos still in my hands and walked over to the bed to look down at the map. At first, nothing seemed to appear before my eyes and then numbers began to flash, 55, 10, 49, 65, and 20. I looked more closely at the map and the numbers corresponded with the major interstate highways in the area.

"Do you see the pattern?" I asked.

"It's the interstates isn't it?" she said.

"All of the locations where victims came up missing are within five miles or so of one of major highways or interstates," I said.

"Most commonly fifty-five, sixty-five, and twenty," Blair said. "It isn't uncommon for a serial killer to be a long-haul truck driver or some type of traveling salesman, and this would seem to fit that profile." She remained silent for a few minutes and then said, "As far north as Birmingham and as far south as Slidell. I wonder where he goes and for what type of business? None of the victims were taken from or near a truck stop, so that doesn't fit, and we know he has used a white van and a red pickup in at least two areas."

Blair was about to say something else when her cell phone rang. She stood up and walked into her room to answer the call. I went over to the window to sit in the window seat. Bright fingers of lightning raked down from the heavens to light up the sky. I leaned back against the wall as static electricity ran through my body raising the hairs on my arms. I felt the darkness beginning to form. The faces in the shadows swirled as I concentrated and called each one by name. Lisa walked forward, followed by each of the women I recognized from the photographs.

You are doing great, Tally, Lisa said. You are learning more and more about him every day.

Not nearly enough, though, I said with an exasperated sigh.

You will find him, I just know you will, Tally, and we all appreciate your efforts.

I watched as a slight young woman pushed forward. I recognized her as Barbara Turner from Slidell. *You're Barbara, yes?*

She smiled a heartwarming smile. Yes, I am. I wanted to tell you something that may be of no use, but all the same it might help.

What is it, I asked.

The first night he had me in some old abandoned shack he dropped a keychain, she said. I got a good look at it before he reclaimed it, but unfortunately it appeared broken. It was one of those with initials on it. The first letter was a J, but the second letter was broken, so I couldn't tell if it was an R or a D or an L or any other letter with a strong left-hand post.

That is very interesting, I said, showing appreciation for the information she provided. I need you all to think as hard as you can about any other facts and let me know if you come up with anything, and I do mean anything. We have got to catch him soon. I looked over to Lisa and smiled. We think he may be some type of traveling salesman, someone who frequently travels the interstates on business.

It could be seafood, another woman sounded off from the group. I remember his truck reeked of something fishy smelling.

Yes, now that you mention it, I do too, several others agreed.

That's it, ladies. Think and think hard, I said. A close clap of thunder tore me from the vision. My body shuddered and I turned to find Blair watching me closely.

"You had another vision, didn't you?"

I nodded my head but held up my hand, motioning for her to wait one minute as I walked to the desk and opened my notepad and jotted down, J something, possibly R, L, or D, and seafood.

†

Detective Johnson had sent Tim Boyer to New Orleans to track down the woman who had a flat tire. He had waited outside the address until nearly seven before the woman pulled up in her drive and turned off her engine.

"Mrs. Badu," he asked when she stepped out of her car.

"Yes, may I help you?"

Boyer pulled out his badge. "I'm Detective Boyer from Picayune. May I have a few moments of your time?"

"Yes, but please let me get the kids in the house first."

"Certainly, let me take those bags for you," he said, reaching for the suitcases.

"Thank you," she said and turned to walk to the house. "You two head upstairs now and get ready for bed."

"Yes, Mama," the kids said and bounded up the stairs as Boyer set the bags down at the foot of the stairs.

"What can I do for you, Detective?" she asked as she ushered him to a seat in the living room.

"Did you have car troubles earlier today?"

"Why, yes I did," she said. "Did I do something wrong? I offered to pay the nice man," she added.

"No, you did nothing wrong at all, ma'am. Actually, we're looking for the man who stopped to help you and hoped you might be able to help us out."

"He was the nicest man, but had the most hideous scar down his face. I was scared at first when he stopped, but he was such a gentleman, and wouldn't take a penny from me for changing the tire."

"Do you have any idea who he is?"

"No, I never did ask him his name or where he was from. May I ask why you are looking for him?"

"We need to talk to him about a case we have open," Boyer explained. "Do you remember what he was driving?"

"A big, shiny red pickup truck, one of the Ford F-150s I believe, with a camper on the back. My husband had one like it a few years ago."

"Where is your husband?"

"He is working offshore on the oil rigs," she said.

"Did you notice anything else about the man that stood out?"

She seemed to think hard for a few seconds. "He had some type of tattoos on his fingers, but I didn't want to stare so I don't know what they said. Is he in trouble or something?"

Sensing he would not get any more information from the woman, Boyer decided to be frank with her. "He is a person of interest in an open case I'm working. He could possibly be a very dangerous man."

The woman turned white, and for a brief moment, he feared she would faint.

"I think you were a very lucky woman today if this is indeed the man we are looking for." Boyer pulled a business card from his pocket and handed it to her. "If you can think of anything else, please call me right away. If by chance you see him again, get to safety immediately and call the police."

"You don't think I'm in danger do you?"

"You didn't tell him your name or any other personal information did you?"

"Only that we were on our way home to New Orleans," she said, her hand moving to her throat.

"I don't think you have anything to worry about, but please keep your doors locked and your eyes open," he warned.

She nodded, her voice failing her as his warning sank deep.

Boyer stood to leave. "Thank you for your time, ma'am, and stay safe."

"Thank you, Detective," she said and walked him to the door.

Boyer stepped outside and waited until he heard the deadbolt slide shut to secure the door, then returned to his car.

✝

"That was Johnson. Boyer just called him from New Orleans. The woman was able to confirm he was driving the red truck with the camper and that he has tattoos on his right hand. That was all the information he could get from her though."

"I hope she realizes how lucky she was today," I said.

"Did you see anything new?"

"I learned two more pieces of the puzzle from the women." I opened up my notepad and looked at my notes. "He has a keychain that is one of those with initials. The first letter is a J, but the second was broken, but could have been an L, R, or a D."

"That's interesting," Blair said. "What else."

"I told them we thought he was some kind of traveling salesman or businessman and several of the women thought he may be a seafood salesman."

"Based on what?"

"They all said the truck reeked of a fishy smell." My eyes fell upon the word I had jotted down earlier in the day. "Does the word pirogue mean anything to you," I asked.

"No, it doesn't ring any bells, why?"

"That word came to me earlier today, but I haven't put any meaning to it," I explained.

"It sounds like some kind of New York deli sandwich," she said with a grin.

"Very funny," I answered with a smile.

"That was nice."

"What?"

"Your smile, it's very nice to see."

Her comment caught me completely by surprise and I felt myself blushing furiously. "Thanks," I said. I turned back toward the window to hide my face.

"We will ask around the task force tomorrow to see if they know what the word stands for," Blair said as she folded her map and started toward the door. "Have a good night, Tally."

"You too," I said, barely turning from the window. I watched as she slipped through the adjoining door, leaving it cracked as she disappeared.

I was exhausted and pulled down the sheets to climb into the welcoming bed. I didn't bother turning on the television as I pulled the covers tightly under my chin. The lightning flashed brilliantly outside the window, and I closed my eyes hoping sleep would come soon. The falling rain was like a lullaby. I felt myself drifting off to sleep almost instantly.

†

Blair stored her files and then climbed into her bed. She stretched out and turned off the lamp to watch the storm rage outside. A strange new sensation ran through her veins as her thoughts drifted to the young woman in the room next door. Many people would turn away from Tally's strange eyes, but she found herself drawn deeper into their depths.

†

JD sighed with relief when he parked his truck in its usual spot. Dropping the bundle of bloody clothing in the bottom of the boat, he began untying the boat from the small dock and stepped onto the craft. The lightning lit up the late afternoon sky as he climbed in and pushed away from the dock. Sane people would be rushing to get off the water to escape the approaching storm, but he welcomed its arrival. He knew the lightning couldn't touch him and the rain would wash his soul clean. He cranked the engine and started for home.

The bayou warmed his heart. The uninhabited swamps and dark bogs was the one place he could hide from everyone, except the voices in his head. There were times when he would go weeks without seeing another human, and he notched those up as some of his better times. He would hunt or fish for his meals, beholden to none to survive.

He looked down at his right hand as he maintained his grip on the throttle. JD had once had a dream in which the voices told him he should tattoo the word Death on his fingers so the creatures he killed would know that death had come to claim them. The following day he had used his ingenuity to tattoo the letters on his fingers. It had hurt like hell, but he was extremely pleased with his handiwork. The next day as he pulled up the first of his lines to harvest a gator, he shook his right fist in the reptile's face and screamed, "Death has come to claim you," and then laughed hysterically as he lifted the gun and pulled the trigger.

If JD had friends, they would have been able to see how quickly he spiraled out of control. But, other than an occasional brief visit with his mother, and a monthly visit to a grocery store, JD remained a recluse, preferring the solitude of the bayou. His only close friend, Tommy Jon Fitch was a little slow, but he worshipped JD as a hero. Tommy Jon was the best gator skinner in the state and helped JD set up his customer base. Even the customers he saw regularly would have noticed the difference in him if they had taken a moment to notice the strange man who brought them goods.

JD killed the engine once he entered the slough and picked up a long pole. As he poled through the canals, he heard the deep bellow of a bull gator off in the distance and saw small animals skittering through the bog to find refuge from the coming storm. He lifted his face to the sky, allowing the cool rain to caress his face with a lover's touch. Yes, the bayou had stolen his soul, and as he pushed deeper into the cypress canals, JD knew he was home.

When he tied up to his small dock, he pulled a rope to lift a fish trap from the water. Captured inside were several large fish that would make an excellent meal, but tonight JD only wanted to sleep and heal his weary body. He draped the bundle of clothes over the wooden railing on the small porch to allow the rain to wash them clean and entered his home. He had neither electricity nor running water, but JD had learned to live without them. He stripped out of his clothes and collapsed onto the bed. He fell into an exhausted sleep filled with troubling dreams.

At first, JD dreamed of his life on the bayou. He poled his pirogue through the sloughs checking his fish traps and the lines he had baited for gators. He smiled a wicked grin as large gators slithered down the banks and took to the murky waters to escape the glare of his evil eyes. He was happiest here far away from civilization and the responsibilities he left behind.

A vision of his mother invaded the peacefulness of his dream. His mother had no mortgage and she had a small sum of cash leftover from his father's insurance, but that was not enough for her. As soon as he returned home from the hospital, she had harassed him about finding work and paying rent. He rapidly grew to hate the woman that had brought him into this world. It would be almost too easy to send her to an early grave, but he knew that he would be at the top of the list of suspects if she were to be murdered. So instead, JD packed up his meager belongings and moved to the bayou.

His dreams changed gears and he began reliving each of the gruesome murders he had committed. The faces of the young women flashed in front of his eyes like a kaleidoscope. His body twisted on the bed as he relived each perverted action had he taken with these women and the last remnant of remorse released from his body. He settled in to a deep, restful sleep and dreamed of the women yet to come.

✝

I slept deeply for a short period, until I felt my body begin to vibrate with ethereal energy and I knew a vision was coming. I wasn't prepared to be thrust into his dreams, forced to watch the horrors he committed against the innocent women. After one especially brutal murder, I cried out in my sleep and sat up in bed. I was unable to break the contact with him to escape the horrible dreams.

Blair heard Tally cry out and rushed to her room. She found her sitting up in the middle of the bed, locked into a vision and unresponsive to her calls. She climbed into the bed and wrapped her arms around Tally's waist, holding her close, resting Tally's head softly on her shoulder.

I sensed a depression of the bed and then felt an aura of warmth surround me, providing comfort and protection. Strong arms circled my waist as Blair enclosed my body within her own. I shivered with the revulsion from the images he forced me to witness as she held me close.

"Tally, can you hear me?" she whispered into my ear.

I could feel her warm breath caressing my neck, but I could not pull away from his dreams. The warmth of her infused me with positive energy and I felt his power begin to release his control. She pulled me tighter as she continued to whisper to me.

Suddenly, I released from the dream with an audible pop in my head. I squeezed my eyes shut, forbidding the images to return and took a deep breath, exhaling a long sigh. I felt encased in protection, and allowed my eyes to steal open and adjust to the darkness. I felt a warm body pressed into mine and heard a soothing voice comforting me.

I forced my head to turn toward the sound and found her watching me.

"There you are," she whispered and I could feel her breath caress the bare skin of my shoulder.

My eyes flew open when I realized I was naked, and my hand flew to the covers to pull a sheet over me.

Blair chuckled softly and the heat of embarrassment flushed across my face. I felt her soft lips on my neck as she planted a tender kiss just below my ear. She made no effort to pull away from me, content to hold me close as I continued to shiver. "You are so precious," she whispered into my ear.

The sound of her voice and the feel of her body was a sharp contrast to the evil and hatred I'd felt in the dream. I turned slowly toward her and wondered if I was still dreaming. Our lips were mere inches apart. I could taste her sweet breath as she leaned in closer and brushed her lips across mine. My eyes snapped closed as a surge of electricity flowed into me loaded with a pleasant hunger as my lips parted and Blair deepened the kiss.

A soft moan echoed through the room, and I was unsure which of us issued the sound until I felt it vibrate throughout my body. I was flooded with peace as her fingers snaked into my hair, pulling me closer.

A shockwave slammed into my body and I felt the evil invade my brain as I lurched on the bed.

"My, my you are a naughty little girl," JD's evil voice filled my brain. "I wouldn't mind a taste of that myself," he growled.

My head reeled with fright as I realized he had somehow managed to invade my thoughts, just as I had done to him. My hands pressed to the sides of my head in agony as I used all of my energy to push him from my mind.

"No. Get out. Now," I shouted. "You are evil. Leave me alone."

"Now, sugar, I have played nice, and shared with you, it's the least you owe me," he said with a wicked laugh deep in my brain.

"Be gone," I shouted.

"I'm sorry," Blair stammered, thinking I was talking to her. Before I could stop her, she had flown from the bed.

I was successful in driving him from my mind, but once more my body collapsed on the bed, exhausted and powerless to move. No matter how badly I wanted, and needed, to rush to Blair, I found I could not move. I closed my eyes and succumbed to the paralysis of exhaustion.

†

Blair hurried back to her room and sat on the edge of her bed, her face buried in her hands as tears gushed from her body. Headstrong, stable, Special Agent Blair Cooper reduced to a blithering idiot. She did not understand what had come over her to kiss Tally. It had felt so perfect and natural. Then it had turned into a nightmare when Tally realized what she had done, leaving her feeling like one of the deviants she chased in real life. She curled into a ball and rocked her agonized mind to sleep.

✝

An hour later I woke, still weak from the encounter but knowing I had to get to Blair to explain.

I had never had an encounter of an intimate nature from either gender, but somehow I knew Blair was destined for me. I had dreamed of her since I was a child, but still the suddenness of all the emotions I was experiencing overwhelmed and confused me. The kiss had been heavenly until the monster had encroached on my thoughts. I had no clue what I would say to Blair, but I had to explain to her that my reaction was meant for him, not her.

Painfully, I drew my body out of the bed and walked across the room to the adjoining doorway. The moonlight drifted through the window illuminating her body as she lay curled up on the bed. I realized I was still naked and stepped back into the room to put on an oversized T-shirt. I entered her room and stepped quietly to Blair's bed and sat beside her sleeping form. I took a deep breath to steel my courage then reached over to touch her arm, gently shaking her awake.

She moaned softly as she moved away from the encroaching touch. I became more insistent and pleaded, "Blair, please wake up."

At the sound of my voice, she sat straight up in bed and looked at me with fear in her eyes. She began to move her lips to speak. I leaned forward to cover them with my own, to swallow the words with a kiss. I could feel her body stiffen and then relax as her hand stroked down my face. When I broke the kiss, she looked at me with startled green eyes.

"Oh Blair, I wasn't shouting at you," I said. "Somehow the killer got into my mind, and he saw you."

"What?"

"I don't understand it, but somehow he was able to invade my mind and he saw and felt us kiss."

"Oh my God, Tally, are you okay," she asked.

"It was disturbing, and now he knows what you look like," I said as worry crept into my voice. "I was able to push him out, but I'll have to remain vigilant to make sure he doesn't return."

"I will protect us," she said as her face softened. "I was afraid my actions had upset you."

"That was the best kiss I have ever had," I said. "Until now." I grinned and leaned into her for another kiss. That one led to many more before the night pulled us back to sleep, wrapped comfortably in one another's arms.

I awoke startled to be lying next to a warm body, until I remembered coming to Blair earlier that morning to explain my odd behavior. I had never kissed anyone like Blair before and I quickly felt my lips aching for more of her sweet kisses. We had yet to mention or discuss what had occurred between us, leaving me to fear that our attraction was a once-in-a-lifetime moment.

The night was still dark as I sat up to leave the bed. I felt Blair stir and looked back to find her green eyes watching me. "Good morning," I said.

"Good morning."

"Thanks for letting me stay with you last night."

Her smile widened as she looked at me. "I enjoyed you being here." She looked at the clock beside the bed. "We have time, if you want to stay a little longer."

I stretched out beside her and propped my head in my hand. "I like the way your eyes sparkle when you look at me."

Blair turned on her side and reached up to move a strand of my wayward hair. "You make me feel peaceful inside. I can't explain it, but I feel like we are meant to be together."

"I think you are right, we are destined to be a part of one another's lives," I answered.

"It's going to be terribly complicated to start a relationship. Can you handle that?"

I took her hand and brought it to my lips. "I'd sure like to find out."

Blair pulled me close and smiled even brighter. "Careful what you ask for," she said and leaned in to kiss me softly.

Chapter Eleven

Nearly a year earlier, JD had gone into town to grace his mother with one of his infrequent visits. When he pulled his truck into the driveway, Mr. Oliver, his mother's neighbor for almost twenty years, met him.

"JD, son, I need to talk with you," he said.

"Hey Mr. Oliver, are you okay?"

"I'm fine, JD, but I'm sad to tell you your mama has passed."

"What?" JD said, barely suppressing a smile.

"We tried to find you, but had no idea where you were. Your mama fell in the shower and struck her head. When I didn't see her out on the porch for a few days, I went inside and found her," he said. "The medical examiner said she drowned, but she did not feel anything as the fall broke her neck."

What a shame, the bane of his existence didn't suffer as she left this world he thought to himself. Fate had done what he had couldn't force himself to do.

"When we couldn't find you, her lawyer, Tandy Nelson, made arrangements for her burial down at the church," he explained. "I imagine he will want to talk to you to settle her estate," Mr. Oliver said, but JD's mind had drifted elsewhere.

"Thank you Mr. Oliver," JD said as he walked to the house and used his key to open the door.

He closed the door behind him and let out a shout of joy, one that, if overheard, could have been mistaken as a cry of grief for dear old mommy dearest. This unexpected turn of events left him in the mood to celebrate the old witch's passing. JD walked to his boyhood room and flipped on the light. He pulled some of his nicer clothing from the closet, took a long hot shower, then dressed in his best and drove to the church. Behind the church was an old cemetery. It wasn't hard to locate the fresh grave that now held his dearly departed mother. A thin metal nameplate confirmed that it was indeed her gravesite. As the sky darkened and the humidity weighed heavily in the air, JD let loose with a bizarre-sounding laugh and urinated over his mother's grave. "Rest in peace you old bitch," he growled and walked to his truck.

His recent elation brought the hunger to him. JD stopped at a bank to withdraw several hundred dollars from his mother's account then he headed north to New Orleans to celebrate his newfound freedom.

After consuming a seafood feast fit for a king and several deep glasses of Jack Daniels, JD paid his bill and left a generous tip for his server, a beautiful Creole woman in her mid-twenties. If the hunger hadn't been so strong in him, JD probably would have waited for her to get off work. Instead, filled with the need to possess, hurt, and kill, he drove toward Bourbon Street. It was a muggy Saturday night and the streets were filled with partygoers making his hunt easy. He had hoped he would run across a drunken co-ed making her way back home by herself after her money ran out, but a storm moving in sent revelers scurrying around in pairs huddled under large umbrellas.

JD turned his truck south to a darker part of town. His hunger blinded his common sense and he pulled over when he saw a young black woman strolling down the street sporting a small umbrella. She turned when she saw his truck slow and graced him with a beautiful smile. He rolled his window down and she approached his truck.

"Hey, sugar," she slurred in a slow southern drawl. "Are you looking for a date to party with?"

"I sure am, honey," he said as he lifted a full bottle of Jack he had purchased. "My friend Jack and I are looking for some company."

The woman had already crashed from her latest hit of crack. An hour or two with this john would give her enough cash for a few more hits, and she would get a buzz from his whiskey. "What do you want, sugar?" she asked, leaning in the window.

"The works," JD said.

"That will cost you sixty."

JD reached into his pocket for a wad of bills and pulled off three twenties, showing them to her. With a grin and an invitation he dropped the bills into his unused ashtray.

"Where can we go?"

"Let's take a ride out to the battlefield, and we can enjoy some Jack," she said as she slipped into the truck and slid over next to him. Her right hand rubbed up his thigh and he felt his dick swell into a steel rod. "Mmm, this feels promising," she said, cupping her hand over his crotch.

"I will promise you a ride to die for," JD said with a grin and handed her the bottle.

She took a long drink from the bottle and began to feel an immediate buzz from the strong liquor. "It's been ages since I've had me some Jack," she purred, taking another drink. "What's your name, sugar?"

"JD," he answered.

"Like Jack Daniel's," she said with a chuckle.

"Yeah, like Jack Daniel's," he said as he turned off the main road into a dense copse of woods. "Is this good for you?" he asked, turning off the engine and killing the headlights.

"This is perfect," she purred, giving his crotch a squeeze. "Gimme some JD," she said as her fingers manipulated his zipper.

He took from her for hours, sparing her no pain as he choked her to unconsciousness, and then when she revived he took her again.

"I've got to pee, sugar," she slurred, still drunk on the liquor, and left the truck to go stumbling into the bushes.

When she returned to the truck, JD grabbed her by the hair, slammed her head into the hood of the truck. Dazed, the woman made a futile attempt to fight. He easily overpowered her and with a purely evil-sounding laugh, he thrust into her, pinning her against the truck. JD loved the power of control and when his body exploded, he drew the sharp knife across her bare throat. He dropped her to the ground and foraged through her handbag and took the bills he had given her. "You won't need this now," he said as he tucked the bills deep into his pocket and tossed the bag toward her then returned to his truck.

He spent the rest of the weekend at his mother's, and then met with her lawyer the following Monday to settle her estate. He was surprised the old broad had more tucked away than he expected as he signed the papers to execute her will. She was his only family and now he was alone, except for the voices growing stronger in his head.

JD paid little attention to the infection that started in his groin. Left untreated, it began to slowly eat away at his already twisted mind. He had taken the whore's life, but she had given him more than the pleasure he sought.

†

As normally happened, my internal clock woke me before the alarm clock. I woke disoriented until I looked next to me and found Blair still sleeping soundly. At least that part of my strange evening had not been a dream I told myself as I watched the gentle rise and fall of her breathing. Completely relaxed during her slumber, I could see just how beautiful she really was. The soft lines that surrounded her eyes from intense concentration were invisible as she slept, and a cute smile played across her face.

Moving carefully, I rolled on my side and propped myself up on my elbow and watched her sleep. In just a few minutes her alarm sounded and she reached behind her to shut it off without opening her eyes. She pulled the covers up and her hand settled on my naked thigh. Her eyes flew open and gleaming emeralds swallowed my heart as she too remembered back to a few hours earlier. She smiled warmly. "Good morning."

"Good morning," I answered.

"How long have you been awake?"

"Not long," I answered. "Just long enough to see how beautiful you are when you sleep."

"And what do you think now that I'm awake?" she teased.

I leaned down and kissed her breathless. When I broke the kiss, I looked into her sparkling eyes. "You are just as beautiful awake."

Blair pulled me down onto her and we kissed as her hands explored my body. .

I wanted nothing more than to spend the morning in Blair's arms, but we had arranged to meet Joe for breakfast. After several long, slow kisses, we parted to shower and dress for the day to meet Joe.

When we joined him for breakfast, he looked up and smiled as we approached. "Good morning, ladies. I hope you slept well."

"We had a very busy night," Blair surprised me by saying. "But we did get some rest."

"What had you so busy?" he asked. I could feel my face blushing furiously and was grateful for the shades to hide my eyes.

"We think we have solved a few more pieces of the puzzle," Blair said.

"You came up with a name and address?" he teased.

"No, Joe, we were waiting for you to come up with that," I said.

"Do I get a preview or are you going to make me wait until we get to the Task Force?"

"I think we should make him wait," I said, and he immediately began to pout.

"I do too, but we could use his opinion on our theory," Blair said.

"Well, you are in charge, Special Agent Cooper," I said. She gave me a warm smile and her eyes lingered a little longer than normal.

Joe did not miss her look and softly cleared his throat.

"Tally had more luck with her visions," Blair said proudly. "Then I asked her to look at some of the photos of the other potential victims and she was able to connect twelve of them to terminal events."

"Terminal events," I questioned.

"That's Fed speak for death," Joe said.

"Ah, I got it," I said.

"Anyhow, she was able to contact several of the women and they came up with a few more facts for us. Then we really got to thinking."

"Blair got a road map out and we started plotting the locations and dates for the disappearance of the twelve women that I recognized from my visions," I said.

"Tally was the first to recognize it," Blair said.

"What?" Joe asked as the waitress delivered coffee.

115

"Each of the victims was abducted within five miles of an interstate or major highway," she said, pulling out her marked map. "Since none of them were taken in or near a truck stop we have somewhat ruled out a truck driver, but we do feel he is a businessman or someone else who travels frequently."

"Aren't a lot of serials long-haul truck drivers?" he asked.

"In many cases yes, but it just doesn't feel right," Blair answered.

"One of the victims shared with Tally that he had dropped a key chain and she saw the initial J, but the other letter was broken, so it could be almost anything, but probably a L, R, or D. Several of them also mentioned that his truck smelled like seafood."

"Wow, you two really were busy last night."

"We also got a call from Johnson. The detective he sent to New Orleans didn't come up with anything new, so that was a dead end."

"Maybe, but it was worth a shot," Joe said.

Their waitress brought their food and they finished breakfast and headed off to meet the rest of the Task Force. Blair gave the group an update of the information they had, and then went around the room to ask each member for an update. Suddenly I remembered a question I wanted to ask so when a detective finished his report I piped up.

"Does the word pirogue mean anything to any of you?"

Toma laughed a deep laugh. "A pirogue is a Cajun type of boat. A type of canoe, but wider and flatter across the middle, used to maneuver sloughs and canals a motorized boat can't get through. The operator usually stands and uses a pole to propel the boat. Most Cajun children can sneak up on you almost silently by the time they are six years old," he added with a chuckle.

"I don't know why, but that word came to me yesterday."

"It could be telling us he's a swamp man. That would go with the seafood theory," he said.

A young woman walked in and handed Johnson a report. He read over it quickly and his shoulders sagged with the weight of the news. "The good news is that the lab got two great prints off the stool. The bad news, though, is they don't match anyone in the system."

"Still, it will be helpful when we do capture him," Blair said to lighten his mood. "I know this is a long shot, but I think we need to pull the registrations on all the red F-150s in Louisiana and as well pull business licenses for seafood vendors."

"Holy cow, that's a tall order," one of the men said. "I'll take the truck."

"I will do what I can on the licenses," Toma said.

A young officer came in carrying another report. "This just came over from the ME's office." He was unsure who to give the report to until Blair nodded to Johnson.

Johnson took the report from him. The cause of death or the numerous other injuries Brianna had suffered were no surprise. There was one fact that caught his attention. The rape kit taken revealed that the killer was suffering from an advanced stage of syphilis.

"We are dealing with a sick puppy here," he said.

"Tell us something we don't know," Joe said.

"I'm serious, our boy is suffering from advance stage syphilis," Johnson said.

"So there may be a chance he sought treatment at a clinic or hospital at some time," Joe suggested.

Two of the agents volunteered to search for medical records.

I watched as Blair, Joe, and Johnson scoured the files, reviewing evidence from the latest crime scene, desperately trying to reveal any clues they may have missed. I listened to them and found my eyes repeatedly drawn to Blair, taking in her soft beauty as a feeling of warmth entered my body.

She must have felt my eyes on her. She lifted her head, looked at me and smiled. I knew from that brief contact my fears were unfounded as her eyes glowed with attraction, and a slight blush rose to her cheeks.

While she and I seemed so different, the attraction that was growing between us was obvious to anyone who caught the glances and soft smiles that we shared more and more often. Joe looked at me and I knew that he had caught the interaction between Blair and I. He smiled his acceptance of the situation and then turned back to the report he was reviewing.

†

JD climbed from the bed and stumbled to his knees as the pain threatened to rip his head wide open. He had raided his mother's medicine cabinet during his final visit and found a plentiful supply of painkillers. He opened the bottle he had placed by his bedside and took two of the pills, gnashing them to a bitter powder with his teeth in hopes they would begin to work faster. Then he took a long drink of water from a plastic jug he kept by his bed.

As the pain in his head began to ease, JD walked out to his small dock and pulled up a fish trap. He pulled out a large catfish and impaled the fish on a long spike sticking out from a post on the dock. He picked up a sharp filet knife and made a light cut behind the fish's head then a long incision down the fish's belly to disembowel the creature. He dropped the knife back on the cleaning table and took up a pair of pliers to begin skinning the catfish. JD cut long, thick filets from the fish's body and tossed the carcass into the muddy water. He pulled a string to open a valve on a bottle of water to rinse the gore from his hands and the filets that he would fry for his breakfast. He would need to visit the spring to replenish his water supply he thought as he closed the valve and walked back inside.

He opened the valve on a propane tank and ignited a small four burner camp stove he used for cooking then coated the filets with corn meal. He poured some water in a pot and set it to boil as the oil heated in a frying pan.

JD portioned out a cup full of grits and shook a healthy dose of garlic salt on top. He tested the oil and then dropped the first of his filets into the hot grease as the water started to boil.

After eating a breakfast of fish and grits, JD gathered his water bottles and placed them in his boat. He walked back inside and cinched a holster around his waist then checked to ensure his pistol was fully loaded. He never knew when an opportunity too good to pass up would present itself in the swamp, and he wanted to be prepared.

He poled his small boat through a narrow canal then tied it to a cypress stump as he tossed his jugs onto solid ground. JD made the short hike to the spring with an armful of bottles and filled each one, making several trips back to his boat with full bottles. The morning sun bore down on him as he stepped back into his boat to head for home. JD slipped the shirt on and tried to ignore the whispers in his head. After he returned home and stored his water, JD would make his way to a small inlet where he stored a larger canopied aluminum boat that he used for his harvesting. If good fortune shone on him, his gator lines would be full and he'd take a nice load of gators to Tommy Jon's for processing.

JD had gone to school with Tommy Jon until Tommy dropped out at fifteen to take over his dad's processing business. He knew of no one that could skin a gator faster or with more accuracy than Tommy Jon did. He was also the man who had set up the customers for JD in Birmingham and Jackson that had brought in good money for him and JD.

Tommy Jon had left a note on his truck that the customers needed gator meat and crawfish, as much as he could harvest and deliver by Thursday for the coming weekend. JD had smiled when he read Tommy's note, knowing the activity would help to occupy his mind.

JD filled his boat with a dozen gators and delivered them to Tommy Jon to begin processing while he returned to the sloughs where he had his crawfish traps. His honey hole was paying off as he filled two fifty-gallon tanks with the lobster-like crustaceans. He checked several of the lines he had baited, and took in another five gators as he headed back to Tommy Jon's place.

"You've had a great day, my friend," Tommy Jon said as he helped JD unload his bounty.

"The swamp was good to me today," JD said as he used a dolly to roll one of the tanks up a small ramp. "I will get these babies on ice and go get my truck," he told Tommy.

"I should have these other gators processed and on ice by the time you make it back," he answered. "You got some really nice hides that should bring us good money this week. I will run them up to Pierre Part tomorrow to market."

"Sounds good to me," JD answered. "I will make my run and be back in a few days. Pick up a few new crawfish traps at market for me," he said as he closed the lid on a large cooler.

"Man these are some pretty steaks," Tommy Jon said, holding up a thick slice of meat he had harvested from a ten-foot gator.

"Hold us a couple back and when I return we'll grill them and have some beer," JD said.

His suggestion brought a nearly toothless grin from Tommy Jon, "Sounds good to me."

"I will see you in a couple of hours," JD said and headed back home to trade out boats and get his truck for his trip north.

When he returned just before dark, Tommy Jon helped him load the large coolers into the bed of his truck. "I got them steaks soaking in some apple cider," he said. "Should be tender as a mother's love by the time you get back."

"I will see you Saturday afternoon," JD said. "Have that beer good and cold."

"I will JD," Tommy Jon said and then watched as one of the few friends he could rely on drove slowly away.

JD planned to drive to the outskirts of Jackson and then sleep in his truck. He would be at the market early the next morning, and if they didn't buy all his harvest he would head over to Birmingham to sell the remainder. He hoped the buyer in Jackson would take the full load so he could start hunting a different kind of prey. His smile deepened as he felt himself grow hard at the thought of his next woman.

†

By late afternoon, I was feeling restless. I felt like my time was wasted, sitting around listening to the others as they tried to piece together the puzzle the killer had left for them. He was a crafty hunter, and had left little behind for them to use, adding to the group's growing frustration. Following the need to escape the tension in the room, I took out the cell phone, and stepped outside the war room to call home.

"Hey Mama," I said when she answered the phone.

"How are you Tally?"

"I'm doing fine, Mama, and you? Everything going okay at Laura's?"

"Yes, baby, we have taken advantage of our time together to prepare some pies, and stick them in the freezer. I swear I haven't peeled that many apples and peaches in my whole life."

I chuckled at my mama's response. She sounded happy and safe and that was all that mattered to me now.

"How is your business going?"

"Slow, but everyone is doing what they can to find him."

"Are you eating and getting plenty of rest?"

"Yes ma'am. Joe is taking good care of me," I answered.

"He sounds like a good man."

I couldn't help but smile. "He is mama. He has me hired on as a consultant so they are paying my expenses, and he even says I'll get a small paycheck for my work here."

"That will be nice. You should be paid for your efforts."

"I almost feel guilty though, Mama," I said.

"Why on earth would you feel guilty?"

"Because I feel like most of the time I'm sitting around just getting in the way."

She sensed my frustration. "Is it time for you to try to enter his mind again?"

I shivered at the thought. I knew she was probably right, but the thought of entering his diseased mind made a chill rush up my spine. "Yes, ma'am, it probably is."

She could sense the hesitation in my voice. "Baby, are you okay? You know you can come home anytime you're ready."

"I know, Mama. I just have to stick this out. I don't think I could stop now even if I wanted to."

"Have faith that you will find him, Tally. I do, and I know you won't rest until that happens."

"I will find him, Mama. I have to," I said with assurance in my voice. I could hear the crowd noise in the diner picking up and looked at my watch to find that it would be time for the supper rush. "It sounds like you will be getting busy soon so I will let you go."

"Call me anytime, baby, day or night," Shelby said.

"I will, Mama. I love you."

"I love you too, and stay safe, my baby."

"Goodnight." I hung up the phone, and stepped outside for some fresh air. The familiar humidity welcomed me like a blanket. The sun was beginning to fade from the late afternoon and the daily rumble of a late afternoon storm threatened in the distance. I could feel the electricity in the air as I walked back inside.

There was a different buzz when I stepped back into the War Room. The group clustered around Johnson, who was reading a BOLO report. I crept closer to the group and asked Toma, "What's going on?"

"We just got a fax from a small town east of here about a missing boy," he said. "He disappeared from his backyard four hours ago. They are requesting all available resources to help with a search."

"You don't think this could be connected do you?" I asked.

"No, I don't think so at all. Hopefully he is just a curious six-year-old that has wandered away from home and gotten lost." He handed me a copy of the fax. A brown-eyed, freckle-faced kid smiled for a school photo, and I felt a pull deep in my mind.

"How far away is it?"

"About ten miles, according to one of Johnson's men," Toma said. "Why?"

"I feel useless here," I admitted. "I wonder if I could take a break and maybe see if I can help."

"Mind if I join you?"

I smiled up at the big man. "Well, I do need a ride."

"Consider me at your service, ma'am," he said with a grin. "We will be back in a while," Toma said to Blair.

She looked at me and smiled. I nodded to her as she turned back to the group.

Toma closed the passenger door behind me then climbed in behind the wheel and started the car. "So how does this work for you?" he asked as he turned the AC on high.

"If it works for me, I usually need something of the person's to establish a contact. So far I have only been contacted by those experiencing a terminal event," I said, proud that I had used some cop lingo. "Hopefully I can tap into his energy. If it works, it will be like looking through his eyes. Sometimes, I can actually hold a conversation with the person."

"It's worth a try, and we get to escape the War Room for a while," he said.

He drove directly to the child's home address. A crowd of people milled around the yard as searchers returned from assigned grids with no success. I noticed a woman sitting on the porch, staring out into the yard, looking like she was in shock, and knew this was the boy's mother.

Toma walked over to check in with the local authorities as I made my way to the porch. I slowly sat beside her on the swing. "My name is Tally, and I would like to help."

"It's almost dark and my baby is out there all alone," she said as tears threatened to steal her voice.

I noticed she was clutching a child's toy in her hand. "Is that your son's toy?"

"Yes, it's my Bobby's favorite toy, a Transformer or something," she said, gripping it tighter.

"Would you mind if I take it for a few minutes?" I asked with a soft, gentle voice.

She seemed hesitant to release the toy, as if she were holding onto her baby. "Please," I persisted, "I promise to give it back."

Reluctantly she handed me the toy, and I stood and walked from the porch into the backyard. I could feel the boy's energy through the toy and I reached out with my mind to search for him. I could feel the path he had taken to leave the yard and started walking in that direction.

Toma watched me leave the porch. As I left the yard, he followed me, along with one of the local officers. He trailed behind me and made no effort to speak to me or break my concentration. The dark was growing, but I had no reservation about the trail I traveled, drawn by the child's fear. "Bobby, can you hear me?" I asked with my inner voice.

No answer in the growing darkness. "Bobby, can you hear me?" I repeated.

"Who are you?" I heard a weak voice reply.

"My name is Tally, Bobby."

"Mama says I shouldn't talk to strangers," he said.

I smiled at his response. "I just talked to your mama. She is very worried about you and wants you to come home, Bobby."

"I can't," he cried. "I don't know how to get down."

"Where are you?" I asked.

"I saw a bunny rabbit in the backyard, but when I went to him he hopped away. I started chasing him so I could take him home for a pet," he said. "I wanted a puppy, but Mama said I'm not old enough for a puppy yet."

"I like puppies too. Did you catch the rabbit?" I asked to tease him.

I could feel the laugh from the little boy. "No silly, he was too fast for me."

"Where did you go after you lost the rabbit?"

"I walked around for a bit but I couldn't find my way home. I saw a white ladder and started to climb. I thought I could see my house," he said. I could feel his fear. "I couldn't see it, and now it's getting dark. I'm scared."

I could feel the tears as they ran down his cheeks. "What does the ladder go to?"

"It looks like a big ball," he said. "I climbed as high as I could, but I got tired, and now I'm scared and can't get down."

"Just stay right there, Bobby. I'm coming to get you," I said.

"Is Mama mad at me?"

"No baby, she just wants you to come home," I said as I whirled on my heels and headed back to the house, stopping to talk with Toma.

I looked at Toma and the female officer with him. "Is there a water tower around here somewhere?"

"About a mile north of here, why?" she asked.

"That's where Bobby is," I said.

"Let's go," Toma said and turned on the run.

"We need to hurry, Toma, he's stuck on the ladder."

"Oh my God," he said.

The chief of police was sitting on the front porch trying to comfort the distraught mother, and heard us approaching at full run.

"He's at the water tower," the female officer shouted to him as we ran past to her cruiser.

"Let's go," he said to the woman still seated on the swing.

Toma and I piled into her cruiser as she tore out of the yard, barely missing a large oak. "Whoa, missy, we need to get there in one piece," he teased.

"Yes sir," the officer said and brought the cruiser under control.

It took only three minutes for us to arrive at the water tower. There was dim lighting around the top, and I could barely make out the child's small form clinging to the ladder about forty feet in the air.

"Damn," Toma said, loosening his tie.

"What's wrong?" I asked.

"I hate heights," he grumbled.

"Do you want me to climb up there?" the female officer asked.

"No, I will get him." He began the climb as the chief's cruiser skidded to a halt.

Bobby's mother climbed from the car, her hands covering her face to hold back her scream of fright as she watched Toma climbing toward her son. I approached her and handed the toy back to her. "He's going to be just fine," I said to assure her.

"How did he get up there?" she asked.

"He was chasing a rabbit he wanted to make a pet. When the rabbit disappeared he realized he was lost, and began climbing to see if he could find his way home, but he got scared," I explained.

"How do you know that?" the chief asked suspiciously.

"Bobby told me," I calmly answered. "I would also recommend getting him that puppy he wants."

His mother stared at me. "How did you know that?"

"He desperately wants a pet. That's why he chased after the rabbit and left the yard," I explained.

"I have a litter of puppies ready to go," the chief said. "Bobby can have first pick."

I turned back toward the tower. Toma was making his way slowly up the ladder.

✝

"Bobby, my name is Charles and I'm coming to get you," he said. "Just sit tight until I get there."

"Yes sir," Bobby answered. "I'm scared."

"I will get you in just a second. I hear from my friend Tally you want a puppy," he said.

"Yes sir, I do," Bobby said, suddenly excited. "I would take really good care of it."

"I'm sure you would, son," Toma said. He was nearly close enough to reach the boy. His shirt was soaked with sweat. He really did hate heights but refused to look down.

"Hey Bobby," he said, finally climbing up behind the frightened child.

"Hey Mr. Charles," he said with a quivering voice.

"I'm going to take you down with me, but I need you to be brave for me," he said. "I want you to turn around, wrap your arms around my neck and hold on."

"I will fall if I let go," he cried.

"No, you won't," he reassured him. "You were very brave to climb this high. Just let go one hand at a time and we can go home."

"Will I get a spanking?" he asked.

"No, son, I can assure you that you won't get spanked," he said with a chuckle. "Your mama is down there waiting for you now."

Bobby leaned backward to try to see his mama, and one hand slipped from the ladder rung. Toma quickly caught it and placed that hand around his neck. "See, we're already halfway there," he said. "Just let go."

Bobby held his breath and reached back for Toma. When he was certain the boy had a good grip on his neck, he started to descend. "Hang on tight and we will be down in just a few minutes."

He had an excellent grip, Toma thought as the child's arms threatened to cut off his air. He climbed down as fast as he could. As he got closer to the ground he could hear people running toward the tower, shouting encouragement. It was a huge relief to feel solid ground under his feet. He handed the child to his mother and with a deep breath leaned back against the ladder.

✝

"You did it Toma," I said, very proud of him.

"Yes, we did," he answered. "Now I think I need a stiff drink."

"Thank you both," Bobby's mother said.

"Thank you, Tally," Bobby said as he reached out for a hug from me.

I took him in my arms and hugged him tight. "Don't chase any more rabbits okay?"

"He won't be chasing rabbits," his mother said. "Tomorrow he's getting a puppy."

"Really Mom?" he cried out as he squirmed in my arms.

"Yes, I think it's time," she said.

"I already know what her name is going to be." He shocked everyone by saying this.

"Oh really, what will you name her?" the chief asked.

Bobby grinned up at me. "Tally, my protector," he said proudly.

The small crowd erupted in laughter, and I felt tears come to my eyes. "You stay safe," I said as I handed him back to his mother.

"Thank you again. I don't know what I would have done," she said.

"Enjoy that puppy," Toma said as he messed up the boy's hair.

We walked back to the cruiser and slipped inside. "The first round is on me," he said.

After picking up his sedan, we drove back to Picayune, back to the War Room. Everyone was relieved and impressed that we were able to rescue the child. After a round of applause, we decided to head out for drinks.

Blair enclosed me in a hug and whispered in my ear. "I am very proud of you."

"It feels good to finally find someone alive," I answered.

"You did something really good, Tally."

We ended up back at the steak house, this time in the bar for several drinks. Not much of a drinker, I nursed a glass of red wine for several hours until she suggested we get some food, and head back to the hotel. I was hoping that she seemed eager to get back to the hotel for some alone time.

We left Joe in the bar still sipping beer with the boys, and ordered salads to take back to the hotel. We ate at the small table in her room in a comfortable silence. When we finished eating, I walked back to my room and returned with a small bottle of bubble bath.

"Care to join me for a soak?" I asked brazenly.

Blair smiled up at me. "I like the way you think. The garden tub is larger in your room," she added.

"I'll get it started then."

She joined me in the bathroom a few minutes later, covered by a plush robe. I was still dressed except for my shoes. She looked at the tub full of bubbles and then pulled me into her arms.

"I have wanted to do this all day," she said as she lifted my chin and lowered her lips to mine for a slow, all-consuming kiss.

When she broke the kiss, I felt breathless and frozen in place. She chuckled softly and said, "I better help you out of these clothes before our water gets cold." Her fingers worked quickly to unbutton my shirt and then unfasten my jeans so I could step out of them. I stood in front of her in a bra and panties as my fingers untied her robe and pushed it off her shoulders.

My breath caught in my throat as my eyes caressed her body. "You are so beautiful," I said as my hands followed my eyes. Her skin was perfectly smooth and soft. I felt her shiver as my fingers traced the curves and hollows of her body. "Are you cold?"

"Not in the least," she said as she lowered the panties from my body and I unfastened my bra. "Do you want front or back?"

"I'll take the front," I said as she helped me into the tub and slipped in behind me.

The lights flickered as we settled into the tub. "We may end up in the dark," she said.

"That won't bother me in the least," I said as I lay my head against her shoulder as her arms encircled my body.

Blair wrapped her legs around my body pulling me into her center as her hands explored my body. I moaned softly as her hands cupped my breasts and her lips nuzzled into my neck. The lights flickered and then went out completely as lightning filled the night sky.

When the water ran cold, we dried our bodies and crawled into my bed. Our bodies entwined as we watched the storm through the picture window. As the storm began to fade, Blair turned to me and kissed me deeply. I sensed her need and felt my body responding to her kiss. Her touch sent tendrils of electricity through me and I felt myself losing control of my thoughts. Panicked, I broke the kiss and turned away from the hurt I saw in Blair's eyes.

"Tally, what's wrong?"

"Oh Blair, I want nothing more than to make love with you right now, but I'm terrified of losing control and allowing him back inside my head. I've struggled to keep him out, and I wouldn't want to ruin our first time together with my mind occupied with the fear of his interference, instead of on you."

Blair lifted my face so she could see my eyes. "I don't want to wait, but I can understand how you must feel with the constant threat of him entering your thoughts. I've waited this long to find you, so a little more time may not be easy, but we can wait, for now." She grinned and kissed me sweetly before wrapping me in her arms.

"Thank you Blair," I whispered.

Chapter Twelve

JD turned into a truck stop a few miles south of Jackson and pulled into a parking spot as raindrops began to fall. He could see lightning flashing in the distance and knew the storm would be upon him soon. He reached over to pull a small duffel bag onto the seat to use as a pillow and kicked his feet free of his boots before stretching across the seat. He watched the clouds passing in front of the moon until the rain on the truck roof lulled him to sleep.

The blast of a truck's air horn jolted him awake the next morning. He looked at his watch to see that he had slept until seven. He couldn't remember the last time he had slept so soundly. He lifted his duffel and walked through a light fog to the truck stop for a hot shower and a change of clothes. JD ate a hearty breakfast while he waited his turn in the rented showers.

An hour later, JD pulled onto the highway to make his first delivery. He was disappointed that the buyer only took half of his harvest, but the price was exceptional. So, after unloading the meat and returning the empty cooler to his truck bed he climbed behind the wheel to head for Birmingham.

Twenty minutes out of Jackson he took an exit and turned right onto a two-lane road. He took another right on a small path, which led to an abandoned house. He had scouted the area on a previous trip. The wood-framed house looked like it had been a sharecropper's house, with dirt floors and remnants of cotton fabric in the windowsills. Regardless, whoever had lived there hadn't had much in the way of possessions, and the only thing left behind was a worn cot, a small table and a chair with the back broken off. JD was surprised that some homeless person had not stumbled across this find. It wasn't much to look at but the tin roof, while rusted, still protected the small house from the elements.

Content that the house had remained undisturbed since his last visit, JD returned to his truck and drove onward. He made it to Birmingham in record time, finished his delivery, and got back on the interstate before the sun began to set. He took a planned detour from the interstate and drove into Tuscaloosa. Students would be plenty as the new semester was underway, and he felt his hunt would be successful. He drove past many women, but most walked in small groups as they rushed to classes or home for the day.

On his second trip through the campus, his luck changed. He slowed his truck as he approached a single young woman walking down the sidewalk. He rolled his window down as she turned her head to look at him.

"Excuse me, miss. Could you tell me where Tutwiler Hall is?" he asked. "I'm trying to surprise my daughter for a visit, but I'll be danged if all these buildings don't just look alike."

She smiled at JD and he knew then that she was his. "That's very sweet of you," she said as she approached the truck. "I hate to tell you, but you are on the wrong side of the campus though."

He put his most disappointed look on his face. "I was hoping to catch her before she went to the cafeteria and take her out to dinner."

She leaned down and began giving him detailed directions on how to weave through campus to find the dormitory.

"I will never remember all those turns," he said. "Would you consider showing me the way?"

She looked down at her watch. She had an hour before she was supposed to meet Greg at the library. "I guess I could," she said.

"Hop in," JD said with a grin.

The woman climbed in. When he pulled away from the curb, the doors locked automatically, causing the woman to jump and look at JD.

"It's one of the new model safety features," he explained. "When you put the car in gear the doors lock."

"That's a good feature to have," she said. "Turn left here." She pointed to a street sign.

He allowed her to direct him through a few other turns, and when he was sure no one was looking he pulled over to the curb. She looked toward him and was about to ask something when his fist struck her in the face.

He quickly cuffed her while she was out and held her down on the seat as he drove back to the interstate, away from prying eyes.

✝

The following morning I was still riding the high of finding Bobby and spending a glorious night with Blair. The team had just finished making their morning reports when I felt a familiar buzzing in my head. The rumble of voices in the room dimmed and then exhausted altogether as I slipped into the darkness. Lisa was there immediately.

He's on the move, Tally, and has taken another. Try to enter him to see where he is, she suggested.

135

I covered my ears with my hands and propped my elbows on the table as I focused on entering his mind. A wave of nausea flowed through my body as I felt my mind moving. Suddenly, I was in his mind, and I had to force myself to not gasp as the revulsion rose like bile in my throat. I could feel the pain in his head when he turned to look down at the dark-haired woman, who was still unconscious, lying on the seat. As his eyes came back to the road I searched desperately for any sign of where he was. I knew his location immediately when he passed Bear Bryant Boulevard. He was in Tuscaloosa, and near or on the campus of the University of Alabama. With great joy, I left his mind and felt myself reenter the room.

"He's in Tuscaloosa and he has another woman," I said. The room fell silent.

"What else can you tell us?" Blair asked.

"She's dark-haired, probably brunette. She was unconscious and handcuffed in his truck. I think she's a college student. He just passed over Bear Bryant Boulevard."

"Johnson, get on the phone and see if the locals can put out a net; let's try to catch him before he leaves Alabama," she instructed.

"I will call up the state patrol and get them to issue a BOLO for all red trucks," Joe said.

†

JD wove through traffic until he reached the outskirts of town and found a state road that would cross over into Mississippi. His experience told him to stay off the interstate and other main highways until he was well away from Tuscaloosa. He pushed the speed limit, eager to flee possible detection and begin his fun. He stopped at a crossroads and gagged the young woman. She would be waking up soon; the last thing he wanted to hear was her begging and whining.

He turned on the radio to drown out any noise she may make and sang along with the radio.

He was twenty minutes out of town when the radio announcer broke in for a rush hour traffic report: *"All major routes leading out of the city are experiencing severe delays as authorities search for a particular vehicle."* The DJ did not describe the vehicle they were searching for, but JD knew they were hunting for him.

It may be time to change vehicles for a while, he thought as he drove down the highway. If they were looking for him, they were getting too close for comfort. There was only one way they could have known where he was so quickly. That woman had managed to slip inside his mind again. He didn't feel her, but the pain in his head could have masked her arrival.

"Two can play this game, sweetheart," he spoke aloud. His head was already pounding so what was a little more pain. He pulled to the side of the road, out of view of oncoming traffic, and put the truck in park. He squeezed his eyes closed causing the pain in his head to worsen shortly as he searched for the trail she would have left when she abandoned his thoughts.

†

I took a sharp intake of air and sat bolt upright as I felt him enter my mind. You think you are pretty smart, don't you, bitch? he snarled. Well, I too can play your game of hide-and-seek.

I'm going to hunt you until you are caught, I answered him.

He laughed that wicked laugh. Better hunters than you have failed to find me.

I won't fail, so why don't you let that young woman go and end this now?

And spoil all my fun? No way, I have such special plans for her, he taunted. She felt him flinch from the pain.

I hope your head bursts from all the pain, you crazy son of a bitch, I said as I projected as much energy toward him as I could. I felt him howl in pain. There, how did you enjoy that?

Not as much as I'm going to enjoy you. Maybe I should just come for you and end your miserable life, freak, he growled. Or maybe I should just take your red-haired friend and show her a good time. I hear redheads are hot in bed. Is that true?

His threat took me by surprise for a second. *Bring it, asshole,* I growled back at him.

In due time, missy, he warned, in due time. I felt him take a deep breath against the pain. Come find me in the bayou and I will teach you how to play this game, little girl.

Consider me on the way.

With a sound of completely insane laughter, I felt him leave my brain. I immediately ran to the bathroom to purge the contents of my stomach. Blair rushed in behind me.

"What happened, Tally?"

"He entered my mind and we had a rather aggressive discussion, but I confirmed he's in the bayou somewhere."

"You cannot personally challenge this man, Tally," she warned. "It is way too dangerous. He has nothing to lose."

"I won't back down from him," I told her as I rinsed my face with cool water.

"Tally, promise me you won't do that again," she pleaded.

I remained silent until she stepped forward and took me in her arms. "Please, baby, I don't want to lose you when I've just found you."

She crushed me into her chest so tightly that it was hard to breathe. I pulled away to stare up at her. "I promise I won't incite him further, but I will find him."

"*We* will find him," she said "to end this all."

"He's somewhere in the bayou," I said. "He challenged me to come find him." I did not share the vile threats he made against her.

"I need to get you armed for your protection."

"I've never shot a gun in my life," I said.

"There's no time like the present then. A small handgun around your ankle should suffice," she said. "A knife, pepper spray or other device would be useless. If he gets that close to you, you are dead already," she warned.

I really had screwed up by challenging this man. Blair's warnings sank to the bottom of my soul as the realization hit that I had marked not only myself, but her as well for danger.

"Come with me," Blair said.

Blair stormed across the room to where Joe and Toma were sitting. "I want you two to get your hands on the most detailed maps of southern Louisiana that you can. Concentrate on areas below New Orleans," she instructed. "This is getting way too personal. I have to get Tally armed and trained on using a firearm now."

"Let me handle that," Johnson said. "We have a stash of confiscated weapons, and I am sure we can find something to suit her there."

"Something small with an ankle holster, preferably automatic," Blair said.

"That won't be a problem. I will get her hooked up tomorrow, and then take her out to our range for a few lessons with our instructor. We have the best in the area," he added.

"Thank you," Blair said. "He's threatening Tally. We have to find him before he finds her."

Both men nodded their understanding of the situation.

"Let me go get started on those maps," Toma, said and excused himself from the table.

"Are you okay?" Joe asked.

"Just worried for Tally, she is way too valuable for us to lose her."

"Yes, she is," Joe, agreed. "Be careful not to allow your personal feelings to blind you to the investigation though."

Blair looked at him with her deep green eyes afire. When she saw the smile of acceptance from Joe, her body relaxed. "I won't," she answered.

After several more hours, we left the War Room and headed back to the hotel. It had been an emotionally exhausting day.

Neither Blair nor I had much of an appetite, so we showered together and curled up in my bed. As predicted, the evening thunderstorm was approaching. We could see the flash of lightning in the distance. Blair wrapped her arms protectively around me and when the next bolt flashed, I said, "One Mississippi, two Mississippi, three Mississippi, four Mississippi, BOOM," as the thunder echoed in the air.

"I haven't thought of that since I was a little kid afraid of the storms," Blair said as she hugged me tighter.

"That's how I always know how close the lightning is," I said as I snuggled into her warmth.

Another flash lit up the sky and I heard her say, "One Mississippi, two Mississippi, three," and then the thunder roared inside my head.

I was in no mood for any more visions today. I squeezed my mind shut as my body relaxed and drifted off to a dreamless sleep.

Blair wrapped her body around Tally as she slept. Fearing that Tally's rest would be ravaged by visions, she held her close until the storm passed and then she drifted off to sleep too.

✝

JD used his large right hand to choke the woman on the seat beside him back to unconsciousness the moment she began to stir. Another twenty minutes on the county road and he would feel safe enough to wind his way back to the interstate. Then it would only be two more exits to the sharecropper's house and his fun could begin.

JD felt himself grow hard as he pulled next to the building. The woman was beginning to stir, so he rushed around the truck to carry her into the building before she could struggle against him. He kicked the door closed behind him and located the cot.

JD wasted no time securing the young woman to the old, stained cot in the sharecropper's house. He used his pocketknife to slice the clothing from her body at a snail's pace, deliberately adding to her terror. The bandana muffled her screams as she struggled against her bindings.

"You have one fine body there, missy," he said, allowing his fingers to trail down the soft skin between her breasts and panties. "I bet you love to tease the boys with this fine piece of ass," he said as he sat down beside her. "I might even be tempted to wager that you're still a virgin," he said as his knife sliced the right side then the left of her panties. He saw her shiver beneath the cold steel's touch. He took the ruined fabric and ripped it off her body.

"Not for much longer though," he said as he stood and started undressing. In his excitement, a button ripped loose from his shirt and rolled beneath the cot, the sound covered by the girl's muffled screams and his distraction with his growing arousal. He lowered the zipper on his jeans and dropped them to the floor.

✝

The next morning, Blair asked, "Have we heard anything from Tuscaloosa?"

Johnson reported that Tuscaloosa PD had received a missing persons report on a college sophomore, Lynn Browning, from nearby Demopolis. Her picture circulated around the room, and when I saw her face, I knew immediately that she was the woman he had taken. I felt a shiver run through me as I now had a name to go with her face.

"Now that they have received a missing persons report maybe they will take us seriously," he said.

"Maybe if they act quickly enough, they will find something on the truck."

"We can only hope," Joe said.

"First thing I need to do is get Tally armed," Johnson said. "Come Tally let's find you a gun you're comfortable using."

†

After they left, Blair started rifling through the file folders in the middle of the table.

"Are you looking for something in particular?" Joe asked.

"I just had a thought. Tally can use personal objects to track people, as she did with the lost boy yesterday. Has our killer left anything of a personal nature behind that she could focus on?"

"Nothing but his DNA and the useless prints as far as I know, but give me half of those files and I'll search too, it beats sitting here twiddling my thumbs until something else comes up."

She gave him a warm smile and passed him a stack of folders.

"What makes you feel he is south of New Orleans?" he asked.

"Just an educated guess," she said. She looked up from the file she was searching. "Most serials don't hunt close to home for fear of recognition, especially once the media starts getting information. Unfortunately, we both know the media will eventually get involved. Besides there has to be thousands of acres of swamp land south of New Orleans, so, what better place to pick if you wanted to hide?"

"Especially if he is an avid outdoorsman," Joe said. "He could be right under our feet and we'd never know it."

"That is a rather daunting thought, so we better find some hard evidence, and soon," she said.

✝

"Hey Sarge, this little lady needs a handgun," Johnson said as they stepped into the gun range office.

"Hey Johnson." He gave me the once-over. "I think I have the perfect weapon. Let me see your hand, darlin'," he said. I offered him my right hand.

"Do you have an ankle holster as well?"

"I will have you hooked up in a matter of just a few minutes," Sarge said and left the room.

"He truly is one of the finest shooting instructors in the area," Johnson said. "Even the state police send trainees to him."

Sarge walked back into the room and handed me a gunmetal blue pistol. "This is a Ruger LCP 380 Ultra Compact pistol," he told me. "They don't make a small gun any finer than this. Lightweight, has a small traction grip, perfect for tiny hands, and a clip that holds six with one in the chamber."

I took the gun and weighed it in my hand. It did fit well and was very light. "If I can't hit him in seven tries I deserve to be a goner," I said to Johnson.

"Have you ever owned a firearm?" Sarge asked.

"No sir, I haven't."

"Why don't you leave the little lady with me, and I will drop her by the station on my way to lunch," he suggested.

"That okay with you Tally?" Johnson asked.

"Yes, Detective."

"Okay, Tally, take a seat here and we'll get started. My name is Greg, by the way."

"Nice to meet you, Greg."

"The pleasure is all mine," he said. "Word travels quickly around these parts. I appreciate what you did to find that lost boy, and helping us find Brianna. She went to school with my baby girl. I swear, I don't know what I would do if someone took her or any of my kids," he said.

"I understand how you feel, and I don't even have kids."

"You can do me a big favor then." He smiled.

"What's that," I asked.

"When you find that son of a bitch, put a bullet in his head with this gun," he said.

"I would love nothing more than to do just that," I said.

"Well, let's get to work then, and I'll show you everything you need to know."

Greg showed me how to take the gun apart and reassemble it, how to clean it, how to load the clip and chamber, and how to most comfortably wear it on my ankle. I knew almost everything except the craftsman who built the gun. He looked at me. "Are you ready to shoot?"

"Yes sir," I answered, and followed him to the indoor range.

Greg explained the art of shooting to me, and within an hour, I was clustering shots within inches on the paper target.

"You are a natural, Tally," he said with a warm smile. "Just remember to breathe and squeeze gently. If you ever have any doubt about hitting your target, aim for his gut. You have the best chance of hitting something. Trust me, no one is going to go far with a 380 round in his gut. A head shot is a guaranteed kill, but any decent contact will slow him down until you can aim, and take a better shot."

"I understand," I said and safely holstered the pistol.

"Wait for me in the office if you will, Tally."

I walked back into the office and waited for his return. When Greg entered, he carried a small carton of ammo and several empty clips. "This will probably be more ammo than you will ever need, but better to be prepared. Keep these clips full and always keep a spare close. The holster I gave you has a slot for a spare, so make use of it."

"Thanks Greg. Do I need to fill out any paperwork or anything?" I asked.

"No, not for you," he said with a grin. "Just remember that favor if you get a chance."

"I will, I promise."

"Let's get you back to the station then," he said and opened the door for me.

"Thanks for everything," I said as I stepped from his vehicle at the station. The weight of the ankle holster would take some getting used to, but it brought a feeling of comfort to me as well. I hoped I never had to shoot anyone, but if I needed to, I had all the tools and training to do it correctly.

†

I walked back inside just as Joe was asking, "What about the stool?"

"We don't know if it was something he brought with him or if it was already in the barn," Blair said. "It's worth a shot."

"I'll have it brought over from the crime lab," Johnson said. "Hey Tally, welcome back. Sarge called to report you're a natural with a handgun."

I smiled at him. "Thanks, he's a great teacher." I looked at Blair. "What are you working on?"

"We're trying to find something that belongs to our killer to see if you can track him that way, like you do with the others," she said.

"That's not a bad idea. Do you think the stool was his?"

"We don't know. Are you willing to try it?"

"Of course I am," I answered.

†

"You know reducing the geographical area has dropped down the listing of red F-150s to not quite five hundred," Toma said.

"Was that the only damned color they made that truck?" Blair asked.

"No, but it was by far the most popular color."

"Can we trim it down to white males in their forties?" she asked.

"We can certainly try. Let me get on it. Those maps should be delivered this evening too."

Johnson walked in carrying the small three-legged stool processed from the crime scene. It was still in the heavy plastic evidence bag. I noted it did still have droplets of blood on its top surface as I carefully opened the bag. "Is there someplace quiet I can go for a bit?"

"You can use my office," Johnson said. "Just close the door behind you. That's about as quiet as you can get around here."

"Thanks," I said.

I closed the door to Johnson's office and sat behind his large desk. The overhead light was off, and a small desk lamp softly lit the room. I sat the stool on the desk in front of me and placed my hands on the legs before closing my eyes.

☦

The pain behind his eyes was horrifying when JD awoke the next morning. He had spent the night on the dirt floor after he had taken his pleasure from the woman. He also realized he was hungry, unable to remember the last meal he had eaten.

He stood and, with tremendous effort, got dressed. His bottle of pain pills was in the truck along with his pint of Jack. He looked at the woman and met her terrified eyes. "I'm going to get us some food. Don't plan on going anywhere," he said with a dark chuckle that made his head hurt worse. He made his way out the door to the truck, confident the handcuffs had her restrained. His hands trembled violently as he picked up the bottle of painkillers and pried the lid free. He chewed three pills before taking a deep draw from the pint to wash the bitter taste down. The pain was growing worse each day and the pills were becoming ineffective in dulling it. He would soon have to go to a doctor or find some other way to kill the pain.

He started the truck and pulled down the overgrown drive to the paved road. He had remembered seeing several fast-food restaurants at the last exit, so he turned north onto the interstate in search of food.

☦

The woman groaned with pain as she turned her head to watch her captor leave. She knew her time for escape was limited and if she was going to survive, she would have to act immediately. The metal cuffs were solid, but she had noticed the previous night that the frame at the head of the cot seemed loose. She was lucky he had failed to secure her legs so with all the might she could muster she brought herself up off the bed onto her feet. The cuffs had been attached to the top bar of the bed frame, and were free to move the length of the frame. She examined the metal cot closely and saw a small stress fracture at the main joint. If she could break that joint, she could free her wrists. She picked up the frame and slammed it down on the hard-packed floor several times before she felt the metal begin to give way. Her ears remained vigilant for any sounds of his truck returning as she pounded the frame against the floor.

She nearly collapsed with joy when she felt the metal finally separate from the frame, but she knew her time to escape was rapidly ticking away. There was no sense in taking her ruined clothes, so she searched the small area. There was a small duffel bag with clothes, but her stomach lurched at the idea of placing any of his clothes on her body. She was moving toward the door when her foot kicked another bag and she heard metal clanking inside.

She opened the bag and gaped at the collection inside. This was his kill bag. She quickly reached for the biggest item in the bag, a long, sharp cane knife. If she was going to die today, at least she could use this weapon to take part of him with her. She grabbed the knife and ran from the building into the small copse of woods behind the sharecropper's house. All night long, she had listened to the sound of traffic on the interstate, and knew it was her best hope of finding help before he returned to find her missing.

She ran as fast as her bare feet would take her through the woods, briars and low-slung branches digging into naked skin, but she didn't care. She was already covered in blood and bruises so what did a few more scratches count. She could see the traffic as it moved quickly on the four-lane highway and her hopes soared.

A hog wire fence topped with barbed wire was the last remaining obstacle to freedom. She knew she needed both hands to climb the fence, but she was terrified to release the knife that was her only source of protection. She looked back toward the house with wild eyes, searching for any signs of the devil that had taken her prisoner, and then dropped the knife through the fence. She gritted her teeth against the pain of the barbed wire as it chewed into her hands and legs, but she finally made it over the top. Her handcuffed hands were soaked with blood as she bent down to retrieve the knife and then ran wildly toward the interstate.

A female trucker locked up her air brakes and nearly jackknifed her rig when a blood-covered, naked woman ran out in front of her truck. The trucker sent up a silent prayer of relief when she pulled into the outside lane barely missing the crazed woman by less than a foot.

She swung open her door and ran around the front of her truck, stopping dead in her tracks when she saw the bloody cane knife in the woman's hand.

"You have to help me," the young woman cried. "He's trying to kill me."

"Okay, honey, I'm going to help you, but you need to put down the knife first." The woman had a long-sleeved button-up shirt open over her T-shirt. She slowly took it off as she approached the terrified woman.

The young woman had a death grip on the cane knife even though the sharp blade had cut slashes in her abdomen. She looked back the way she came, and then back at the anxious woman who had stopped to help her.

"That's it, just drop it on the ground, sweetheart," the woman said. She carefully approached the injured woman, her eyes never leaving the woman's until she heard the ring of metal on the pavement. The trucker draped the oversized shirt over the woman and pulled her close in an embrace.

"Just relax now, you're safe and we're going to get you some help. Can you make it up to my truck?"

The woman nodded her head and allowed the trucker to assist her into the passenger's seat. The driver carefully closed the door behind her, then climbed down and cautiously picked up the cane knife. She had no clue what had just transpired, but she wanted to preserve the knife as evidence for the authorities.

She placed it behind her seat and climbed back into the cab of the truck to pull the truck off the road and call for help as the woman shivered uncontrollably in the seat.

✝

JD smiled when he saw the familiar golden arches. He was starving and now that the pain in his head was beginning to ease, he was hungry. He placed his order and drove to the first window to pay for the food. He pulled a credit card out of his wallet and handed it through the window.

"I'm sorry sir, but our credit card machine is down. Do you have cash?"

JD realized he did not have the cash to cover the meals. "You have got to be kidding me," he growled. "Do you at least have a goddamned ATM machine inside?"

The woman blanched at his question. "Yes sir, we do, but unfortunately it is tied into the same system as the credit card machine so it's down too," she said.

"You have to be fucking kidding me?" JD said, on the verge of going ballistic.

A pimply-faced young man stepped into the window when he heard JD shout. "Calm down mister, there's an ATM at the bank down on the corner," he said as he pointed out the direction. "Get some cash and we'll keep the food hot for you."

JD released a string of obscenities as he put the truck in gear and exited the drive through. He needed to be more careful of drawing attention to himself he thought as he pulled up to the bank. He slipped his ATM card inside and pushed the buttons for a cash withdrawal. He waited impatiently as the machine spit out crisp twenties, a receipt, and his card.

Bitterly impatient, he drove back to the restaurant, paid for and received his food. He was driving back to the interstate when he heard the shriek of sirens. His heart raced in his chest as he slowly entered the on-ramp and blended into the flow of traffic.

†

The truck driver climbed back into the sleeper cab and pulled a blanket out of a cabinet and wrapped it around the woman's body to help with her shivering.

"What's your name, honey?" she asked.

"Lynn, Lynn Browning," she spoke softly through lips that quivered so uncontrollably it was amazing she could speak.

"Just hang in there, Lynn, help is on the way."

"Where am I?" she asked.

"Just north of Jackson, Mississippi, where are you from?"

"Home is in Demopolis, but I was at school in Tuscaloosa when…when he took me."

"Is there someone you need to call?" she asked, pulling out a cell phone.

"My mama, please."

"Give me the number and I will dial it for you."

"Thank you, ma'am," Lynn said, giving her the number.

The woman handed Lynn the phone before stepping from the truck to give her some privacy. In the distance, she could hear the rapid approach of sirens.

†

"Fuck, fuck, fuck," JD said as he pounded the steering wheel. Traffic had slowed to a crawl as drivers gawked across the median to see what was going on. He saw a semi-truck pulled off to the side of the road, but there was no obvious sign of an accident. JD looked beyond the truck and saw the roof of the sharecropper's house just above the trees.

The blood in his veins turned to ice water as he saw paramedics leading a woman wrapped in a blanket to the rear of an ambulance. JD recognized the swollen face of the woman he had taken captive. The pain in his head returned with a vengeance as his blood pressure soared to stroke levels. He remained in the flow of traffic fighting the urge to break free and drive down the median to escape the nightmare that was quickly unfolding. Torn between returning to the house to remove any evidence or to go into hiding, JD chose the latter so he could think through his dilemma. He knew one thing for certain he had to get off the interstate as quickly as possible.

Chapter Thirteen

"Holy shit," Johnson said as he rushed back to the War Room. "We finally got a break," he said as the group crowded around him.

"What is it?" Blair asked.

"He made his first mistake. The college kid managed to escape from him this morning, just north of Jackson."

"You have to be kidding," Joe said.

"Nope, a detective from Jackson just called to say the victim was being admitted to Jackson Memorial under police protection. She was held captive in an abandoned building not far from where she was found. Jackson PD already has the place cordoned off."

"Joe, Tally, and I will go interview her while the other agents go to the crime scene. Johnson, I want you and Toma to get on the phone lines. Talk with everyone you can to set up as big a net as quickly as you can around Jackson. And renew the BOLO on red F-150s," Blair instructed. "Call us if you receive any more updates."

"Yes ma'am," Johnson said as he and Toma hit the phones.

She spoke to the other agents, giving them specific instructions before they all walked to their vehicles and drove north.

"He must be unraveling quickly to have let a victim escape," Joe said on the way to Blair's car.

"Let's just hope he continues making mistakes," Blair said.

"Amen to that," Joe said.

✝

JD took the exit, turned in the opposite direction of the sharecropper's house, and drove the speed limit. He could not risk returning there to retrieve his kill kit. He cursed his luck as he mentally reviewed the contents. Satisfied there was nothing in the kit that could identify him, he decided he had no choice but to abandon it. He had used the same kit for years now and was frustrated that he would have to begin his collection again.

He had to think, but for now, he had to put some distance between himself and the sirens that continued to arrive. He took a county road and continued south. He hoped the activity would distract the locals and he could sneak through unseen. JD supposed they would expect him to head due south, so he took a route to the east that would put some miles between him and Jackson. Then he could find a remote spot to lay low until after dark and then continue his journey home.

✝

"Back off, boys," Detective Tony Hooper said to the group of officers gathered in front of the house. "I just got a call from the Feds and they are taking over the scene as soon as they arrive. We are to tape it off and prevent anyone from entering before they get here."

"Not even a quick look, Hooper?" one of the men asked.

"Not a one. I hope I don't need to remind any of you about contaminating a crime scene," he warned. "Tom, you and Harry stay with me. The rest of you clear out. We have already ruined any possible tire tracks with all this traffic and I'll be damned if I want the Feds to think we are a bunch of country bumpkins."

There were audible grumbles, but the men slowly dispersed and returned to their cars.

"Let's get the tape up," Hooper said as he popped his trunk.

✝

Blair placed a magnetic bubble light on the roof of her SUV and wasted no time in breaking the speed limit as she drove north to Jackson. Joe had gotten on the phone to find directions to the hospital and navigated for her as I rested in the backseat.

I smiled as I realized just how badly the killer had screwed up. It would be very interesting to find out how the victim had escaped and where he had erred in his planning. This type of behavior seemed very out of character, and I wondered if he was beginning to really suffer mentally due to his illness. He had seemed so very under control, and had left very little evidence behind to this point.

Hopefully her escape had caught him completely off guard and there would be items left behind that would help them discover more about him, and if possible, something she could use to track him. I rested my head back against the headrest and reviewed the facts discovered so far.

✝

Special Agent Jerry Thompson, Blair's second in command, pulled into the crime scene. Hooper updated him on the victim's condition and the efforts to track down the perp. He was relieved to find that, while emotionally and physically traumatized, Ms. Browning was physically safe and receiving the medical attention she needed. He was also disappointed to learn that there had been no sign of the red F-150 they were desperately seeking. The man was a regular Houdini when it came to evading detection, but it appeared his luck was fading fast.

"Has anyone been inside yet?"

"No sir, we taped her up and waited for you to show. It's amazing, but even the media hasn't gotten wind of this. I kept a few officers onsite to handle any news crews, but we've been lucky so far." He grinned up at the much taller Thompson. "Hopefully you will be done with your investigation before we get bombarded."

"Let's pray you're right," Thompson said. "There's very little worse than news hungry television crews."

"Ain't that the truth. Do you think this is the serial killer that we've been hearing about through the grapevine?"

"I think it is very likely he is one and the same. Maybe he is starting to make mistakes. Up to this point he's been pretty clean."

"I will wait out here. Just holler if you need anything."

"Thanks Detective," Thompson said and joined his men preparing to enter the house.

The smell of blood reached them before they opened the front door. The heat certainly helped to exacerbate the odor as they approached. "Let's get a lot of photos before we get company," he told one of the men.

A short burp of a siren alerted Thompson to the approach of another vehicle. He turned and saw a Mississippi State Trooper cruiser pulling into the yard and walked toward the vehicle.

"Are you Special Agent Thompson?" the young trooper asked.

"Yes, I am," he replied.

"My supervisor asked me to deliver this to you," he said as he handed over an object wrapped in an evidence bag. "The truck driver that found the young woman gave this to us. She said the victim was carrying it as she approached the highway."

Thompson opened the bag and smiled broadly. He was looking at a cane knife that he felt sure was the murder weapon for at least one victim. The knife still had a substantial amount of blood on it.

The trooper saw him looking at the bloodstained blade. "The blood is all hers. She tore her hands up pretty good making her escape. We had it typed already, and there are no prints except hers," he added.

"Thanks for the delivery," Thompson said and turned back to the house. He felt like he was carrying a priceless artifact and smiled at the potential break the knife represented. He wiped the smile from his face as he gently pressed the door open and stepped inside.

The first thing he noted were the droplets of blood near the bed that had soaked into the hard-packed dirt. There was evidence of obvious injury, but not one that involved massive blood loss. Thompson assumed the blood he was viewing was a product of the repeated sexual assaults perpetrated on the young woman based on their location on the mattress. At least he hadn't had the time to start cutting on her, he thought as he scanned the scene. It was apparent that he had secured her to the small metal cot. From the scars on the metal bed frame, he used handcuffs. He also saw the broken joint and smiled at the ingenuity the woman showed in breaking free of the metal frame. Across the room from the bed sat a small broken chair. Thompson nearly fainted with delight when his eyes came to rest on a small bag, and the contents of the killer's kill kit.

"Well I'll be damned," he said as he knelt down next to the bag to visually review the contents. The killer had left a prized possession behind and he would be distraught that he had lost his kill kit.

✝

I sat across the room from the hospital bed and listened carefully as Blair and Joe interviewed the young woman. Blair questioned her about how she met her captor and the woman went into extensive detail describing his ruse of a loving father, arriving to surprise his daughter and take her to dinner.

"He just looked so harmless and disappointed," she said. "I took pity on him and willingly entered his truck."

Tally watched her closely. The woman had visible cuts and bruises, but at least she had not been in captivity long enough for him to brutalize her like his previous victims. She had suffered through multiple sexual assaults, but with time and therapy, hopefully those wounds would heal. She had escaped with her life, which was more than twelve or more women had. That didn't make it any less painful to listen to her recount the horror she had survived.

A woman burst through the door and I knew immediately her mother had arrived. Blair excused us from the room after a brief introduction, saying that we would be back later.

I followed her and Joe from the room and Blair's cell phone began ringing.

"You're kidding," Blair said after a few seconds. "That's fabulous news. We have finished at the hospital for now so we will head out there," she said and ended the call.

She looked at Joe and me with a huge smile.

"What's the good news?" I asked.

"He must have gotten wind of her escape and he fled the scene without going back to the house. He left his kill kit behind."

"That must have been traumatic for him," Joe said.

"I certainly hope so," Blair answered.

"So, this means we have some personal items?" I asked.

"We have a bag full of them, and the best piece is the cane knife he probably used on Brianna."

I felt myself shiver at the memory of the fatal blow I witnessed. If there was an item that should hold some of the killer's energy, it would definitely be that knife. I sent up a silent prayer that it would be strong enough for me to use to track him down.

✝

JD drove for an hour before he had to find a place to hide. The pain in his head was blinding. He had to find a safe place to park and take some action to relieve the pain. On a whim, he took a small side road and followed it deep into a wooded area. The road did not look like it was used very often and he was fortunate to find an abandoned barn next to a winding stream. The door to the barn was long gone, so JD was able to back inside to conceal his truck in case any aircraft were employed in the search for his vehicle.

The heat inside the barn was stifling, so JD took his duffel bag from the truck and walked down to the stream. He opened the bag and chewed three of the pain pills, chasing the bitter taste with a long drink of Jack Daniels. Then he pulled off his boots and socks, rolled up his jeans, and waded into the cool water. His body felt like it was an inferno and the cool water helped to ease the pain running through him. He felt the pills begin to take affect and waded back to the bank. He sat down on the soft grass and took out the food that was now beyond cold and ate what he was able to choke down.

JD stretched out, using the duffel for a pillow. He gazed up dreamily at the late-summer sky, watching the clouds take on different forms as he succumbed to the effects of the narcotics. His dreams were filled with the woman who had escaped her captivity. In his dreams, she had turned into the monster and was now stalking him with deadly intentions. JD found himself running through the bayou with her hot on his heels. No matter how fast he ran or what shortcuts he took, she was always there, clawed hands and sharp teeth glaring at him through a wicked smile. Her eyes burned with passion as she chased him until he feared his heart would pound out of his chest. Just when the woman creature finally reached him and was pulling his prostate body toward her gaping mouth, he was jarred awake.

His body was soaked with sweat even though a cool breeze blew across the stream. The white fluffy clouds had turned into dark thunderheads as he slept and he could smell rain on the way. He was surprised to find he had slept for nearly four hours and the sun was on its way to the horizon. The rain would help to disguise him because he knew small-town law enforcement would be less likely to venture out of their dry, cool cruisers. He walked into the barn and tossed his duffel in the back just as the first drops began to fall. Thunder rumbled in the distance as JD pulled out of the barn and took a county road south.

He couldn't help but chuckle to himself as his route would take him right back through Picayune. JD knew enough about law enforcement to realize that being the last site of his handiwork there was probably a small task force gathered in Picayune desperately trying to find him and bring him to justice. Even though the woman's escape had been a major blunder on his part, he was confident they would be unable to learn much about him from her. It was a shame he had to leave his kill kit behind, but he would begin to create another when he made it back to the bayou.

He planned to pick his way south through back roads and small towns. With luck, he could be home before midnight. He glanced down at his fuel gauge and knew he would have to stop in the next hour so he searched for a remote station. JD planned to use his mother's credit card to pay for his purchase to eliminate having to go inside where his face might be recognized. He would have to do it soon he thought. These little towns rolled up their businesses at dark, and the building storm would only serve to encourage them to close up shop earlier to head for their own homes.

JD was relieved when he approached a modern convenience store, and pulled up to the pumps to fill his tank. He slid the nozzle into the tank and began fueling while his eyes searched for the store attendant. He saw a couple of teenage kids, one mopping the aisles while another stocked shelves. They never even took notice of him as he filled his tank, grabbed his receipt, and pulled back onto the road.

As he drove, JD tried to figure out where he had erred with the woman. He was certain the cuffs were secure around her wrists and the metal frame of the bed. He regretted not being able to return to the scene to determine how she managed the escape, but lady luck had frowned upon him. He would guarantee his next woman would have adequate restraints to ensure he did not repeat his mistake.

JD smiled when he saw a road sign announcing his return to Louisiana. Just a few more short hours and he would be safely at home. When he reached Highway 90, the tension in his body began to fade. This part of the trip he could complete in his sleep, having traveled it all his life. He felt he knew the location of every tree on the route through several little sleepy towns.

He had decided a change in vehicles would be a good idea, knowing everyone was looking for his red F-150. When he reached his mother's house he pulled the truck inside the garage out of view of any prying eyes. He would switch back to the white utility van when he left his mother's the following day. Right now, all he wanted was a hot shower, more drugs, and a soft bed to sleep in. He used his keys to unlock a back door and slipped inside his deceased mother's home.

JD could still smell the reeking odor of the sweet-smelling perfume his mother used to bathe in all her life as he walked through the house. He passed through the small living room, where she had spent so much of her time, into his even smaller bedroom and closed the door behind him. He walked to the bedside table, pulled out an incense burner and lit a small cone with a smile, thankful his stash was still there. He had started burning the incense when he was in high school to hide the sweet smell of the pot he used to smoke in his room. JD wished he had one of the strong joints now to help dull the endless pain in his head. He stripped out of his clothes and headed into the bathroom for a long hot shower. Scrubbed clean, he downed two more pills and collapsed naked on his bed.

†

I sat up in the backseat when I felt Blair slowing the SUV in preparation for a turn, then I heard her swear aloud. I looked up to see what made her curse and saw the field surrounding the sharecropper's house filled with a frenzy of media vehicles. The cat was definitely out of the bag and the circus had begun.

Blair flashed her credentials to a young man who barely looked old enough to wear a police officer's uniform and he pointed to an area cordoned off for official vehicles. Several other officers maintained a barricade that prevented the press from encroaching on the crime scene.

I could feel the evil aura of the killer as we stepped inside the door. His presence was still very strong in the small house. I tried to ignore it as I followed Blair into the small room. The young woman's pain lingered in the energy of the room as I imagined her torment. My eyes flew to the droplets of dried blood soaked into the packed dirt floor. She had suffered, but she was fortunate to have escaped with her life. Still, she was way too young to have to experience that type and depth of trauma.

My eyes were drawn to an object wrapped in a plastic bag. I knew if I opened the bag, the cane knife would be gleaming up at me. Blair caught my glance and when I looked up at her she nodded her head.

"Take it if you are ready."

I took a deep breath and reached for the knife. I lifted it in my hands, surprised how the weight distributed throughout the knife. There were still spots of blood along the blade from her hands and body as she clutched the knife to her abdomen. I remembered the terror in her voice as she described forcing herself to drop it through the fence so she could have her hands free to climb. It would have been impossible for her to accomplish with her hands still cuffed while holding the large knife.

"His energy is very strong in the knife," I said. "He must have owned this for a very long time."

"I think it would be safe to say that it was one of his prized possessions and it pained him greatly to have lost it," Blair said.

I placed my hands around the smooth wooden handle and immediately felt the knife begin to glow with warmth. I could feel the dark energy emanating from and flowing through the knife. "I can feel him," I whispered. I got a vision of him holding the knife in his hand, slowing stroking a moonstone across the edge of the blade with the gentleness of caressing a lover's face. "This is a very treasured object for him. I think I will be able to use this to find where he is located."

"I sure hope so," Blair said. "We have every interstate in the area covered, but there has been no sighting of him yet."

"He didn't take the interstate," I said. "He figured we would assume he would head south and he has taken a circuitous route home."

"There's no way we can cover that many roads," Joe said, frustrated.

"Could we go to Louisiana?" I asked.

"Isn't that like finding a needle in a haystack?" Joe asked.

"I think if we follow Blair's instinct to focus south of New Orleans we can get close," I answered. "I know we won't find him in Picayune."

"I agree with you there. I'm just not sure I can get clearance for you and me to go," Joe said.

"Do you think you could if I could get Tally on as a federal consultant, so Birmingham just has your expenses?" Blair asked.

"That's a possibility. Do you think you can get her on the Fed payroll?"

"Not a problem," she answered.

Joe called his supervisor and was able to gain clearance for three more days of travel expenses. "If it lasts longer than that, put me on vacation," Joe told his supervisor. "I have to see this through to the end." When he closed his phone, he looked over at Blair. "All settled."

Chapter Fourteen

They all were lost in thought as Blair drove toward Picayune.

"It's going to be late when we arrive back in Picayune, so let's get a good night's rest and head south in the morning." Blair could feel her own exhaustion kicking in and had witnessed Tally nodding off several times in the rearview mirror. Even Joe, who had been as tough as steel, was starting to form dark circles under his eyes from the lack of rest. "I would like to meet with the Task Force prior to our departure to give everyone an update, and to continue following up on assignments."

"I will give Johnson a call and arrange a meeting for seven," Joe said.

†

JD woke up terrorized and coated with a cold sweat. He could feel the fever scorching through his body as the pain thundered in his head. He had been dreaming and the visions he had seen had left him gasping for breath. JD stumbled from the bed to down more painkillers and finish off the bottle of whiskey on the bedside table. He really didn't want to return to his horrid dreams, but sleep was his only escape from the pain. He climbed beneath the covers and pressed pillows over his head like a vise to help provide some relief.

✝

I could feel my head nodding again so I reached down, and picked up the cane knife that had been stored in the rear floorboard. I could feel the faint stirring of a connection as we drove south. It would take a tremendous amount of faith and energy, but I was certain I could hunt this man down. My mind relaxed, and I focused on slipping into his wicked mind.

My skin tingled with energy as my mind reached out to find the killer. The buzzing of a thousand bees filled my ears. I felt my mind slip into his and my body convulsed with horror at the evil images flooding his mind.

I could almost taste the sourness of the whiskey in his mouth as I began to enter his mind. The man was in agonizing pain, making it difficult to remain inside the turmoil in his head. I could tell he was trying to sleep and was self-medicating trying to relieve his pain.

Get out of my head, you dumb bitch, I heard him growl when he sensed my presence.

You're calling me dumb? You're the bastard who doesn't even realize how sick he is. You have syphilis and it's eating away at your brain, I taunted.

What are you talking about?

The horrible headaches, the fever that is burning you alive, are all from the infection. I can feel it growing inside you even now.

You are a lying bitch. Get the fuck out of my head, I heard him scream. Deep down though, he knew I was right. He couldn't deny the torture his body was going through. It must have been that crack head whore in New Orleans, I heard him thinking as he searched his addled brain for a possible source of infection.

Is that another one you killed?

Damned straight, if I could do it again I would, for making me sick.

I'd say you are beginning to reap some of your just rewards, I said.

Get the fuck out, I heard him roar in pain, and then felt a door slam inside his head to block me out.

"What was that?" Blair asked from the front seat.

I hadn't realized I had spoken aloud. "Our killer is dreaming again. He is really sick," I said.

"Could you tell where he was?" she asked.

"No, nothing except that he was inside, and in a bed, not sleeping in his truck. He's close to home if he's not already there. I can sense a feeling of comfort in his surroundings. His body is burning up with fever, though, and the pain in his head makes it very difficult to maintain a focus, for both of us probably."

"I hope the bastard suffers unbearably until one of us can put a bullet in his brain," Joe said with absolute venom dripping from his words.

Blair looked over at Joe. "I agree with you there, Joe. I know the Bureau would prefer we bring him in to stand trial and help to close some other cases, but I don't think he will give us that option when we finally stand toe to toe with him."

"You're probably right, but I would love to be the person to put a bullet between his eyes."

"You might have to stand in line for that," Blair answered.

✝

I was exhausted by the time we made it back to Picayune and had a late dinner. When we arrived back at the hotel all I wanted was a hot shower and Blair's arms around me in a comfortable bed. I looked up at her as we unlocked our doors. "Would you like to come over after we've showered?"

She smiled at the invitation. "Unlock your side of the door and I'll be there soon."

I nodded and entered my room. Clothes disappeared like magic as I made my way to the bathroom and turned on the shower. I walked back to my suitcase and pulled out my last clean nightshirt. Either I was going to have to do some laundry or buy some new clothes I thought as I walked back to the bathroom. I made a mental note to call home before it got too late, then looked at the clock and noticed the time. It was already way too late to call mama. She would have been in bed at least two hours by now, so I decided to call first thing in the morning.

My eyes came to rest on the cane knife safely tucked into the evidence bag. "Rest assured, I will find you," I said to the empty room.

The shower was as close to heaven as I could imagine. The warm water cascading down erased the tension from my body and I felt stiff muscles begin to relax. When the water started to cool, I rinsed one last time and stepped from the shower. I reached for a towel and felt my stomach clench with fear. I knew the killer was dreaming again, and in this dream he was searching for a connection with me. I focused all my energy in blocking him from entering my brain. I'd had enough of him for one day, and I needed a peaceful night to reenergize. I dried off and slipped into the nightshirt before brushing my teeth and hair. As I stared into the mirror, I wondered how much longer this nightmare would continue but knowing it would last until at least he was captured. Weary from that thought, I left the bathroom and found Blair already snuggled under the covers.

She reached her arms out to me as I entered the bed. I gladly rested my head on her shoulder as her long arms wrapped protectively around me. "You feel so good," I whispered against her skin.

"I have been waiting for this all day," she admitted. "I so wanted to kiss you earlier today."

"Well there's nothing stopping you now," I teased as I looked up into her sparkling eyes.

"You are so right about that, Ms. Rainwater," she said and lowered her lips to brush softly against mine.

Blair's kisses reminded me of the love that was growing rapidly between us, and for a short time I could forget the horror of the man we were pursuing. I felt my eyes closing as I drifted off to sleep, still wrapped in her arms. I felt her arms tighten around me in a protective move and then relax as she too began to drift into sleep. I knew then that I was wrong about the shower. This was as close to heaven as I could imagine.

✝

It was nearing five o'clock when I woke with a scream. Blair's body reacted immediately to cover me from any intruder as her eyes searched the room. "What happened?" she asked when she realized there was no one else in the room.

I was still trying to catch my breath when a knock sounded on my door. "Tally, are you all right?" Joe asked.

My scream had apparently awakened him as well. Blair and I looked at each other with panicked eyes as we scrambled to find our clothes. She rushed to her room and tossed back her covers as I started for my door. She gave the impression of coming through our adjoining door, gun drawn, as I opened the door for Joe.

Joe stood at my door in a white T-shirt and boxer shorts, his gun drawn as his eyes scanned the room for intruders. I stifled a laugh and then remembered all three of us were dressed for bed.

"I'm sorry I woke you, Joe, I was having a nightmare."

"I think that bloodcurdling scream took a few years off my life," he said. "Are you okay?"

"Yes, I think I'm fine," I said.

"You scared me too," Blair said. That was not a lie as she reacted to immediately protect me from impending harm.

"I'm sorry. I didn't mean to scare either of you."

"No need to apologize. Do you want to talk about it?" he asked.

"Not now, Joe, I need to write some things down first before I forget," I answered. "Maybe we can meet for an early breakfast, now that I have everyone wide awake."

Joe smiled at her. I knew he was pleased that I was following his direction in writing facts down while they were fresh.

"I'll shower and meet you two in the dining room at six," he said before turning away to return to his room.

Blair closed the door behind him as I had already walked over to the small desk where my notepad and pen were lying. I sat down and began writing while Blair sat on the edge of the bed, remaining silent until I looked up. She looked worried, and I was sure the same look crossed my face. The visions I had received in my dream were very disturbing, one more so than all of them together. I had seen an image of my mama's face in the vision and I struggled to make sense of it. That had been the face that had jarred me awake screaming at the top of my lungs.

"I don't know what is happening," I said, on the verge of tears.

Blair rushed over and pulled me up into her arms. "It's going to be okay," she whispered as her hand stroked my hair. "Everything will be all right, I promise."

I could feel my body shaking violently in her arms. "I need…I need to call my mama."

She hurried to find the cell phone I had charging and handed it to me. "Do you need me to dial?"

"No, I think I can manage."

"I'll go shower and dress then to give you some privacy, unless you want me to stay."

"Go ahead, and I will join you as soon as I can."

Blair nodded and kissed me softly before returning to her room.

Without her arms to hold me upright, I collapsed into the desk chair. My knees were still shaking from the visions in my dream. I had seen the man do horrible things to the women in my visions. What startled me the most was seeing the image of my mama. I did not understand why she would be in his vision, but I had to hear her voice to know that she was okay. It was still early in Georgia, but I knew Mama would be awake and already at work. With fingers still trembling from fright, I pushed the number to Laura's diner.

"Hello Laura. I'm sorry to call so early but I need to talk with Mama," I said.

"No worries, Tally, hang on and let me get her."

The silence was terrifying until I heard Mama approach the phone. "Hey baby, is everything all right?"

"Yes Mama, I'm doing fine I just needed to hear your voice to know you're all right."

"I'm doing well. I was getting a customer coffee when you called. Are you sure you're okay? How is your project coming?"

"We are making slow progress, but we're making progress," I said. "I even helped find a missing little boy."

"That's great news, baby. I'm so proud of you. Are you taking care of yourself? Eating well and getting your rest?"

"Yes ma'am. We will be going down to New Orleans later today and I wanted to call before it got too late to call again." I sighed deeply. "The last few nights have been late nights and before I knew it time had flown by until it was too late to call."

"Don't worry at all about me, Tally. Laura is taking very good care of me. You stay focused so you can catch that bad man and come home."

"I'm trying my best, Mama."

"I know you are, honey, just trust in yourself and your gift. You will find him and bring justice for all those women."

"I wish I had all of your confidence," I admitted.

"I know you, Tally Rainwater. You won't quit until the job is done."

Mama had a way of knowing when I was smiling. "You just keep that smile on your face and get him," she said.

"Thanks for the boost, Mama, it's just what I needed."

"Be careful, and call me again when you can to let me know how you're doing."

"I will. I love you."

"I love you too, Tally. Don't ever forget that."

"Yes ma'am. I will call you again soon."

"Goodbye, baby," Mama said and hung up.

I was relieved to hear her voice and to know that she was all right. I still had no idea why her face came to me in the killer's dream, which left me feeling uneasy. There was no way he could have learned who I was and ultimately known about my mama, so maybe I was projecting my worry for her in my dreams. For the life of me, I could not fathom any other reason.

I took a quick shower and dressed. I packed the remainder of my items in my small bag in preparation of checking out of the hotel. I knocked on her door and waited for her to open it.

"Hey, baby, are you all set?"

"Yes, I'm all packed and ready to check out after breakfast."

"Are you okay?" she asked, the worry plainly written across her face.

"Yes, I was much relieved to hear Mama's voice. I needed to make sure she was okay."

"Has something happened that had you concerned for her?"

I took a deep breath. "I saw her image in the dream I was sharing with the killer."

"No wonder you were freaked out. Do you know why?"

"The best explanation I can think of is that I projected her into my dreams, and thus into his."

"You don't think there's any danger for her do you?"

"I can't think of any way he would even know she existed."

"I don't know how he could. I'll have an agent put her under surveillance."

I thought for a second. "I don't think it is necessary just yet."

"Maybe not, but I'm not taking any chances with the mama of the woman I love," Blair said.

"Thanks."

"I don't want you to worry for her safety."

"That means a lot to me."

"You mean a lot to me," Blair said as she lifted my chin to look into my eyes. "Don't forget that either."

"I won't," I said.

"Good. Now let's go have some breakfast."

†

After breakfast, I told Blair and Joe about the painful images I had seen in my dreams. I didn't feel I needed to worry Joe about the image of my mama in the dream so I left that part out.

We checked out of the hotel and left for the meeting with the task force. It was agreed that Johnson would remain in Picayune to continue following up on the leads they were getting from the latest victim, while Charles, Joe, and the other agents accompanied us to New Orleans.

"I have a feeling he was infected by a prostitute in New Orleans. He mentioned a whore he killed, and I believe it was there," I said.

"I will make contact with NOPD to see if they have any unsolved cases that may fit the profile," Johnson said. "Do you really think you will be able to track him?"

"I think I have enough of his possessions that carry his energy to be able to narrow things down quite a bit. That cane knife definitely puts out strong energy," I said.

"Good luck and keep us posted," Johnson said as we finished packing and prepared to leave.

"Thanks for all your help," Blair said as she shook his hand.

"My thanks to you all, especially you, Tally," he said as he placed a large hand on my shoulder. "You are a remarkable young woman."

"Thanks," I said, slightly embarrassed.

"I hope I can count on you in the future if I need your help."

"Of course you can," I told him and gave him a quick hug.

The convoy left Picayune and headed south to New Orleans. The plan was to cross over the river south of New Orleans and begin hunting for a suitable hotel to set up shop. As we rode, I flipped open my notebook and reviewed the notes I had scribbled earlier.

Every time my eyes wandered across my mama's name in the notebook a prickle of unease ate away at my stomach. There was something there, but I couldn't put a finger on it. Joe remained quiet until I closed the book and began staring out the window at the endless swamps and bridges.

"Is there something you aren't telling me?" Joe asked.

"Why would you think that?"

"You just seem unusually distracted."

"My mama's face was one of the images in my dream this morning."

"That's really odd isn't it?"

"Yeah, I can't figure out why she would be in his dreams. I did go to bed thinking about calling her this morning so the only thing I can think of was that I projected her into the dream."

"Did you call her?"

"Yes, I did, and everything is fine with her."

"I can have a protective detail placed on her if you think she's in danger," he said.

I smiled at Joe. "Blair said the same thing. She already has someone watching over mama."

"You two seem to be getting quite close," Joe said with a grin.

"She's a beautiful, intelligent woman," I said, surprising myself by how easy it was to talk about Blair. "She has taught me a great deal, along with you."

"You have taught us a great deal too, about having faith in a fellow human being and about being more open-minded when it comes to psychics," he said.

"Do you think we will catch him soon?"

"I sure hope so, Tally. He seems to be unraveling. Hopefully his failure in Jackson will be the beginning of the end. He is already making critical mistakes."

"I hope it ends soon before he takes another victim."

"Maybe. It will take him a while to assemble a new kill kit. I heard someone say that serials take a lot of pride and detail in making their kits, so hopefully that will buy us some time."

"That would be very nice," I said as I saw a Welcome to Louisiana sign beside the road.

"Not much farther now," Joe said.

†

JD woke with a start from the dream. He had always heard that people near death see their lives flash before their eyes and his latest dream certainly qualified for that. His visions flashed from his days as a traveling salesman through all of his kills up through his recent failure. It left him wondering if his days were ending. Then there was the interference of the woman who seemed to have free access to his world through his eyes. Her presence increased the pain in his head and he desperately hoped he would have an opportunity to share some of that with her before his time was over.

He stretched and was relieved that the sleep and medications had eased the pain he had suffered the previous night. He was looking forward to spending a relaxing day drinking beers and having a cookout with Tommy Jon.

He searched the room for his watch and found it was nearly noon. He dressed in fresh clothes and then located the keys to the white van. He searched his mother's medicine cabinet and found a bottle of antibiotics. He popped a couple in his mouth then tucked the bottle into his pants pocket. He wasn't sure they were the type of antibiotics he needed to clear up his infection, but he figured they couldn't hurt until he could get into a clinic to see a doctor.

It pained him to leave his prized truck hidden in the garage, but he was sure it had become a critical point in the hunt for his location. He rummaged through the garage until he found another small tool bag that he would use to begin his new collection. He would assemble his tools of trade and when he had everything in place, he would hunt once more.

He smiled brilliantly as he backed the van out of the garage, slipping a pair of dark sunglasses over his eyes to shade them from the bright sunny day. He drove slowly through town, stopping to allow traffic from one of the small churches to merge onto the highway. He smiled and waved at several drivers as he made the trek to Tommy Jon's home.

An hour later he walked through the door to Tommy Jon's place. "Hey JD, I'm glad you made it back okay. Did you have a good trip?"

"Thanks Tommy Jon. It wasn't bad at all. I got a good price for the catch, and the weather held out."

"I got my airboat running again while you were gone. Would you care to take a quick spin while the beers get icy?"

"I could use some time on the water," JD said. "I hate being landlocked, even if it's just a day or so."

"I know what you mean. I took a trip to see some family up near Nashville once, and I swear being away from the bayou made my skin crawl."

"Yeah man, that's about the size of it. I don't see how them city people stand it."

"Me either, brother," Tommy Jon said. He clapped JD on the back. "Let's go make some waves."

JD and Tommy Jon spent several hours riding through the bayou. JD noted several sloughs that held promise to some good-sized gators and he made a mental note to set out some bait soon. He had plenty of license tags left and when those ran out, he and Tommy Jon would continue to work the black market that welcomed fresh gator meat year round. They were swamp men, and they would continue to live the way their relatives had for hundreds of years, making a living and surviving on the bounty of the bayous.

When Tommy Jon tossed him a line he secured the airboat to the dock. "Let's pop some tops," JD said.

Tommy Jon lit the charcoal in a homemade grill while they drank some of the ice-cold beer. "Thanks for taking a ride with me."

"I enjoyed it," JD said. "It's nice to sit back and unwind a bit."

"You have been pushing pretty hard lately. When's the last time you had you a vacation?"

"It's been a mighty long time," JD answered.

"Why don't you take off and go somewhere then?" Tommy Jon asked.

"Don't know where I'd go." JD hung his head and his friend knew he had touched on a sore spot. "Now that Mama has passed I don't have any more family."

"I'm sorry to make you sad," Tommy Jon said.

"It's okay, Tommy Jon, I know you didn't mean any harm."

"I will always be here when you need a friend, JD."

"I know that, and I really appreciate it. I can always count on you."

"You've been looking kind of peaked lately. You feeling all right, JD" he asked.

"Naw, I'm gonna have to go see the doc. I think one of them girls in Nawlins gave me the clap or something."

"Good lord, man, you got to get that seen to," Tommy Jon said with a sheepish grin. "You don't want nuttin' falling off."

JD looked at his friend and just shook his head. "You ain't doing too good at cheering me up," he teased.

"I'm sorry, man, let me get us a fresh beer and shut up."

JD laughed at his friend's response and the cold beer he offered. "I reckon I will stay in town tonight, go see a doctor then go home, and get ready to tag some more gators."

"Let me know if you want some help. Things are kind of slow around here right now."

"Head on out to my place Monday morning then. You can help me hang some bait in a couple of those sloughs we passed today."

Tommy Jon broke out in a huge smile. "You want to take the airboat back out?"

"Sure, that will work just fine." JD propped his feet up and relaxed while Tommy Jon prepared the meal for grilling. He dozed off for a bit, his body snapping to attention when the warm beer can fell from his fingers with an audible thud.

"You're more than welcome to stay here tonight," Tommy Jon said. "You look really tired."

"That is probably a good idea," JD said, getting up to get another cold beer.

"Let me go get the guest room ready then while the food's cooking."

"Don't go to any trouble," JD said.

"It's no trouble at all," he said. It had been years since he had an overnight visitor so he was excited to have the company. "I'll be right back."

JD watched his friend disappear into the house and smiled. He was probably the only friend Tommy Jon had. The type of work he did, the constant smell of fish that seemed to flow through his pores, repulsed most people. JD was used to the smell and appreciated the hard work his friend provided for his customers. He lifted the cold beer can and rolled it across his forehead to soothe the heat burning inside his brain.

✝

"This one will do," Blair said as they located a small chain hotel. She sent one of the agents to inform the locals that they were in the area, and to inquire about the availability of a room for the task force. The hotel had a small conference room, but Blair did not cherish the thought of some curious maintenance worker or housekeeper walking in on something so horrible.

"Let's check into our rooms and get settled in. Joe, can you give Johnson a call to see if he has any other information for us?"

"Sure thing, Blair," he said and carried his small bag to his room.

"I need to do some laundry. Is there a guest laundry?" I asked.

"Down on the first floor, according to the front desk," she said. "Let's get settled in and I'll go with you. I need to wash a load too."

We were in the process of folding the last load when Joe rushed into the laundry room.

"There you are," he said, wearing a huge grin.

"You look like you have good news," I said.

"Johnson just faxed this to the hotel," he said, handed Blair a piece of paper.

"The boys in Jackson got Lynn to settle in with a sketch artist and they have a composite of what our killer looks like."

Blair and I studied the face that looked out of the page. There were also notes at the bottom of the page providing a physical description: brown hair with light graying, six foot tall, one hundred eighty pounds and blue eyes with a tattoo of DEATH on the knuckles of his right hand.

Blair looked up at me. "What do you think?"

"It feels right," I said. I had never seen his face, but I had a notion that the description was close.

"Johnson has already sent this out to locals in the surrounding area in hopes that someone will recognize him," Joe said.

"Good job. Thanks for getting this to us. When we hit the local PD tomorrow let's make plenty of copies we can use in our manhunt."

"I will take care of that first thing," Joe said.

"Let's put these clothes away and round up the rest of the gang for dinner," Blair said, her mood definitely lifted by the new information.

†

When we returned from dinner, I decided to take a shower. Blair said she would do the same and then join me afterward. I turned on the television for the news, freezing in my tracks as the composite sketch flashed onto the television screen. I rushed over to the adjoining door and banged my fist on it. "Blair, come in here quick."

She came through the door half undressed as I leaned down to turn up the volume. A local talking head reported that authorities were seeking the man in the sketch for questioning. An 800 number flashed across the bottom of the screen, encouraging viewers with information on the man's identity to call.

"Damn," she said in obvious distress.

"What? Isn't this a good thing?" I asked.

"It will either be a blessing or a curse," she said. "I don't know who authorized this release, but I will definitely find out tomorrow."

"Okay, explain that to me," I said.

"It will be a blessing if we luck out and someone recognizes the image."

"Yes, that would be nice. So what's the downside?" I asked.

"It will turn into a curse if the hotline receives thousands of calls. Each one requires manpower to follow up and most of them will be crackpot calls." She looked deep into my eyes. "Even worse, if the image is even remotely close and the killer sees it, he may go even deeper into hiding."

Blair's cell phone rang. "Yeah, I saw the television spot," she said with a hint of anger still in her voice. "We will deal with that tomorrow," she said and hung up.

"Are you okay?" I asked.

"I'm tired, in need of a hot shower, and a good snuggle with you," she said with a grin. "We need a good night's rest. Tomorrow is going to be a really long day."

"Go shower and then get your cute tail back in here," I said, watching her leave the room before heading off to my own shower.

Chapter Fifteen

JD and Tommy Jon had finished off the feast and the larger part of a case of beer. JD chewed a few more painkillers, added a couple of antibiotics and chased it all with the last swallow of beer in his can. "I think I'm done for the night," he said as he tossed the empty can in a large metal drum.

"Come on and let's get you settled in," Tommy Jon said. "I don't have no television, but I can turn on a radio for you if you want," he added.

JD laughed softly. "Ain't nothing good on TV these days anyhow, I will just let the sounds of the bayou lull me to sleep."

"There's nothing better in my book," Tommy Jon said.

It wasn't long after my body slipped into REM sleep that Lisa came into my shadow world.

That picture is very close, she said. I feel like you will have him soon. Just be very careful, Tally, he is a very dangerous man.

You can see through my eyes? I asked.

Sometimes yes, does that bother you?

No, it's just a little eerie, especially since I don't feel your presence. When he enters my mind, I know immediately.

That's because he is a wickedly evil man. I died still an innocent, Lisa said with a grin. I will ask permission before entering if that would make you feel better.

Just let me know when you're riding around, I requested.

I will, Lisa answered.

Can the others do that too?

Not that I am aware of, why?

Because I don't have room in my head for all of you at once, I teased.

I think I am the only one that has ventured so far, Lisa answered.

Has anyone thought of anything else that would help us find him?

Lisa sighed deeply. *Not yet.*

Don't worry, Lisa, we will find him.

I know. I just hope he doesn't kill any other women before you do.

It's been like finding a needle in a haystack so far, but I think we are in the right hayfield now at least.

You are doing all that you can, Tally. Rest now and be ready for tomorrow. I have a feeling it's going to be a big day.

Do you know something you aren't telling me?

No, I just have this feeling.

Keep your fingers crossed then, I said. Goodnight Lisa.

Goodnight, and stay safe Tally.

Thankfully, the rest of the night was dream free and my body received the rest it desperately needed.

†

JD woke to the smell of frying bacon. "Damn you got this place smelling good, Tommy Jon," he said when he wandered into the kitchen.

"I wanted to send you off with a good breakfast," he said.

"I appreciate that. I think the clinic opens at nine."

"Do you want me to come out later today so we can hang some bait?"

"Yeah, plan on coming out around lunchtime. I'll let you know if I'll be longer at the clinic."

"Sounds good to me, man."

JD finished his breakfast then drove to town. He debated trying to see his mother's doctor but decided the clinic would be a much faster option. All he needed was a few tests and some stronger drugs to make him better.

He was the first in the door of the clinic, but still had to wait twenty minutes before a doctor could see him.

"What seems to be the problem, Mr....Walker?" the young doctor asked.

"I think I've got some kind of infection," JD said.

"What type of infection?"

"Of a sexual nature," JD said.

The doctor listened to JD's description of his symptoms then suggested a few blood tests. "Hopefully it won't take long to get the results," the doctor said. "Take a seat in the lobby and I'll let you know when we get the results."

JD mumbled something under his breath about having to wait, but strode back to the lobby and plopped down in one of the uncomfortable chairs. He searched through the meager magazines but found nothing that struck his interest. There were no Serial Killer Digests or Mass Murderer's Monthly in the magazine rack he chuckled to himself as he settled back in his seat.

✝

Rex Corbin was the Chief of Police in Raceland, the small town off Highway 90 where they had set up shop. He welcomed Blair and her crew, ushering them into the room her agents had confiscated to use as the Task Force War Room.

Blair looked at Toma. "See if you can track down who gave the composite on the television media, and see if we can get tapped into that eight hundred number."

"I'm all over it," he said.

Within the hour, they had begun to receive tips from the hotline that were in the general vicinity of their location. Toma tracked the television coverage to the police in Jackson, and Blair vowed to call them later and give them a piece of her mind for their interference. The only saving grace would be if the tip line brought them some useful information.

"I have an idea," Joe said. "It may be a long shot, but maybe not."

"What are you thinking?" she asked.

"I don't have a great medical background, but don't physicians and clinics have to report sexually transmitted disease cases?"

"You may have something there, assuming our killer is aware he is sick," Blair said.

"He's aware, I made sure he knew he was infected," I said. She whipped her head around to look at me in surprise. "Sorry, I couldn't help myself."

"Okay Joe, why don't you get started on that project. Let me know if we are going to need a subpoena to access the records as soon as possible."

I felt useless amidst all the activity in the War Room. Everyone but me seemed to have an assignment. I felt a need to be away from the activity so I could concentrate. I looked up at Blair. "May I borrow your vehicle?"

"Sure you can. Are you all right?"

"I just need to get some fresh air and find a spot where I can concentrate."

"Do you want me to send someone with you?"

"No, I think I need some downtime, and you all have so much to do," I said.

"Be careful and don't do anything that places you in any danger."

"Yes, Mama," I teased as I took the keys she offered.

"There is a map in the console and a built-in GPS, so don't get lost. It could take us days to find you."

"I will be back before dinner and I promise to call you to check in," I said.

Blair sent me the sweetest of smiles. "I will miss you," she whispered as she leaned in close.

"See you soon," I said. As I walked from the room, I could feel her eyes on me as I left but dared not turn to see the passion in them.

I walked out to the parking lot and found her SUV, pushing the key fob to unlock the doors. I climbed inside and locked the doors before reaching for the cane knife. I closed my eyes, and waited for the energy to swarm and enter my hands. I felt the warmth intensify and I suddenly felt an urge to drive south.

My hands shook a little when I replaced the knife on the passenger's seat. I could sense an increase in activity, like a storm surge building. I knew we were getting close to finding the killer. I turned the key in the ignition and adjusted my sunglasses before putting the SUV in gear to begin driving south.

The road was more of a string of unending bridges as I drove deeper into bayou country. My mind could sense the peacefulness of the sloughs and bayous. Centuries old cypress trees grew like fingers toward the sky, their delicate arms draped with gray Spanish moss that blew gently in the breeze. I was amazed at how identical everything looked and understood how easily one could become lost, or hide in the bayou without fear of discovery.

Thirty minutes later, I saw a sign for a wayside park and turned on the blinker to make an exit from the road. I hadn't seen another vehicle on the highway for twenty minutes and wasn't surprised to see the park empty of visitors. I pulled to a stop in front of a covered concrete picnic table and picked up the cane knife from the passenger's seat. I exited the SUV, slipping the keys into my pocket.

Sleep overtook JD in the waiting room of the clinic. At first, the dreams stayed away, and he rested peacefully though the fever burned through his body. When they did come, the dreams were of his childhood. His grandfather was there in the dreams with him. They were at a powwow. He could remember his father telling him stories of their Indian heritage as they watched colorful dancers performing to the beat of heavy drums. The war paint on one particular dancer's cheek, a red crawfish, enthralled JD. His dream flashed forward to his life in the bayou after he woke from his coma following his accident. He had bought a can of red paint and painted the image on his aluminum boat. He remembered being very pleased with the symbol's appearance and began to think of it as his personal mark. A thought came to him as he slept in the chair that maybe he should begin to mark his prey with the symbol as a final stamp of ownership. They were his after all, and should carry his mark.

He was still thinking this thought when a hand on his shoulder shook him awake. The heavyset nurse that had checked him in earlier was standing over him, speaking to him.

"Mr. Walker, the doctor will see you now," she repeated impatiently.

JD startled awake and then looked up at her with his cold blue eyes.

Undeterred by his glare the nurse said, "Follow me," and turned to lead him back to an exam room.

JD took a seat inside the room and continued his wait. His acute hearing picked up the sound of a chart sliding from a pocket on the exam room door and he knew the doctor would arrive soon. A knock came to the door and a concerned-looking doctor stepped inside and sat across from JD.

"Your test results have returned, Mr. Walker," he said while studying several pages of laboratory results. "I'm afraid it isn't good news, I have to report."

"What is it, Doc?"

"The tests revealed that you have late-stage syphilis," he said. "You're a very sick man, but I suppose you know that if you are here today."

"I know I haven't been feeling right for some time," JD said. "Even my hair seems to hurt some days."

"That's the infection running through your body. Your lack of treatment has made it worse to deal with. I would like to admit you to the hospital for some IV antibiotic treatment."

"I ain't going to the hospital," JD insisted. "What other treatment can you do?"

The young doctor scratched his head. "We can try some heavy doses of oral antibiotics, but they won't work near as well or as fast as the IVs could."

"I'm sorry, Doc, but I just can't go into the hospital," he repeated.

"I strongly advise it as the best course of treatment."

"That may be, but I can't be cooped up in a hospital room," JD insisted. "Just give me a prescription and I will deal with it."

"We can try that, but I want to see you again in a week. If you seem to be getting worse, get to the hospital immediately," he said as he scribbled on a prescription pad. "I really don't feel good about the oral treatment."

"I'm a strong man, Doc. I will work my way through this," JD said.

"Be back here next Monday," he said as he tore off the prescription and handed it to JD. "I would also recommend abstaining from sexual contact, and you need to inform any sexual partners to get tested."

JD grinned at that comment, knowing that all but one of his sexual partners were dead. "I will do that," he said and left the exam room. He paid his bill and left the clinic, drove to a pharmacy and filled the prescription. He popped the first two pills in his mouth and washed them down with a Coke.

He climbed back into the van and drove for the bayou. He sensed the peacefulness welcoming him home as he drove deeper into the bayou until he reached his spot and parked the van. He smiled when he saw his boat safely secured to the small dock. His eyes came to rest on the brightly painted red crawfish. He went to work untying the boat from the dock and pushed off.

JD felt a small breeze come up as he pulled the handle to start the engine and begin his journey deeper into the bayou, to his home. He watched gators slip into the water as the purr of the engine reached them and they sought the concealment of the dark waters. His nose picked up on the smell of the ancient cypress that dotted the bayou. He could sense the rain that would arrive later in the day or early evening. He hoped he and Tommy Jon would finish hanging bait before the storm arrived. He never relished the thought of being on the water in a metal boat during an electrical storm, and with the record heat they'd been experiencing, lightning was sure to accompany the rain.

He guided the small boat expertly through the route he had traveled hundreds of times, maneuvering around cypress stumps and fallen logs that could easily destroy his motor if he came too close. JD smiled when he made the last right turn, seeing Tommy Jon's airboat tied up to his dock and his friend sitting on his porch smiling like the Cheshire cat.

"Hey Tommy Jon," JD said as he cut the motor and glided over to the dock. He tossed his friend the rope and Tommy Jon began securing the boat.

"Welcome home, JD. I got the bait all loaded up and ready to go."

"Just let me get a few things and I'll be ready," JD said as he stepped from the boat and walked inside. He downed two more pills and changed into a pair of waterproof work boots. He pulled on his ball cap with the red crawfish on it and smiled as he stepped back outside into the early afternoon heat. "Let's go bait up some lines," he said to a smiling Tommy Jon.

"All right, let's get some gators," Tommy Jon said excitedly as he watched his idol step onto the airboat.

✝

I walked over to the picnic table and sat on the top of the table with my feet resting on the bench. It was a very peaceful morning, broken only by the sounds of a bird or animal across the water. Perplexed by the lack of human presence—I had seen only one or two vehicles on my drive—but it was nice to have the little park all to myself. It would have been impossible to concentrate if playing children or rowdy teenagers had been at the park.

The cane knife rested in my lap and I allowed my mind to relax to the sounds of the bayou. Birds and insects called to one another. On more than one occasion, a large heron took flight as it moved from one hunting spot to another. A giant osprey roosted in the top of a large cypress, and I watched it as it dove into the murky waters and returned to the nest carrying a small catfish in its talons. I could hear the hum of mosquitoes and was thankful they had not yet picked up my scent. There was a faint purr of a boat motor in the distance, but I could see no signs of any other humans in the area. I heard a large splash deeper in a slough and could imagine a gator thrashing with its prey held tightly in its powerful jaws. A rash of chill bumps covered my flesh at that image so I quickly erased it from my mind.

I closed my eyes and focused on the dark. I could feel the static energy surrounding my skin as a vision slowly began forming behind my eyes. My nose filled with the heavy smell of the bayou and the lighter smell of approaching rain as my eyes blacked out my current surroundings.

The visions in my mind floated by like a movie as my eyes focused on colorful Native American dancers in full costume performing at what I would later find out to be a powwow, a meeting of tribe members to celebrate together. It was night and several young men danced around a large bonfire, twisting and turning to the beat of drums that I could not hear. One of the young men carried a shield that held a colorful symbol, but he was moving too fast to determine what it was. As their performance drew to an end, I could clearly see the image of a red crawfish painted onto his shield and a smaller crawfish image on his left cheek. The image left me confused by its meaning and I hoped I could later unravel the symbolism behind it.

I was concentrating on the colorful symbols when the reeking smell of rotting meat stung my nostrils and the image shifted. The killer was on a fast-moving airboat and I rode with him as he made several stops along the canal. I watched as he picked up a line with a large hook on the end and forced the sharp head of the hook through rotting chicken flesh. I felt the movement of the hook as it embedded inside the rancid meat. I watched as the line was secured from a tree and the meat hung barely twelve inches above the water. When he had finished hanging the bait, he turned his head toward the driver of the boat.

The driver smiled at him with a grin missing most of his teeth. He nodded back at the killer and started forward to the next stop. I could feel a sense of complete relaxation in the killer as he was comfortably back on his home turf, his domain, the bayou that nobody knew as well as he.

I was tempted to make my presence known but decided to ride along with him to see what other information I could gain. I could still feel his pain but it seemed dulled, probably by medication to a point that he could function. The infection was still there. I could feel the fever ravishing his body as sweat poured down his back. I rode with him for another hour until the boat rounded a turn and a small wooden shack came into view. He stepped from the boat and waved at the driver as he spun the boat in the dark water headed for home. I watched as he bent down and picked up a fish trap and smiled at the fish caught in the metal cage. He dropped the trap back into the water and walked inside.

The furnishings were sparse. A small table and a couch that looked older than I did sat in a small front room. He walked into a small kitchen area, poured a mason jar full of water, and then picked up a pill bottle from the counter. He poured out two pills, and popped them into his mouth. I could taste the bitterness of the pills as he chewed them and washed them down with sweet-tasting water. A buzzing feeling filled my head and I knew he had taken some form of narcotic. The pain had increased as the day had worn on and his vision had become blurry. He kicked off his boots and collapsed across a disheveled bed and closed his eyes.

My connection with him snapped closed. I heard a sound that seemed to echo in my ears. When I opened my eyes, I could see that I was dripping droplets of blood onto the bench. I had cut one of the fingers of my left hand on the cane knife. I stared at the splatter of blood on the concrete, and had a flashback to the barn where he had killed Brianna, and of the blood-soaked walls. The coppery smell of blood reached my nostrils and I had to fight the urge to vomit as I shook the vision from my head. I used a small cloth I found in the SUV to dab the blood from my wounded finger.

The cut was long but seemed shallow. I did not think it would be anything that required stitches. I wrapped the cloth around it and squeezed to staunch the flow of blood. I placed the knife under my arm and held my finger as I walked back to the SUV and climbed inside. The blood flow had slowed, so I made a fist to keep pressure on the wound as I drove back to Raceland. I stopped at a small store and walked inside to buy first aid items.

The small woman behind the counter eyed me closely as I approached, the cloth soaked through with blood.

"Good Lawd, chile, what you done did to youself?"

"Just an ugly cut," I said.

"C'mere and let me hep you with that," she said.

I was grateful for the woman's assistance, placing a bottle of peroxide and Band-Aids on the counter.

"Let me get a clean paper towel while you douse some of dat peeroxide on that cut," she said before waddling off to a small food counter.

I opened the bottle of peroxide and poured a small amount in the cap. A drop of blood escaped the cut and splattered on the counter. I fought against the vision that threatened to flood into my mind of the blood-spattered walls. The peroxide burned as it entered the cut and began to bubble furiously.

The woman returned with a handful of paper towels. "Here, you can dab it with this," she said as she handed one of the towels to me.

"I'm sorry, I got some blood on your counter," I said as I dabbed the bubbles away and poured more peroxide on the wound.

"Don't you worry none, this old counter has seen much worse, I promise you. How did you get that cut?"

I struggled for a quick story. I didn't want to tell her I had cut it on a cane knife while I was having a vision, even though the wise look in her eyes said she probably would have understood. "I'm not sure, I must have caught a sharp edge on the car door," I lied.

"Make sure you clean it good," she said. "Won't do to get an infection. Those danged doctors charge an arm and a leg these days."

"That's true," I said as I watched the bubbles end.

"Did you get some of them new Band-Aids with the antibiotic cream already in 'em?"

"Yes ma'am."

"You dry that off good and I'll put one of 'em on for ya," she said as she opened up the box, careful not to lose the price tag from the top.

I watched the woman and my thoughts went to my mama, and how many times in my childhood she must have performed this very task. I had always been an active child and frequently had cuts, scrapes, and bruises that would require her attention.

"I bet you have done this plenty," I said as her tongue darted to the corner of her mouth as she concentrated on getting the Band-Aid on straight, but not too tight.

"I raised four boys, so I've probably used a dozen cases of Band-Aids over the years," she said with a warm smile.

"I can only imagine then," I said with a chuckle. My stomach announced that it was empty at that moment. I looked at the woman and smiled. "I guess I missed lunch."

"I've got some cooked hot dogs, and fresh buns on the steamer that are two for a dollar," she said.

"That sounds great to me. You got any Sun Drop?"

"Back in the cooler in the right," she said, pointing in the general direction.

She wiped off the paper scraps and the blood spot from the counter as I turned and walked to the cooler. "What do you want on your dogs?"

"Some ketchup and mayo if you have it," I said. "Any chopped onions?"

"What kind of dog would it be without unyuns?" she teased.

"Good point."

"It ain't much, but there's a little table just outside the front door iffin you want to eat there," she said. "I use it for my smoke and coffee breaks."

"Join me then?" I asked.

"Don't mind if I do. Take your drink out and I'll bring your dogs."

I carefully opened the door and located the table surrounded by two chairs. I sat down in one and twisted the top off the soft drink and took a long drink. It was icy cold and the citrus taste filled my mouth.

"Name's Lily, by the way," she said as she pushed her way out the screened door.

"I'm Tally," I said. "Thanks for all your help."

"Not much else going on today so you gave me something to pass the time, the traffic has been even slower today than usual," she said as she stared down the empty highway.

I could feel the emptiness swarm through her. "Do you run this place all by yourself?"

"I have for the past ten years since the old man passed," she said with a note of sadness.

"I'm sorry for your loss."

"He was in so much pain from the cancer he was ready to go."

"Still doesn't make it any easier on you."

"I survive," she said proudly. "It's not always dead around here."

"Do you not worry about being robbed way out here?"

She chuckled at my question and I cocked my head at her curiously.

"I have a bit of a reputation round these parts so no locals will mess with me for fear of getting cursed. And I have my finger on the trigger of a double-barreled shotgun when a stranger pulls up till I get a feel for 'em," she said.

I smiled at the small feisty woman, certain she could hold her own if challenged.

"I'm glad I didn't get welcomed with buckshot then," I said.

"You're a gifted one," she said. "I felt it as soon as you stepped on the ground. I bet if I looked behind those dark glasses I would find two different colored eyes." She fished a pack of unfiltered cigarettes from her pocket and lit one.

I was shocked at her knowledge. "How did you know?" I asked, still in awe.

"I tole ya, I have a reputation round here. I have a few gifts of my own. You're hunting someone aren't you?" she asked.

I dropped the hot dog back on the paper plate. "Yes, I am. A very bad, bad man."

"What's he done to stir up your ire, sugar?"

"He's killed many women," I said.

"You know what dis man look like?"

"I have an idea," I said as I took the composite sketch from my pocket and unfolded it.

She studied the drawing for several minutes while I finished eating the hot dogs.

"I've seen dis man. He stopped by and wanted to sell me some crawfish, but I didn't get a good feel from him so I passed." She dropped the burnt cigarette to the ground and used the heel of her house shoe to grind out the cinder.

I nearly choked on the last bite when she said she had seen him. "When was this?"

"A few weeks back. He pulled up in here for some gas in a big red truck, and wanted to know iffin I wanted to buy some crawfish for the store."

"That was definitely him then, he drives a red truck."

"I never forgets a face, and dat scar he carries makes him unforgettable."

"You don't know a name or where he's from by chance?"

"No, sugar, I don't. But I've seen him pass many a time so he must be fairly close."

I took a sip of the drink and remained silent for a few minutes. "May I ask you one more question, Lily?"

"Shore, sugar, ask away, I ain't got nuttin' pressing me."

"Do you know the symbolism of a red crawfish?"

"Saktce-ho'ma," she said with a grin.

"Come again."

"Saktce-ho'ma is the Houma Indian word for red crawfish. It is a powerful war symbol for their tribe. Why do you ask such an odd question of an old lady?"

"The red crawfish was in a vision I had today," I said. "I had no clue as to its meaning."

"Do you think this has something to do with the killer?"

"I think so, but I can't be sure. Why?"

"Because dear one, Houma is only fifteen miles down dat road you were on," she said with a chuckle.

My head whipped back around to the road I had been traveling. "No wonder I was being pulled in this direction."

198

"His energy is pulling you in, sugar. Be careful. His power is mighty strong and you know what he can do to a woman already," she warned.

I was excited to get back to Raceland and tell Blair and the others of the information I had found. I cleaned up my mess and walked with Lily back inside. I paid her for my purchases and was surprised when she walked around and hugged me before I left. "Be careful and wise to him," she said.

"I will," I said and rushed back to the SUV. I was driving along when I heard the cell phone ringing.

"Hello," I said after picking up the phone from the seat next to me.

"Finally, I have been trying to get you for a good half hour," Blair said.

"I'm sorry I stopped for a late lunch and left the phone in the car."

"We have some new leads I want to share with you. Are you on your way back?"

"I should be there in no more than a half hour, and I have some new information too," I said, wearing a broad smile.

"Be careful, but hurry back," she said.

"I'm on my way."

†

Tommy Jon walked into his house and saw that he had a message on his answering machine. He pushed the button to retrieve the message as he went to his small kitchen for a cold beer. One of the priests from Raceland was calling to see if he could get two hundred pounds of crawfish delivered for a crawfish boil tomorrow night. His normal fisherman had caught a case of the flu and he needed a supplier quick. Tommy Jon's face widened with a grin as he called to inform the priest the crawfish would arrive by early afternoon at the latest. He knew JD always had his crawfish traps out, and with his help to set more traps they could easily bring in two hundred pounds.

He walked back out to his boat, topped off the tanks and then loaded five large coolers onto the boat and secured them. It may take them all night but they could fill the order, he thought as he cranked the engine to head back to JD's.

✝

JD had awakened from his nap and walked out to the dock, preparing to select something for his dinner when the buzz of an airboat engine caught his ear. It was still far away but heading in the direction of his home. Tommy Jon was the only person with an airboat that would dare enter his slough this close to dark so he dropped the fish trap back in the water and took a seat on the railing. It was odd for Tommy Jon to come out so late, so he figured it must be something important.

Five minutes later, JD saw the headlight of Tommy Jon's boat as he entered the last turn toward his house. His friend's face lit up when he saw him sitting on the dock.

JD caught the towline and pulled the airboat toward the dock. "What's up for you to be out this late?" he asked.

"I got an SOS call from a priest up in Raceland. They have a crawfish boil scheduled for tomorrow night, but his fisherman's took ill. He needs two hundred pounds by tomorrow. I figured we could pull that many in tonight."

"Yep, I probably already have a hundred pounds in my traps," JD said. "Let's have some dinner and get to work. I hope you got some rain gear though, 'cause it's gonna be a wet night."

"I'm da man with da plan," Tommy Jon said with one of his toothless grins. "I got my rain gear stowed under the seat, 'sides a little water never hurt nobody," he said.

"I was figuring on some fried shrimp and hush puppies for supper. How's that sound to you?"

"Sounds like good grub to me, man. I'll clean the shrimp if you want to get ready to cook."

"You got a deal, my friend."

Tommy Jon took the basket of shrimp JD pulled from under the dock and placed it on the fish table as JD went back inside to start heating up the oil on the fish cooker. He mixed up some hush puppies and poured half a can of beer in the batter before downing the remainder of the beer. It wasn't cold like Tommy Jon's but it still tasted fine to him.

Tommy Jon worked quickly to peel and devein several pounds of red-tinted shrimp and carried them inside. JD rinsed them in some of his spring water and then dipped them in batter as the hush puppies were cooking.

"Go around back and see if there aren't a couple more beers in that trap," JD said. "They won't be icy cold like the ones we had last night, but they'll do in a bind."

Tommy Jon walked through to the small back porch and fished out the metal cage that held four remaining beers from a six-pack. He carried them inside just as JD was dipping out the last of the hush puppies. He placed them on paper sacks to soak up the excess oil and then began cooking the shrimp.

"Why don't you whip us up some sauce, Tommy," he said. "The hot sauce and ketchup are to the left of the sink."

JD watched with a growing smile as Tommy went to work mixing a bowl of hot sauce and ketchup to make a dipping sauce for their shrimp. Tommy loved the hot stuff. JD was sure it would be spicier than he usually made it, but it would be good all the same.

"Are we eating in the formal dining room?" JD teased.

"That's as good a place as any," Tommy Jon said. "I'll take the sauce and our beers on out," he said, carrying the supplies out to the small table sitting on the front porch. He returned inside and carried a plate full of hush puppies next.

"I'll bring the shrimp out in a minute," JD said. He took two more of the pills the doctor had prescribed and swallowed a drink of water to wash them down. Maybe it was his imagination, but he was feeling better already, he thought as he dipped up the last batch of shrimp and turned off the cooker.

"You a good cook, JD," Tommy Jon said as he bit into a hush puppy.

"Let's dig in. We got lots to do tonight."

They watched the heat lightning flash green across the bayou. "I shore hope that real stuff stays away tonight," Tommy Jon said.

"I do too. I sure don't want to end up like these shrimp, fried up and toasty."

Tommy Jon laughed at JD's response. "Me neither, man, so we will have to be careful."

"That we will, my friend."

When they had finished eating JD said, "Let me go get my rain gear while you drop these scraps off the dock, then we'll be ready to head out."

"You got it, boss," Tommy Jon said, picking up the paper plates and tossing the shrimp tails into the murky water. He could see bubbles in the water through the glow of the moonlight, but had no idea what critter was making them.

The screen door closed behind JD and they walked back to the airboat. "At least we are starting off with a beautiful night," JD said as he climbed aboard and stowed his rain gear.

Tommy Jon untied the boat and hopped onboard. "It's a full moon in the bayou," he said, and then lifted his voice to the slow stirring wind. "Awwwwwooooooooo," he howled.

JD joined his celebration as they slowly floated away from the dock. After they finished laughing, Tommy Jon started the boat and JD directed him to the slough where he had his traps set.

They had barely finished emptying the first four traps when the rain began to fall. They quickly dressed in the rain gear and went about their work. The rain came down hard for a while then settled in with a slow, cool drizzle. "I hope this rain don't waste our gator bait," he said to Tommy Jon. "We set them up high enough, as long as this rain don't raise the water level too much."

Tommy Jon nodded his response. Smaller predators would reach the bait covered by water and they would lose out on that string of gators. He prayed for the rain to stop and after an hour, it suddenly came to a halt. The lightning had moved off far to the north too, which was a huge relief. JD directed him to his honey hole and they began to harvest his traps.

In a little over four hours they had all the crawfish traps emptied and reset. JD planned to send Tommy Jon home with the first load to put on ice, then he would return by eight in the morning and they would pick up the next round of traps. He figured they had well over a hundred pounds in the first batch, but he would get a report from Tommy Jon in the morning. If there was enough left over from their catch he and Tommy Jon might have a crawfish boil of their own. Even though Tommy Jon was four years younger than JD, they had grown to be good friends, and he would do anything JD asked of him.

It was nearly two in the morning when Tommy Jon let him off on his dock. "I'll see you at eight," JD said, then watched his friend slowly maneuver the loaded boat through the slough. For a brief second, JD felt guilty that it would be another two hours before his friend would get any sleep.

"What the hell, he's a youngling still," he said as he turned and walked to his bed.

†

I made it back to Raceland in record time, amazed that I found my way back to the police station without the aid of the GPS. When I walked into the War Room, it was buzzing with excitement.

"Hey, what's going on?"

Blair looked up from the table and smiled at me. "We got some decent leads. It looks like a really good prospect could be living just south of New Orleans," she said. "He owns a late model red Ford F-150, he's in his mid-forties, and he fishes around the Slidell area. And get this, his name is John Rockwell," she said with an excited grin.

The man certainly matched some of the criteria we were looking for, but it just didn't feel right. "So, what's the plan?"

"I'm going to take the agents and the Task Force up to see if we can locate him and begin surveillance on him. If it looks like he's our man, then we will take him down tomorrow. Johnson is coming down from Picayune to help us out."

I could sense the excitement in her voice. "Do I get to go?" I asked.

Her excitement quickly faded into a frown. "No, I want you to stay here at a safe distance," she said. "I know you probably don't think it's fair to leave you behind, but if he's the one, I don't want any danger for you. I'm afraid if you are that close he will sense your presence."

While her logic made sense, I was bewildered by the prospect of being alone and left out of the catch. "I understand," I said but the entire room sensed my disappointment.

"I'm going to stay behind with you," Toma said. "We can still work on some leads in case this suspect doesn't pan out."

"Sounds good to me," I said. "Maybe you and I can work on some things I learned today."

"Let's grab an early dinner, then I can drop you back at the hotel before we head out to New Orleans," she said.

We had a quiet meal at a local Italian restaurant. Back at the hotel, Blair came in to pick up a few supplies and extra clothing. When she returned to my room, she took me in her arms. "I'm sorry if you are upset about being left behind, but really, Tally, it is for the best."

"I understand, just go get the bastard," I said and kissed her softly. "Take care of you."

"I will. I'll call to let you know what is going on."

"Promise?"

"Yes, I promise," she said with a lopsided grin.

I walked her back out to where the Task Force had assembled. Toma and I watched as the group disappeared into the growing night. "I'm in room two thirty-eight," he said. "Just call if you need me. If not I will meet you in the morning for breakfast at eight."

"Sounds good to me," I said and walked back to my room. I was still having difficulty processing what I had learned earlier. Blair was so sure they were after the right man, further adding to my confusion. It just didn't feel right to me.

Chapter Sixteen

I took out my notepad and wrote down the information I had learned today at the park and while talking with Lily. I turned on the TV in hopes of keeping my mind off missing Blair, but nothing captured my attention, so I decided to call my mother and check in with her.

"Hello, baby girl," she said when she answered the phone. "How are you?"

It was great to hear the excitement in her voice. "I'm good, Mama, and you?"

"Never better," she said. "Something tells me you aren't telling me the truth, though."

"Why do mothers always know?" I asked.

"It's called a mother's intuition, honey. What's wrong?"

I gave her the rundown of the Task Force's movement against a possible suspect, and shared my disappointment of staying behind when the rest of the team was on the hunt.

"The worst part of it is I don't think he's the right guy. It just doesn't feel right. I still think he's somewhere down around Houma."

"Did you share this with Blair?" she asked.

"No. She was so excited about the suspect near New Orleans I didn't mention my thoughts on possible new leads to her."

"Well, look at it this way. If the man she's after doesn't pan out, you will have a fresh new direction for her to go," she said.

"That's true," I said and felt my spirits lifting. "Thanks, Mama."

"For what?" she asked.

"For simply being you," I answered.

"Try to get some rest tonight. You sound tired, honey," she said.

"I think I will shower and turn in early. Love you, Mama."

"I love you too, baby girl," she said and hung up.

I took a shower and then sat down at the small desk to look at my notes one last time before going to bed. I felt the crackle of electricity around my body even before the first clap of thunder arrived. A storm was blowing in quick and with it an electrical storm. I closed my blinds to hide from the lightning and then turned the TV back on for a distraction and climbed into bed. I tucked the covers tightly under my chin when a bolt of lightning struck the hotel satellite. The TV, then the power, went out, leaving the room in a haze of darkness. I saw a flash of lightning outside the window and counted, "One Mississippi, two Mississippi," and then a clap of thunder rattled my windows. The storm was nearly right on top of the hotel. I pulled the covers over my head and counted out each flash until the storm passed and the thunder faded beyond my hearing, then I drifted into dreamland.

†

Blair sat in the stuffy SUV with Joe as they watched the building for signs of their prey. The thunder rumbled in the distance and as the first raindrops fell, she thought of Tally alone in the hotel. She felt bad about insisting she stay behind, but she didn't want to place her in any jeopardy.

207

Joe sensed her concern, "Are you thinking of Tally?"

"Yes, I hated leaving her behind, and now this storm worries me. You know how the storms affect her."

"She's a strong young woman," he said. "She's also fallen deeply for you."

"Is it that noticeable?"

"To anyone who knows anything about the two of you." He grinned. "No one cares if that's what you're worried about."

"I'm not worried for me," she said. "I just don't want anyone to say anything to her or hurt her feelings."

"If you hadn't noticed, everyone on the team's as protective of Tally as you are."

"I guess you're right," she said as a flash of lightning lit the vehicle.

"Of course I am," Joe said with a chuckle.

†

The alarm woke me at seven the next morning, and while I felt refreshed I was disappointed that Blair's warm body wasn't lying next to me. She must have sensed I was thinking of her because my phone rang.

"Hey, sweetheart," she said. "Did you have a good night's sleep?"

"We had a terrible storm, but I did sleep well afterward. I missed you when I woke up this morning."

I could hear her soft chuckle. "I would much rather have been snuggled up to you rather than cooped up in this SUV," she said, "but I'm glad to know I've been missed."

"How are things going with the suspect?"

"We have him under surveillance and have tracked down his criminal records. So far just petty crimes that got him a few months in Angola, but nothing as serious as murder, you never know though."

"What will you all do today?"

"We were able to get a warrant to search his place this morning, so several of us will stay and toss his place after he leaves for work and the others will tail him as far as possible."

"How will that work if he's a fisherman and goes into the swamp?"

Blair laughed out loud this time. "Joe and Johnson found a sporting goods store and bought some really cheesy fishing clothes and gear. They are going to rent a boat at the marina where he has his boat moored and monitor him as well as they can disguised as tourists out fishing."

"That will be a Kodak moment," I said.

"I'll take a picture on my phone of them and send it to you," she said with another of her delicious-sounding chuckles.

I found that my heart really ached when she wasn't near and I knew that I had fallen in love. Just thinking of her made my face ache from smiling, and I wondered if she felt the same way. I had grown quiet over the phone as I daydreamed.

"Are you okay, Tally?"

"Yes, I'm fine," I answered. "Be safe today and let me know what you find."

"I will. Take care of Toma," she teased.

My mouth stuttered when I attempted to say "I love you," and she caught the hesitancy.

"Did you say something?" she asked.

"Be careful, and come back soon. I miss you."

"I will be back as soon as I can. When this is over, will you spend a few days with me in New Orleans?" she asked.

"I'd love to," I said with a smile growing on my face. "I'm really looking forward to spending some time with you alone, away from all this chaos. I think we deserve time to get to know each other more intimately," she said.

Blair heard the smile in Tally's voice. "I know exactly how you feel. I don't care if we never leave the hotel," she said with a chuckle.

"Hey, wait a minute. I've never seen the city," I teased.

"Okay, I promise you'll get the grand tour. See you soon then," she said and ended the call.

✝

Even though he was out late, JD woke with the sun peeking in his window. He had time for some coffee before Tommy Jon would arrive. He cranked up his cooker and waited for the water to boil then poured a large mug of instant coffee and walked out to the porch.

The hot sauce in Tommy Jon's concoction had left his stomach feeling achy this morning and the acid of the coffee did little to improve it. He searched through his cabinet to find a pastry that was not yet stale and quickly ate the sugary snack followed by more antibiotics and pain pills. He looked at the rapidly depleting bottle of narcotics and saw that there was one more refill on the prescription. He would take the bottle and find a pharmacy in Raceland to fill it, since every pharmacy locally would know his mother had passed away. That was one of the few downsides to small-town life. Everyone knew everyone else's business. He sighed and propped his feet up on the railing and closed his eyes to rest until Tommy Jon arrived.

Tommy Jon arrived early and JD knew after the first glance that the young man hadn't been to bed yet. "Did you get any sleep," he asked guiltily.

"Naw, it was so late when I got done, I figured I'd just stay up. Went to town and got some breakfast and then headed out here," he said as he handed a paper sack to JD. "Figured I would go home and crash while you made the delivery."

JD smiled and opened the bag already knowing there were fresh beignets inside. "I'd kiss you if you weren't so damn ugly," JD teased. He was glad that Tommy Jon wouldn't insist on going on the delivery run with him. Tommy Jon was a great friend, would give you the shirt off his back, but he also stood out in any crowd. JD didn't need any extra attention drawn to him right now.

"I figured you wouldn't turn down Miss Betty's beignets."

"Hell no, not in a million years," JD answered.

"You are looking better. How you feeling?" he asked.

"Much better, I think the drugs are working."

"That's great news."

JD took a beignet from the bag and bit into the powdered sugar-coated treat. "What kind of weight count did we get last night?"

"A hundert an' twenty pounds," Tommy Jon answered.

"We should have plenty left over to have a boil of our own tonight then," JD stated.

"Damn that sounds good to me. I'll get everything ready and some beers on ice before I lay down," he said. "You're more than welcome to stay the night again."

"That's mighty nice of you," JD said, not confirming or declining his offer. He really wanted to make it home before it got too late so he could get up early and check his gator lines. He wanted to use the rest of his tags while they were still legal. "Do you remember the route from last night?" JD asked.

"Yeah, I think so," Tommy Jon said as he used the toe of his work boot to push the light boat back from the dock.

†

Toma met me for breakfast at eight as planned and then we rode into the station to check for any new information.

He had a good sense of people and knew something was weighing heavily on my mind.

"What has you so deep in thought this morning, Tally?"

His deep voice and question took me off guard as I was looking back at my notes. "I just don't think they have the right man. He just doesn't feel right."

"Why do you think that?"

I began telling him of my adventures of the previous day and when I mentioned the red crawfish, he said, "Saktce-ho'ma."

"Am I the only person who didn't know what that was?" I asked.

He grinned. "It is drilled into every Parish school child by the end of elementary school. The Houma Indians first settled up around the Red River just outside of Baton Rouge, and when the French and British went to war they moved down to Lafourche-Terrebonne Parish to an area we now call Houma."

"That's where I think he lives," I said, "and Lily has seen him come through the area."

"There doesn't seem to be anything going on here," he said. "Why don't we take a ride to see Miss Lily, and see if she can give us anything else to go on."

"That's fine with me, I can't stand sitting around and waiting."

"It is all part of being a good cop," he teased. "You learn to have patience while you're waiting for your prey to peek its ugly head out of the hole he's buried in."

"So let's go," I said.

"Slow down and wait on me," he called out as I headed down the hallway.

We were driving out of town when we saw workmen stretching a banner across the street. One of the local cops had traffic stopped while the workers hung it on two light poles. The banner announced, "Crawfish Boil at St. Anne's, 5 p.m."

"That sounds good," he said. "You ever had crawfish?"

"Not yet, but I keep hearing how good they are."

"They're like little baby lobsters. If we are still flying solo for dinner tonight would you let me treat you to some craw daddies?" he asked.

"Aren't you a married man?" I teased.

"Yeah, but she wouldn't mind me treating you to some craw daddies," he answered. "My wife knows I would be too full of beer and crawfish to be up to no good," he said with a deep laugh.

"It's a date then," I said. I really hoped Blair would be back by then, but if not it would help to kill a few more lonely hours without her.

"What happened to your finger?" he asked, noticing the fresh Band-Aid.

"I nicked it on the cane blade yesterday. That's why I stopped at Miss Lily's place for some first aid supplies."

"Those things can be wicked sharp," he said and let his warning drop there, figuring I knew just how sharp that particular blade was.

I gazed out the window until we started getting deeper in the bayou. I knew Miss Lily's store should be coming up on the left at any time so I sat up in my seat and searched out ahead of us. When I saw the little store, I frowned and told him, "Pull over here, this is it."

He looked at me a bit strangely. "Are you sure?"

"I know it is," I said. "Just pull over."

He parked his sedan and we walked to the front of the building. The store was vacant, obviously closed for a long time, which left me dumbfounded by the discovery. I knew I had just been here the day before, and while it wasn't a thriving business, the store had been open. I looked inside at the bare shelves and then slumped down in the same chair I had sat in yesterday.

Toma calmly sat down across from me, sensing my distress. "Are you sure this is the right place? We can drive down farther and see if there's another store."

"No, Toma, I know this is the right place, but I'll be damned if I know what is going on here," I said. "I sat right here and ate my hot dogs while we talked, and Miss Lily smoked a cigarette right where you are sitting."

I glanced down between his feet and saw the glitter of a white cigarette butt. His eyes followed my attention and looked down at the freshly smoked butt.

"An unfiltered butt isn't it?"

He looked up at me, eyes wide in amazement and nodded his head. "What the hell is going on here, Tally?"

"I wish I knew, Toma. I wish I knew."

A local parish officer drove by, saw us sitting on the porch of the store and whipped his cruiser around. He rolled down his window when he pulled up next to the table we were sitting at. "Something I can help you folks with?" he asked.

Toma lifted out his badge and flashed it to the officer. "How long has this place been closed down?" he asked.

"Miss Lily died three or four years ago," he reckoned.

"Lily Solet?" I asked.

"That's one and the same. She was a feisty little woman with a Cajun temper and a bit of the magic, or so people say," he said. "Why do you ask?"

I lifted my hand and just shook my head. He would think me totally bonkers if I told him I had been sitting here with her just yesterday, I thought to myself.

"Just curious, Officer," Toma said. "Thanks for your help."

The man tipped his hat to me and smiled. "Anytime." He pulled his cruiser back onto the road.

"You must think I'm completely nuts," I said.

"Quite the contrary, the cigarette butt is a bit of evidence that can't be disputed easily, but I must admit I'm baffled."

"That makes two of us," I stated.

"Do you think she could have been a part of your vision?" he asked.

"I honestly don't know, Toma. Everything seemed so real."

"Well, you obviously received first aid somewhere before you got back," he added with a shrug of his shoulders. "'Tis the bayou," he said, "home to many strange and wonderful events."

"You sound like a tourism brochure," I said.

"Maybe I should look into that for retirement income," he said with a wink. "Do you want to continue on down this road a bit?"

"The park should be no more than two or three miles down on the right. Let's go see if that is still there or if it was also a figment of my imagination."

"I don't think it was imagination at all," Toma said as we walked back to the sedan.

He drove us to the park and I felt a sigh of relief escape me when we pulled into the exact spot I had parked the previous day. "There should be blood droplets on that bench," I said.

"It's beautiful here," he said as we walked over to the picnic table.

The rain had washed away some of the drops, but there was still plenty of blood evidence remaining to verify my previous day's accident.

"You still think you're crazy?" he asked.

"Yes, but at least we know I was here yesterday."

My cell phone rang and it was Blair. I walked a few steps away from Toma, who had turned and was watching the wildlife in the slough.

"Hey Blair," I said. "How are you?"

"Tired, stiff, sore, and hungry," she said. "We sacked his house and couldn't find anything that led us to believe he's our guy, but we're going to stick with him the rest of today while he's out in the swamp. If nothing changes we will be back in Raceland by midnight at the latest."

"I'm sorry it didn't work out, but I will be glad to see you."

"What have you and Toma been up to?" she asked.

"Oh, just tracking down some leads. He's going to take me to a crawfish boil tonight," I said.

"That's good. I hope you will enjoy that. Don't wait up for me, but know I will be there as soon as I can," she said and hung up.

"It doesn't look good that he's our killer," I said as I turned back to Toma. "Back to square one."

"No, I don't think so. My gut tells me you are on to something real here," he said. "Let's go back and look at those other two suspects. Maybe we can be a step or two ahead by the time the team gets back."

I was relieved that he didn't think me a total nutcase. Being born and raised in Louisiana I think he knew more about the magic and superstitions of the swamp, more so than anyone else of the task force. More importantly to me, he believed in my conviction that I had met Miss Lily yesterday at her store just as I described. Neither one of us could explain it, but it had happened.

We drove back to the station and began rifling through the files on the other two suspects. Strangely, both men looked very much alike. I wondered if they weren't one and the same with two different names. The first, Jericho Benoit, had a significant criminal history from breaking and entering to poaching gators. His last known address was in Houma and he too drove a red F-150.

The third suspect seemed the least likely of them all at first. He had no criminal record but he drove an F-150 and had a rural route address out of Houma. Again, both men were in their mid-forties. There was something about this man's, eyes, though that looked so familiar. They were a cold, icy blue that seemed to reach out from the driver's license photo. I had a niggling suspicion I had seen the eyes before, but I had no way of confirming that. When I touched the photograph I felt a familiar energy, and I looked at his name. Jimmy Dwayne Walker was the man staring up at me and I knew this was our man.

I decided to wait until Blair was back to share my feelings about Walker with her. I was relieved when Toma looked at his watch and announced late afternoon had arrived. "Why don't we go back to the hotel and freshen up before we drive over to the church," he suggested.

"Do you know where we are going?"

"Darling, it's a Tuesday night in a small town. All we have to do is follow the crowd to the crawfish boil," he said with a grin. "If not, I have the address as a backup."

"You are too funny," I said as I punched him in the arm.

"Ouch," he said and jumped back away from any future blows. "Let's get out of here."

He held the door open for me and we stepped out into the humidity. A breeze had kicked up and I silently prayed it would take the mugginess out of the air. When we got back to the hotel, I showered and put on clean jeans and a fresh shirt with high hopes that it wouldn't be drenched as soon as I walked outside. I thought the humidity in Georgia was bad, but here in the bayou it clung to you like a second skin. I pulled on some socks and then my boots. I hesitated to strap the holster to my leg, but then remembered my promise to Blair. I pulled the strap tight and tucked my jeans over the slight bulge.

Toma had dressed more quickly than I had and was waiting in the car with the AC running full blast to cool it down. He had changed into jeans and a lightweight sport shirt. He looked so very different out of the dress suit it seemed every detective had in their closets. "You look nice," I said. "Very comfortable."

"I prefer the more casual look after hours," he said with a wink as I fastened my seat belt.

"It suits you well," I said as we began the short drive across town. I hated to admit it, but he was right. It seemed every car in town was headed in the same direction. We followed the flow of traffic and entered a dusty parking lot then walked to a large pavilion area behind the church. The event was in full swing. Children with painted faces ran amuck in the crowd and I had to bat several stray balloons out of my face as we made it to the line for crawfish. A zydeco band was setting up on a small outdoor stage. Several cookers were boiling the spice-filled water and the aroma in the air smelled delicious. I wished Blair was here to share this first-time experience, but she would be home later tonight and I could tell her all about it.

When we finally made it to the front of the line, we received two very large portions of crawfish mounded on Styrofoam containers, with a side order of hush puppies and slaw to boot. We passed on the offer of sweet tea and after we found an empty spot at a picnic table, Toma left in search of the beer tent. The crawfish were still boiling hot so I picked up a hush puppy to nibble on as I waited for him to return with cold beers.

I glanced over at the cooking station, my attention drawn to a man in dirty overalls and white rubber boots. The ball cap he was wearing had the symbol of a red crawfish on its bill. This had to be more than just coincidence, I thought as I examined him more closely. He was carrying large coolers filled with ice and crawfish, dumping them into an aluminum-watering trough, like the ones used on cattle farms. He had to be incredibly strong, I thought, to carry that kind of weight alone. I found myself walking in his direction. He carried a final cooler and dumped it, then accepted a check and signed off on a receipt for the priest.

He turned away walking toward a white van parked behind a large white tent when he caught my eye. I continued to walk toward him to get a closer look and when I was within arm's reach, he grabbed me and pulled me beside his van. Before I could get a scream from my lungs he had swung around and clocked me directly on my chin. I remembered seeing stars before my lights went out and my glasses flew from my face.

†

Toma waited impatiently in the long line for beer. It seemed the local Catholic population was full of very thirsty parishioners and the line seemed to move slower for beer than food. He glanced over at the picnic table and saw that Tally was no longer sitting at the table. He looked around for her in the crowd. Maybe she just needed to use the ladies' room he thought as he waited in the crowded line. He wiped the sweat from the back of his neck as the line slowly pushed forward. He could almost taste the cold beer on his lips, and he looked forward to teaching Tally the art of eating crawfish. He looked back at the empty seats at the picnic table once more before stepping underneath the tent flap and out of view of the eating areas. He choked down the urge to panic, believing she was also stuck in a long line at the ladies' room and smiled at his assumption. Ten minutes later, he finally emerged from the beer tent, two icy cold beers in his hands. He felt triumphant until he looked for Tally. She still had not returned.

He looked in every direction until his eyes landed on a young priest that had spoken to them as they took their seats. "Excuse me, Father, but have you seen the young woman I was with earlier?" he asked.

"The young lady with dark sunglasses?" he asked.

"Yes, that's the one."

"I saw her a little while ago, talking to the fisherman who delivered the crawfish," he said.

"Where," Toma asked.

"Right over there behind the beer tent."

They walked quickly to the beer tent and fear wrenched in his stomach when he saw Tally's sunglasses lying on the ground. He knew Tally could not stand to be anywhere outside without them on and would have never willingly taken them off. He tossed the beer to the ground, rushed to pick dark sunglasses up and turned back toward the priest, his eyes glowing with rage. "Who is the fisherman?" he shouted.

"I have no idea. Let's go check with Father O'Grady, he was dealing with the man."

"Hurry, Father, this is an emergency," Toma said and followed the man in a dead run to the back entrance of the church. They burst through the back door together and terrified the older priest.

"What in heaven's name?" he started to ask.

"Father, who was the fisherman who delivered the crawfish?" the young priest asked.

"Some new man, our regular man had the flu," the older priest said as he walked toward his desk. "He brought us some fine craw daddies, though, didn't he?"

"Yes, he did, Father. Do you have a receipt or anything with a name?" Toma asked.

"He was signing a receipt for you earlier, wasn't he?"

"Yes, yes, let me get it. What seems to be the problem? Nobody's getting ill from the food are they," he asked.

"No Father, I think he has kidnapped a young lady friend of mine," he said.

"Oh dear me," he said as he picked up the receipt.

He grabbed the receipt from the man and read the heading: Fitch Seafood Processing. The business had a Houma address. His eyes quickly scanned down to the signature slot and ice water ran through his veins. The signature read J.D. Walker. Toma ran from the room despite the cries of the older priest to return the receipt when he was done. He knew the killer they were searching for had taken Tally and precious minutes were ticking away. He ran for his car and slung up all kinds of dirt and rocks as he sped out of the church parking lot. "How could I be so stupid," he yelled at himself as he reached down to locate his cell phone. He pulled his car onto the side of the road and flipped open his phone, his voice beginning to crack as it filled with tears. He scrolled down his contact list until he got to Blair's number and he hit the send button on his phone. "Please Lord, answer the phone, Blair," he prayed as the phone rang three times before she answered.

"Cooper speaking," she said.

"Blair, this is Toma. I have terrible news," he cried into the phone.

"Toma, relax. Tell me what's going on," Blair said.

"He's got Tally," he said. "I went to get us a beer at the crawfish boil and when I got back she was nowhere to be seen." He stifled a sob. "A priest saw her talking with the man that delivered the crawfish, and it was JD Walker, the last man on our suspect list."

"Are you sure she's not in the crowd somewhere or in the ladies' room, perhaps?" Blair asked, fighting off her own panic.

"Tally's sunglasses were on the ground, close to where the man was parked."

"She wouldn't go anywhere without them on," she said, mimicking his earlier thoughts.

"I'm so sorry, Blair, I royally screwed this up," he said, tears welling up in his eyes.

"You had no idea that he would be at a church event, Toma, so stop beating yourself up and let's start thinking straight," she commanded.

"I have the receipt with the name and the address of the business," he said.

"That's a good start. Give me the address."

Joe was riding with her. He pulled out his notepad and wrote down the address Toma gave her over the phone.

"The suspect in New Orleans was a bust so we are already on our way back. We are maybe twenty minutes from Raceland. Meet us at the Houma PD as quickly as you can get there."

"Do you want me to alert the locals in Houma?"

"No, but stop by and pick up the file on Walker. We need to know everything we can about him. They may know the man, but I doubt they know what he has been up to for twenty years. We can't risk them blundering by not knowing the case."

"I'm heading there now," Toma said.

"We will get to her in time," she assured him, trying to set him at ease, but her ploy was as useless with Toma as it was for herself. She could only hope that Tally would remain safe until they could find her. She hung up the phone and hit the lights and siren. "Call the other units and let them know what's going on and where we are headed," she said to Joe. "And pray, Joe, pray that Tally will be all right." She pressed the gas pedal to the floor as they flew down the highway.

Chapter Seventeen

JD didn't know what had gone wrong. He had finished his delivery and picked up a nice check. He was heading back to the van when a young woman broke from the crowd and approached him. Even through her dark sunglasses, he knew that she was inspecting him closely and had identified him somehow. He knew in that split second that he had to prevent her from alerting the crowd to his identity. As soon as she was close enough to him he punched her and she went out like a light. He was quick, and had her inside the back of his van before anyone saw what was happening.

All he could think about was escaping the large crowd without drawing attention. He had slowly pulled his van out the side alley next to the church and quickly found a deserted side road. He had been so busy since his return that he had not had any time to begin assembling his new kill kit. The best he could do was a plastic zip tie to secure her wrists and a bandana that he tied around her mouth as a gag. Once she was secured, he had the opportunity to inspect her closely. Her dark hair flowed like a halo around her face and her complexion gave away her Native American heritage. The bones in her face reminded him of someone from his past, a woman he had fallen deeply in love with. He shook those thoughts out of his head and climbed back behind the wheel. He had to focus, think about what he was going to do next.

He had vowed to never take a woman to his home, however, the unexpected turn of events left him no choice but to take her there. Tommy Jon was expecting him to arrive within the hour for their crawfish boil. He knew that if he didn't show up Tommy Jon would come out to his place, and that was the last thing he needed right now. He would stow his van in the bayou, use the towline from his boat to secure the woman to the front seat, and then drive the boat like crazy to Tommy Jon's. After they had eaten, he would beg off. He really was tired and not feeling well, so hopefully Tommy Jon would buy his story.

JD turned off the paved road onto the track that would bring him to the edge of his property. He pulled the van into the woods and made a dash for his boat. The woman was starting to awaken as he lifted her from the back of the van and placed her in the driver's seat. He wound the line around her upper body and the back of the seat then secured her zip-tied hands to the steering wheel. "Don't go running off anywhere," he snarled as he finished tying the line.

Her eyes flashed open for just a second while his face was near hers and he gasped when he saw her eyes. "You," was all he could manage to say. He slammed the door and ran to his boat. He cranked the engine and roared across the bayou. The wind whipped into his eyes, blurring his vision, but not nearly enough to remove the vision of her demon eyes from his mind. How could she have found him? he wondered as his heart raced in his chest.

When he pulled up to Tommy Jon's dock, the younger man met him and tied up his mooring line. "I thought you wasn't coming," he said.

"I told you I'd be back," I said. "I can smell them mud bugs from here."

"They are ready, just waiting to be et," he said, then handed JD a beer.

"Thanks Tommy Jon. I hate to admit it but I'm whipped, so if you don't mind I'm gonna eat a bite and then head for home. I need to be up early to check the gator lines."

"I could do that for you," he offered. "Then come by if it would be worth your time to harvest them."

"That's okay Tommy Jon, I'm used to running them myself. I'll come and get you if I need help."

"All right, JD, let's go eat and get you home."

JD could see the obvious disappointment on Tommy Jon's face, but he could not chance him finding out just who he really was. He knew that Tommy Jon looked to him as a hero, and he was JD's only friend on earth. It would kill him if he had to dispose of his friend to keep him from finding out the truth about his hero. He spent nearly an hour with Tommy Jon and then jumped up and said he had to go.

"Are you sure you're all right? You're acting kinda weird."

"It's just these damned headaches," JD said, and it wasn't a lie. His head was pounding. He knew the woman he had tied up in his van was awake and she was riding in his head. He could feel her there, deep inside watching and waiting to learn what he was going to do with her.

"I will see you tomorrow," JD said and pushed off.

†

Get out of my head, you bitch, JD shouted once he was out of earshot.

Not a chance of that, I said, as I struggled against the bindings, trying to free my hands. So far, I had been lucky and he had not found the gun in my ankle holster. If I could only find a way to free my hands, then I could reach the gun and place a well-trained bullet between his eyes. There was no hope of that in my present situation. When he returned, to take me wherever he intended, then maybe I would have a better chance of escape. If I could keep his mind in agony then maybe it would be enough of a distraction to give me the break I needed. A whole lot of maybes I thought.

I heard the rumble of a boat motor coming across the bayou and knew my captor was returning. *What's wrong? Couldn't take facing your friend tonight?*

I said, shut up bitch. I could feel his hand pressed to the side of his head.

Has your penis rotted off yet? I taunted him.

Not even close. You will find out for yourself just how good of shape it's in soon enough, he tossed back.

I quieted for a moment. I knew I was inciting his rage, but I had no other way of sending him agonizing pain.

I would think you're so eaten alive with that disease that you couldn't get it up.

Just you wait and see you crazy-eyed freak.

When he brought up the topic of my eyes, I realized then where I had seen eyes that blue and my mind freaked out for a moment. I saw that shade every time I looked in the mirror. My right eye was the exact shade as his. Suddenly everything began to flow together. My stomach lurched with the thoughts running through my head.

Did you used to be a traveling salesman?

I caught him by surprise with that one, I felt his hand release from the throttle and the boat came to a near halt. *What's it to you?* he growled.

I'm just trying to figure some things out, I said.

Yeah, it was a long time ago, nearly twenty-three years now. I was the best until the accident, he said. I could feel the sadness in his mind. His hand remained off the throttle as he contemplated my question.

Did you ever travel to north Georgia?

What's with all the fucking questions?

I waited for a moment. He still floated dead in the water.

Yes, my sales route covered Georgia, Alabama, Mississippi, and Louisiana, he said. What interest is that of yours?

Do you remember stopping off at a diner in north Georgia and sweeping a young Native American woman off her feet?

He sat in silence for several minutes then I felt his stomach wretch in fear. His mind brought up the image of my mother when she was eighteen years old. It even scared me how much we looked alike at that age. I heard a soft whisper. Shelby. I felt a tear slide down the left side his face and trace the track of the long scar on his face.

My worst fear was coming true. This monster who had tortured and killed so many women was my father.

I could feel his mind starting to put the pieces together too. *Oh no, it can't be,* he cried so loud I could hear his wail across the water.

One night of passion at Tallulah Falls left her pregnant and heartbroken when you abandoned her, I said.

It wasn't like that at all, he said.

What, that you just fucked her over good and left her to raise me alone, I said, my anger rising quickly.

It wasn't like that at all, he repeated. I was in love with Shelby and wanted to ask her to marry me. I was on my way home to buy a ring so I could propose to her when I got in an accident.

Likely story, but I reckon as good an excuse as any, I claimed.

It's the truth. An overly tired trucker ran my car off a bridge. I died several times on the way to the hospital, but the thoughts of Shelby kept bringing me back.

I could feel the pain as he relived the accident, and I knew for once that he was speaking the truth.

So why didn't you come back when you got out of the hospital?

It wasn't that easy. I was in a coma for three years. When I finally woke up it took months to learn how to walk and live again.

That still leaves about seventeen years of my life you could have been a part of, I growled at him.

By the time I could function fairly well I found the world had passed me by. No one wanted to employ anyone with my medical history, and I dropped into a deep funk. My mother drove me crazy, always criticizing me when no one would hire me, and I felt as worthless as she made me feel.

I felt a pause in his brain as he thought back to his younger days.

I couldn't go back with nothing to offer you or your mother, he cried out.

You obviously don't know my mother. She wouldn't have cared if you couldn't bring her the moon. She loved you and her love makes anything possible.

Shelby deserved more than I could give her. I never knew about you. Maybe that would have made a difference, he said, more to himself. I loved her. I really did, but I didn't want her to see me as a failure like my own mother.

But you didn't even give her or us a chance to make that decision.

No, you're right. I did the only thing I could do at the time. My grandfather had an old shack in the bayou he used as a weekend fishing spot. I moved out of my mother's house and started fishing for a living. I could feel a deep sigh leave his body. I knew I was sick, and I thought if I stayed deep in the bayou I could control the voices in my head.

It didn't work though, did it?

For a while it did. Killing gators and other game was enough, but my body started hungering, and that's when I started hunting women.

How many in those twenty years?

I felt him place his head in his hands as a wave of shame rolled through him. *I don't even know anymore. Dozens at least, but I just stopped counting when I stopped caring.*

You ruined so many young lives. Didn't that ever matter to you?

No, they were mine to hunt, he growled and I could feel him slipping back away from reality.

They were never yours, I shouted back at him, my rage growing quickly again.

They were, just as you are now mine.

I will never be yours. Never, ever.

But you are, even of my blood, he said and I watched his hand move back onto the throttle.

✝

Four sets of tires screeched to a halt outside the police station in Houma. The police chief had been called in from home and he offered any services needed to Blair and her team. Blair jumped to action immediately. "Have one of your officers lead my team to the Walker address and you take me to Fitch Seafood Processing."

He barked an order to one of his officers. Toma and a group of the Feds followed the cruiser from the lot. The chief climbed in her backseat. "Take a right out of the lot and then a left at the first light," he said. "We got at least a twenty-minute ride out to Fitch's."

"Got it," Blair said as she flew out of the parking lot.

"What do you want JD for?" he asked.

"He is a prime suspect in a serial murder case, and we think he has kidnapped one of our team," she said.

"You think JD's a serial killer? That seems off base from the boy I used to coach in high school. One of the best damned running backs I ever coached."

"How much do you know about him now?"

"I haven't seen JD in about two years. He was in a bad accident and was comatose for three years. He was never the same man after the accident."

"How so?" Joe asked.

"He went into a deep funk after he awoke. Last, I heard he took off for his grandfather's fishing shack in the bayou. He wasn't even found for his mama's funeral nearly a year ago." The chief took a deep breath. "When I saw him he looked like a truly haunted man. He had lost weight and dark circles surrounded his eyes. I tried to get him to stop and talk with me, but he pushed away and said he had pressing things to do."

Blair sent a knowing look to Joe. She knew the traumatic event could have sent him spiraling into a killing rage.

"How does Fitch fit into this?" she asked.

"Tommy Jon Fitch is probably JD's only friend. They were in high school together before Fitch's old man died and Tommy Jon quit school to take over the family business. He's a little short on intelligence, but he's one of the best damn gator skinners in the state."

"Do you think Fitch would be an accomplice in the murders?" she asked.

"No way. Like I said Tommy Jon isn't smart enough to accomplish something like that. He worships JD as a hero, but would never knowingly be involved in a murder. You'll see for yourself when you meet him."

Joe's cell phone rang. Toma was calling from the Walker address. "Let me put you on speaker. Go ahead, Toma."

"This is definitely our man. We found his truck in the garage and it still had his last victim's college schoolbooks on the back floorboard. There's no sign of him here though."

"Stay there and toss the house to see what you can find," she said. "We should be at Fitch's soon."

"Good luck out there," he said.

"Thanks," Joe said and closed the phone.

"Take the next right and it's three miles into the bayou. Road's kind of rough, though," the chief said as Blair took the turn at a high rate of speed.

"I'd suggest you buckle your belt then," Joe said as his hands gripped the dash.

Blair tried every trick she knew with little success to keep her mind off what the killer could be doing to Tally. She felt her guts twisting with fear for her lover, and the possible torture she would have to endure. Stay strong, Tally, she whispered in her mind.

†

I watched as the small boat approached the dock and the man made his way through the shadows toward the van. I could not make out any details of him until he reached for the door and jerked it open. His eyes were open wide as he stared down at me in disbelief. His fingers still smelled of crawfish as he reached in and lowered the gag.

"Hello, Father," I said.

"I don't even know your name," he said.

"My name is Tally, short for Tallulah as in Tallulah Falls where I was conceived in your backseat."

He noticeably flinched when his mind flew back to that memory. "Shelby was such a pretty young thing."

"She's still a beautiful woman," I said.

He looked at me closely. "You look a great deal like her."

"People used to think I was her little sister when I was a child," I said, reliving the memory. "You know she never married."

231

"I find that hard to believe, she was so pretty."

"She was so in love with you. She hoped one day you would come back and we could be a family," I said.

Mama had never talked about this but I knew I had to do everything I could to keep him talking and distracted while Blair tracked me down. I knew she would come and rescue me, if only I could stay strong.

"I had hoped we could marry and raise a large family together," he said. "The accident ruined all that."

"It would have been nice to have brothers or sisters to play with. It was lonely growing up an only child."

"I know how that feels I was an only child too. My grandfather practically raised me though, and he taught me so much. He taught me survival skills that have come in so handy in my hunting adventures."

"Is my grandmother still alive?" I asked, trying to get him focused on family.

I saw the wicked grin come across his face, transforming him into the monster he'd become. "That old bitch has been dead for almost a year now."

"She wasn't a good mother to you?"

"She was until I couldn't bring her expensive gifts anymore or take her out to fancy restaurants in New Orleans," he snarled. "She didn't even visit me in the hospital when I was in a coma. I guess I was lucky she showed up when I finally awoke in the special rehab facility."

"She took you back into her home didn't she?"

"Only so she could torment me and drive me crazy. She was the first target of the voices in my head, but I never could force myself to kill her."

"So how did she die?" I asked.

"Something made her fall in the shower and she drowned when the tub filled with water. A neighbor found her when he hadn't seen her for a few days. She was already buried before I even knew about it."

"That must have hurt," I said. "She was still your mother, no matter how cruel she was."

Evil flashed in his eyes as he glared at me. "I was glad to see the bitch gone."

He stepped back into the open space of the doorway, and began untying my bindings. "It's time to go," he said.

"Where are you taking me?" I asked.

"I'm taking you home, of course," he said with an evil grin. He grabbed my bound wrists and pulled me toward the boat. He lowered me into the front of the boat and I could make out the image of a red crawfish painted on the bow.

"Saktce-ho'ma," I said.

"What did you say?" he asked in disbelief.

"Saktce-ho'ma, the red crawfish," I said.

"How do you know about that?"

"I saw it in one of your visions," I answered.

"So it is you that has been inside my head, isn't it?"

"Yes, I've had the gift since I was a child. I see shadow people and one of them was a victim of yours who pleaded with me to catch you."

"Oh. isn't that a hoot. Which one of my angels was it?" he asked, genuinely curious.

"Her name is Lisa and she lived in Bogalusa."

"Ah, she was special. She was my first," he said. "So young and beautiful, but she wouldn't love me, no matter how hard I tried to make her."

"I see many of your angels in my shadows. The one in Birmingham became the one that linked me to you psychically. After locating her body and releasing her spirit, I found I could ride along in your head and see what you see."

"Did you enjoy watching the one in Picayune?" he asked.

"It was repulsive, and that child didn't deserve to die like that."

"I did that one just for you," he said and I knew he believed it to be true. "I would have preferred to keep her a few more days but your persistent nagging inside my head drove me to it."

"You might believe that, but you can't blame your depravity on me," I said.

He laughed a loud, evil laugh. "How can you preach to me about depravity when I've seen what you want to do with that juicy redhead of yours," he crowed. "I'd definitely love to have a piece of that."

It was my turn to roar with laughter and the sound stunned him. "It's she that will have a piece of you when she hunts you down for killing me," I said.

"Now who said anything about killing you?"

I smiled a knowing smile at him as he stepped into the boat. "You can't afford to keep me alive. I will make sure you rot in prison if you do."

He stepped forward in the boat and backhanded me across the face. "That's no way to talk to your daddy," he said, then howled with laughter.

I raised my hand to wipe away the blood from a split lip and spit the blood into the water. "That's no way to treat your only child," I snarled back at him, which brought another round of laughter.

He started the motor and guided it deeper into the bayou. It was pitch-black, and impossible for me to see where we were going. As I watched, he seemed to know where every stump and fallen log in the slough was and expertly guided the boat slowly ahead.

The darkness did allow me to 'begin working the leg of my jeans slowly up my calf. I couldn't free my hands, but the position he had bound them allowed me a great shooter's grip. I just hoped by the time I had the opportunity I would still have enough feeling in my hands to squeeze the trigger.

Chapter Eighteen

Blair skidded to a halt in front of Fitch's and she could see the form of a small man out near a roaring fire pit. He was sipping on a beer as she stepped out of the SUV.

"Tommy Jon, it's Chief Potter," he shouted.

"Come on over, Chief, and have a brew with me," he hollered back.

Blair lifted the catch off her gun holster and kept her shooting hand close.

"No time for a beer now, Tommy Jon, we're looking for JD. Is he here?"

"He was here earlier for our crawfish boil, but he said he had to go home, 'cause he wasn't feeling none too good."

She could hear the concern in the man's voice. He was worried about his friend and she decided to play on this emotion.

"JD is very sick, Tommy Jon," she said as she stepped forward into the light. "We need to find him and take him in for medical care," she said. "Do you know where he went?"

"He said he was going home," Tommy Jon said.

"Do you know where that is?" she asked.

"Yeah, but JD said I should never tell nobody where he lives," he said like a frightened child.

"Do you want JD to die?" she said, playing on the disabled man's emotions.

"No, JD is my best friend."

"You have to take us to him then," I said. "Otherwise JD will die."

Blair watched as Tommy Jon tried to reason this out, wringing his hands in indecision. "I don't want JD to be mad with me," he said.

"You will be his hero if you help us save him," she said and knew immediately from the man's excitement that she had hit on the key word.

"I'd like to be his hero," Tommy Jon said.

"Take us then. You might even get a medal," Blair said.

"All right then, but you got to make sure he knows I helped save him."

"I will be sure to tell him myself," she said. "Girl scout promise," she said as she raised two fingers in the air.

"Quit fooling, you're too old to be a girl scout," he said.

"Once a scout, always a scout," Blair said.

The man looked her over and when she smiled warmly at him, she won him over. "Let's go," he said. "It's a long ride in the dark."

"How many can you carry on this airboat?" she asked.

"Only three if you want to go fast," he said.

"Chief, Joe, and I will ride with you then," Blair said. She turned back to her men. "We will be back as soon as possible. Go ahead and call an ambulance out for any needed assistance." She nodded her head so they knew this was a true request. There was a high probability that someone would be in need of medical attention before the night was over. It was better to be well prepared for any possibility.

Tommy Jon was good at handling the boat and they seemed to fly over the surface of the water. It was pitch dark and Blair could barely see a few feet in front of her face. She didn't know how Tommy Jon could see well enough for the speeds he was reaching. Then she remembered he was born and raised in the bayou and could probably make the trip in his sleep, having made it so many times in his life. He drove the boat at what seemed full throttle for about ten minutes before he cut back on the speed.

"Here comes the hard part," he said. "I gotta take her slow to miss the fallen trees and stumps in JD's slough."

The small headlight lit up a white van hidden in the trees. "Is that JD's van?" she asked Tommy Jon.

"Yeah, he said his truck was having some problems so he switched over to his van."

They had barely entered the slough when they heard the sound of a gunshot and then another followed a minute later.

"Can we go any faster Tommy Jon?"

Frozen at the back of the boat, he too had heard the shots and was scared.

"It's time to be a hero," Blair said. "Do this for JD."

It seemed like it took forever for Tommy Jon to respond, but slowly he increased the speed of the boat. They had to grab for safety bars when he brushed a downed log or drove over a hidden cypress stump.

Dear God, let us make it in time, she prayed as the night grew a deeper dark.

†

JD had slowed the boat when he saw the dock come into view. The small boat floated over a hidden stump and I felt my body fly forward as I sat facing him. It was the perfect motion for me to reach inside the ankle holster and remove the gun. My finger instinctively released the safety. As JD stepped onto the dock, he turned back to reach for me. I heard the sergeant's voice whisper, *"If you ever have any doubt about hitting your target, aim for his gut."*

I raised the gun and aimed for his belly button then held my breath as I squeezed the trigger. I heard the gun discharge and fell back against the side of the boat. JD fell onto the dock, dropping to his knees as a large stain spread across his midsection. He stared at me for several seconds and then closed his eyes. I breathed a sigh of relief, and then jumped when he pivoted his body to lunge for me as the boat floated slowly away from the dock. I raised my hands and squeezed the trigger again. I saw the bullet enter the middle of his forehead and watched in horror as the back of his head exploded when the bullet ripped through it. I leaned over the side of the boat and vomited into the water. When I had nothing left to purge, I curled into a ball and watched him, lifeless, half hanging off the dock. I kept the gun still pointed in his general direction in case he came back to life again.

✝

"Can we go any faster?" Blair pleaded with Tommy Jon.

"We're almost there, ma'am, just one more turn and you'll see his place."

Seconds took an eternity to pass as she moved to the front of the boat, closer to the headlight as Blair willed her eyes to find Tally. As they rounded the last turn, the dock come into view and she saw a body stretched out lifeless. As they approached, she saw JD's small boat lodged between a pair of cypress stumps and another figure huddled in the front of the boat.

Blair breathed a sigh of relief when she recognized the male figure lying on the dock. The chief climbed from the boat to check for a pulse then shook his head, but her eyes fixed on the small boat.

"Get me closer, Tommy Jon," she ordered.

Tommy Jon inched the airboat forward until Blair could safely step into the small boat.

"Tally, baby, it's me, Blair," she whispered as she crept closer to her lover. Tally's eyes were unseeing and there was no indication that she heard Blair. Her finger was still on the trigger and it would only take a slight movement to get off another shot.

"It's over, baby, you're safe, so put your gun away," she softly spoke.

Tally felt her finger twitch on the trigger and was about to squeeze when Lisa's image came rushing into her head.

No Tally, that's Blair, she shouted. It's over. You killed him.

Tally heard Lisa's words and dropped the gun into the boat, then collapsed into total darkness.

Blair rushed to Tally and used a knife to cut the zip ties from around her wrists. She pulled Tally into her arms, hugging her close and checking for any signs of injury. Other than a split lip and a rising bruise she found Tally intact and breathed a sigh of relief. Tally's breathing was even as Joe stepped into the boat and handed Blair a wet handkerchief.

She wiped Tally's face with the cool fabric and watched as her eyes began to flutter. "We are going to have to stop meeting like this," she told Tally as she smiled and pulled her close.

"Help me get her into the airboat," Blair said to Joe.

With no help from Tally, Blair and Joe lifted her and positioned her in the boat where she was safe.

"Are you okay to stay with the body?" she asked the chief.

"Yes, I am. Take her and see to her needs. Tommy Jon can bring some of the others back when he returns."

Blair had forgotten about Tommy who remained frozen as he looked at JD's dead body. She walked over to him and placed an arm around his shivering shoulder. "I'm sorry we didn't make it in time to save your friend, but you are still a hero for getting us here so fast," she told him.

"Thank you, ma'am," he said his voice filled with sadness.

"Can you get us back just as quick so we can get this lady some help?"

"Yes ma'am," he said and went back to the driver's seat.

†

I could not remember anything about the ride across the water as I fell in and out of consciousness. I could feel Blair's arms wrapped protectively around me as we raced across the water. The last thing I remembered was seeing the lights of an ambulance waiting at the dock. Toma, Johnson, and others were there to carry me over to the ambulance. Within minutes I was strapped to a stretcher and Blair sat beside me as the ambulance screamed into the night.

"She got him," I heard Blair tell Toma as they wheeled me past.

"Joe can you take over and secure the scene?" she asked.

"I'm already on it," Joe said. "Call and let us know how she's doing."

"I will," Blair said as the back door of the ambulance closed and that was the last voice I heard.

I have no memory of the ride back into Houma to the small hospital or being ushered through the emergency room as a direct admit after it was determined I had no physical injuries.

"I want to keep her overnight for observation and fluids," I heard someone tell Blair.

"That's fine with me," she answered.

"I will check back in later before my shift ends then," the voice said and left the room.

I was still not yet conscious enough to speak with her, but I heard her sit in the chair next to my bed and felt the warmth of her hand slide into mine. "Rest now, Tally, but please know that I love you," she whispered softly to me.

I heard the heart monitor spike at the head of my bed as I listened to her proclamation. We had not yet shared those words and they made my heart soar with excitement. "I love you too," I whispered and drifted back to sleep.

I woke again about two that morning when I heard soft voices. At first, I thought I was dreaming, but as my eyes cracked open I saw Blair standing at the foot of my bed talking to Joe, Toma, and Johnson.

"Yes, the doctor says she will be fine and will be discharged tomorrow. He wanted to keep her overnight for observation and some fluids since she was at risk of shock."

"What are our plans for the next few days?" I heard Joe ask.

"We will need to stay in the area a day or two until the investigation and reports are complete, and then we can all head for home."

"That will be nice," Toma said. "I think I'm still married," he said with a sheepish grin.

Johnson had turned toward the bed and was the first to notice my eyes had opened and I was awake.

"Welcome back," he said. They all turned to look at me as they moved closer to the bed.

Toma reached down and picked up my right hand. I could see he had tears in his eyes. "I am so sorry, Tally."

"You have no need to be sorry," I said. "You did everything to protect me. It was my own stupid curiosity that got me in my predicament."

"I almost got you killed."

"No you didn't, Charles," I said. "But you do owe me one thing."

"Name it and it's yours," he said with a relieved smile.

"You still owe me some crawfish and cold beer," I teased.

"As soon as you get out of here you will have all you can eat and drink," he said.

"Deal," I croaked. "Can I have something to drink now?"

They all reached for the water pitcher. Toma brushed them away, pouring me a cup of water while Blair opened a straw.

"Thanks," I said as I took a long drink. "Man, that's good."

Johnson was standing next to Toma. "I brought you something," he said and reached for my hand.

He opened his hand and dropped two shiny shell casings into my hand. "I found these in the boat with your gun and thought you might want them."

I smiled up at his thoughtfulness. "Will you do something for me?"

"Sure, I will," he said as I handed him one of the shell casings.

"Give this to Greg and tell him I kept my promise," I said.

"Consider it done," he said with a smile.

I looked up at Joe and saw him grinning widely. "I want you to have the other," I said as I offered the casing to him. "If you hadn't believed in me I would never have been able to work with all of you. This is for Beanie," I said as my hand caressed his large paw.

"Thank you," Joe said, "for everything."

"Without you we couldn't have caught him so quickly," Johnson said. "I hope if we need you in the future we can call on you."

"Amen to that," Joe and Toma said in unison.

"Just remember, boys, I have first dibs," Blair spoke up.

I looked into those deep green eyes and smiled. "You heard the boss, but I will always help you any way I can."

"Okay guys, now that you can see our patient is okay it's time for you all to go get some rest," Blair said, shooing them from the room.

"I will see you tomorrow," I said as they left the room.

Blair returned to my bedside and smiled down at me. "How are you feeling?"

"I would feel better if you snuggled in with me," I said as I moved over in the bed.

She smiled and kicked her shoes off and climbed in next to me. She wrapped her arm around my shoulder. "There is one thing I would like to know?"

"What's that, baby?"

"Why are you always fainting on me? You never did tell me why the first time."

I smiled at her. "When I was twelve and had my accident, you came to me in my dreams. I could see these beautiful green eyes of yours and your unruly red hair. Lisa told me that someone would come to help me when I was ready." I rested my head on her shoulder and looked up into her face. "I knew when I saw you in Picayune you were the one sent to help me."

Blair leaned down and kissed the top of my head. "I will be here as long as you want me."

"Tomorrow will be busy finishing up the case report won't it?" I asked.

"Yes, but you don't need to worry about that now. You can write your statement when you feel up to it," she said.

"There is something you need to know now," I said.

"What is so important it can't wait?"

"JD Walker was my father," I said.

"What?" she exclaimed.

"It's a long story and I don't have the strength for it right now, but he was my father," I repeated.

Blair thought for just a moment. "I think we will leave that out of the report. There is no need for anyone to know."

"Especially my mama," I said. "She must never know."

"As far as I'm concerned it's between you and me."

"Thanks, I will tell you everything, but not right now..." I said as I rested my head on her shoulder and went back to sleep.

†

I woke again three hours later from a vision. Blair was curled around my body in the bed. In the vision, each of the women Walker had killed came to me with their thanks. I watched as one by one they faded from my vision. There was no bright light they walked into or a door to pass through, they just faded one by one until they were gone. There were others left in the shadows and I knew that one day soon their images would become more vivid as my next mission would come to light. When the others had gone, Lisa approached, and I felt a sadness wash through me.

You did an excellent job, Tally, she said. I feel so much lighter and free since he's gone.

I am really going to miss you. Your presence and assistance has helped me learn who I really am, I told her.

Lisa smiled and placed a cool hand on my cheek to brush away the tears that had begun to gently slide down my cheeks. *I'm not going anywhere.*

What? I asked. I thought his death would bring you a release from this world so you can go to find your peace.

It did, but I would like to stay with you to guide you, if that is okay with you?

I wrapped my arms around her in the vision and hugged her tightly. It would be great to have you with me. I do not cherish the thought of doing this alone, even though I know that is very selfish of me.

There is not a selfish bone in your body, Tally. Besides, you will never be alone as long as Blair and I are with you.

I smiled brightly at the mention of Blair. Do you think she and I will remain together?

She is your soul mate, Lisa said. The one sent just for you. Are you ready for that?

Yes, I think I am. She means the world to me, as do you.

I would have been lucky to find someone like you, Lisa said. So don't screw it up, Lisa added, with a chuckle.

I will try my best.

You always do Tally. Rest now, and soon we will begin our next adventure.

Thank you, Lisa, I said. She nodded then slipped back into the shadows.

Epilogue

Once the reports were finished, the team spent one final night together to celebrate the closing of the case with a crawfish boil and a keg of beer. Toma made good on his promise and we all ate and drank to our heart's content.

I was saddened to see the men I had grown so fond of disperse, but the time had come to say good-bye. With a last tearful hug, I wrapped my arms around Joe and hoped he felt the words I could not communicate to him.

"I will miss you too, Tally," he said. "Feel free to come for a visit anytime. I'm sure Hope would love to see you again and give you her personal thanks for bringing this nightmare to an end."

"I would like that," I said, getting control over my emotions.

The following morning we all packed up and headed off on separate paths. The men went home to their families while Blair and I drove to New Orleans. I called home to let Mama know the case was over and she could move back home. I told her Blair and I were spending a few days in New Orleans, and then I would be coming home.

†

Blair made good on her promise and gave me the grand tour of New Orleans and the surrounding area during the day. After feasting on Cajun food, we returned to the hotel for the evening.

During our first night together, I became the aggressor, no longer worried about anyone entering my mind as I slowly undressed Blair, kissing every inch of her body as the clothes fell into a pile on the floor. "My God, you're beautiful," I told her as her green eyes locked onto me burning with desire. We kissed deeply as Blair undressed me, breaking the kiss long enough to pull my blouse over my head, before leading me to the bed. With no distraction or fear of interruption, we spent the night exploring one another's bodies and I felt true love for the first time. As my first orgasm ripped through me I cried out Blair's name with such intense emotion, she froze in fear of hurting me. I choked out a laugh and looked into her startled face. "Please, Blair, don't stop now," I pleaded. Needing no further reassurance, Blair made love to me until I could stand no more.

When it was my turn, I rolled her onto her back then saying, "I need to taste you, touch you and I can only pray that I can make you feel half of the love you have given me tonight," I whispered against her skin.

"I have no doubt that you will, my love," Blair said as she guided my eager mouth to cover her aching breast.

It took all the restraint she could muster, but I slowly explored Blair, mimicking what she had shown me earlier, until she was panting with pleasure.

When we finally collapsed in one another's arms, totally spent, Blair brushed the dark hair from my face. "I have never loved anyone the way I do you," she said.

"I love you too," Tally whispered. "I don't ever want to lose you."

"You never have to," Blair promised. "Now that we've found each other, nothing else will keep us apart."

Overwhelmed with emotion, I began to cry. Blair held me close until I finally drifted off to sleep. As I slipped into the darkness, I heard her say, "I will always be there to protect you." She curled against me and fell asleep.

†

During our vacation, I told her everything I learned about Walker during my brief captivity. She held me close as the tears flowed down my cheeks from killing a father I never had a chance to love.

I could do nothing to change the past, but with my gift and Blair's love to guide me, the future was wide open.

About the Author

Ali Spooner

Ali Spooner is a native of Florida, currently living and working in Memphis, TN. Home for Ali is Pensacola, Florida where she has a partner of twenty years, one son and a grandchild that has her wrapped completely around her little finger. Her other children are all four-legged, three dogs and two cats, and her dearest companion in Memphis, Rascal, a rescued tiger kitten named after her favorite country group.

A true daughter of the South, Ali enjoys spinning stories about the South, the strong, but gentle women and creatures that make it a wondrous place to live.

As an "Indie" author, Ali has been writing for many years as a hobby. After a cancer diagnosis in 2010, she decided to take a leap and start self-publishing and has published over a dozen stories. Ali's characters range from cowgirls and psychics, to a healthy dose of supernatural beings. She has written stand-alone titles and series. Ali frequently writes several stories at a time, depending on which characters are bouncing around loudest in her head.

Ali is an avid reader and her other hobbies include photography, outdoor activities and watching college sports.

Other Books from Affinity eBook Press

Arc Over Time—Jen Silver_ Dr Kathryn Moss has job offers flowing in after her exciting archaeological discoveries at Starling Hill the previous year. Now she has choices to make that could jeopardise her relationship with Denise Sullivan, the fiery journalist, who has become her lover. For Denise the choice seems obvious. She thinks they have moved beyond the casual sex stage to something more like a true relationship. However, she's not sure how to handle Kathryn's continuing infatuation with Ellie Winters. Ellie's new career as a promising artist proves to be a catalyst for the simmering tensions in relations between her wife Robin, Kathryn, and Denise. Will Denise persevere in her pursuit of the reluctant professor? Does Ellie have anything to fear from Kathryn's fascination with her art, or is there another motive behind the professor's obsessive interest? This wonderful romantic continuation with the characters from *Starting Over* ties up loose ends. But the question is—does everyone have a happy ending? A must read.

Presence—Charlene Neal After catching her husband red-handed in bed with his secretary, Kayleigh Gibbs takes her daughter and her Jeep and flees across the country. She opens up her own veterinarian practice, and they move into an old, secluded farmhouse in Hoekwil, South Africa. At her best friend's housewarming party Kayleigh meets the beautiful and enchanting Rebecca Steward. Rebecca is instantly drawn to Kayleigh, but is still recovering from a breakup—her girlfriend left her for a man. She's afraid of a repeat performance with Kayleigh, and won't pursue a romantic relationship with her, preferring instead to develop a platonic friendship. When odd, inexplicable things start happening on the farmhouse, a terrified Kayleigh turns to Rebecca for comfort, only to find herself developing unexplainable feelings for her new friend. Rebecca, despite her best intentions, is falling in love with Kayleigh. But when Rebecca moves in with Kayleigh to help her get to the bottom of the haunting, she finds more than she bargained for. Can Rebecca and Kayleigh overcome ghosts from the past and their own insecurities, or will a presence from the past tear them apart?

A Walk Away—Lacey Schmidt   Kat and Rand's daily worlds are 2,100 miles apart, but something about their meeting on the magical shores of the nation's oldest national park east of the Mississippi sparks questions that neither woman can just walk away without answering. Sometimes chance brings you to the right person to help you resolve some of your baggage, and you learn to like yourself a little more. Kat and Rand are smart enough to recognize this chance in each other, but they also find that there is a catch to every opportunity—walking toward something is always walking away from something else.

Love Forever, Live Forever—Annette Mori   No one forgets their first love. For Nicky, that's Sara, who abruptly disappears one day, leaving only a cryptic letter. That day scarred her soul. When the pain starts to diminish, Nicky begins to get her life back on track until it is derailed once again by an unimaginable twist. Changed forever, Nicky becomes a careless, womanizing nomad known as the Little Wild One, until she meets Annie. Thirteen years later, Nicky's finally settled and happy. Fate intervenes and puts her directly back into the path of her first love, Sara, and the corresponding events send her into a tailspin. Now she must decide—who will be the person she ends up living with and loving forever?

Possessing Morgan—Erica Lawson New York City, in the height of summer. Crime seems to have taken a holiday, and Detective Morgan O'Callaghan is bored, bored, bored. Paperwork is mating and multiplying on her desk, and even a jaywalker is starting to look good. Anything to get her out from behind her desk! Enter Andrea Worthington, Charleston socialite and all-around rich girl, right down to the wealthy fiancé. She's also the new Assistant District Attorney assigned to Morgan's precinct. Their first meeting is like two freight trains crashing head on. Then a high profile, career make-or-break murder case throws them together again. The investigation has barely begun when Andrea becomes the target of a nearly fatal hit-and-run. But was it really aimed at her? Can she and Morgan find the common ground they need to solve the case and stop the attacks, or are the gaps just too wide to bridge?

Twenty-three Miles—Renee MacKenzie Talia Lisher has a long family history of lying, about anything and everything. With her father dead, and her mom gone on a quest to start a new life, Talia struggles to keep in touch with her only remaining family, her incarcerated brother. When Talia sets her sights on Officer Shay Eliot, she vows to stop lying. She starts watching Shay, waiting for just the right circumstances and amount of courage to talk to her. Talia might be watching Shay, but someone in a dark van is watching Talia. Is the mystery driver a dangerous part of her family's past, or is it all just a coincidence? Shay Eliot has left the police force because of what she perceives as a hostile work environment. When a brutal double-murder on the 23-mile-long Colonial Parkway puts the FBI's magnifying glass squarely on her, her alibi comes from an unlikely source – a young woman who has been stalking her. Shay wants to keep her distance from Talia, but once she gets to know the younger woman she can't keep feelings from developing. This is a story about community, and how it comes together in dangerous and devastating times. When you don't know who to trust, you better have friends who will rally around you. Will Talia and Shay find the answers they need to the mystery of the murders on the parkway, or will justice be elusive? Will they survive their quest for the truth?

Confined Spaces—Renee MacKenzie Andie Waters spends her days pulling waste samples for environmental testing and at night, she tends bar at The Cave, a popular hangout for straights in a small Georgia town. Serial monogamy has grown stale for her, so she's content working to pay off her debts and hanging out with her old hound dog. Or so she thinks, until a beautiful lesbian drops by The Cave. Andie suspects her involvement with the woman will be only temporary. Little does she know no part of her life will be left untouched. Kara Travis likewise anticipates nothing more than a brief fling upon meeting Andie, especially given her reputation as both a personal ice princess and a corporate hatchet wielder for Royal Environmental. What luck to find a hot lesbian bartender in nowhere rural Georgia. Andie and Kara spend a passionate weekend together and find that their notions of no strings attached are far from accurate. Their supposed short-term ideal diversion of a commitment-free romp hits a major complication when they come face-to-face with one another at Royal Environmental's offices Monday morning. While carrying out her duties, Kara discovers crimes being committed by and against Royal Environmental employees. Will Kara be forced to shut down the Georgia

Division of the company? If she does, Andie will lose her job. Worse yet, Kara may lose Andie before she's really even sure she's got her. Corporate politics, complicated romance, and long distances conspire to keep Andie and Kara all boxed in. Can love triumph despite the Confined Spaces?

Reece's Star—TJ Vertigo Reece Corbett watches over the dancers in her gentleman's club with the blue, razor sharp eyes of The Animal. Few know that resting comfortably in her office is her newest love, a tiny MinPin named Smudge. What happened to The Animal, known for her rapacious appetite for women and danger? Faith Ashford is what happened to The Animal. Faith and Reece have been together a while now and they have settled into something resembling domestic bliss. This bliss alarms Reece. It's one thing for Faith to see her softer side, that's vulnerability enough, but to let her friends see it...no. Not the best plan. Under Faith's guiding, loving hand, will Reece successfully traverse the rocky road of emotion and embrace the positive changes in her life? Or will she panic and be unable to control that Animal part of herself? Will she take that next step to declare herself fully capable of love and devotion? This third installment in the popular series that began with *Private Dancer* continues the passionate and often hilarious romance of Reece and Faith as they both grow in love and in trust.

Flight—Renee Mackenzie It's 1983 and Kate Hunter is a student at a small, private college in Virginia. When Lana coaxes her onto the back of her beat-up scooter one night, Kate's education starts to encompass more than just her pre-vet studies. Kate has always done as expected of her, so when she starts staying away from home on weekends to spend time with her new lover it's way out of character for her. Lana is secretive, but Kate accepts things as they are and gives Lana her space. When she feels the sting of betrayal, will she be able to continue giving Lana her privacy? Kate's sister April is a high school student playing with fire as she parties with her older boyfriend, Boyd. After finding someone overdosed the morning after a big party, April grows weary of all the drugs and alcohol. Will she be able to convince Boyd that they should slow down? Will she be able to pull it together before it's too late? Kate and April are forced to face up to events from their younger years, their mother's desertion, and their long-deteriorating relationship with one another. Some lives will be lost and others changed forever when the sisters' lives intersect. Will they be consumed by the wreckage, or will they be able to pick themselves up and take flight?

Reflected Passion—Erica Lawson   Where passion, reality, and destiny combine. Dale Wincott is a 27-year-old woman born into Bostonian wealth and groomed to marry into the social hierarchy. Her mother is a hard-hearted society matriarch, but her father feels for his daughter and helps Dale find a life on her own as a furniture restorer. Françoise Marie Aurélie de Villerey is a 28-year-old Countess, born into the French aristocracy and forced to marry a count much older than herself. For ten years, she was his trophy wife, forced to endure his perverted desires, until the day he finally died. He had broken her emotionally and she no longer cared for what life had to offer, slipping from one sexual partner to another as often as she changed her clothes. Until... that one night when Françoise looked up during a sexual encounter and saw Dale watching her from the mirror. A veritable angel, full of innocence and curiosity, who touched her very soul. Through the mirror, Françoise embraces life anew, while for Dale it is a powerful awakening, forcing her to discover not only her sensual nature, but the inner strength she possesses.

The One—JM Dragon Phil (Philomena) Casters loves her work as a pilot, above everything else in her life except Ming, her married lover. Phil needs to enhance her status in the community before asking Ming to leave behind her wealthy husband. Rosa Moran a teacher, raised by missionaries in China after the death of her parents. She loves the country of her birth and the people. Her English grandfather desperately wants her to live with him to atone for the guilt he feels about the death of her parents. He sends her a letter requesting her to come home. When Phil flies to the mission to deliver the letter to Rosa, neither can envisage the chain of events about to take place. It starts as a collaboration to save four children, leading them to the surreal private paradise of Langshow. Could this be the perfect place for the children and Rosa to settle? Phil is not so sure. Chang, an old friend from Rosa's childhood lives in Langshow and makes no bones about the fact that he wants Rosa. All thoughts of Ming disappear as Phil tries to fight her attraction to Rosa. However there is the little matter of an innocent misunderstanding—Rosa thinks Phil is a man. *The One* is a romance with everything, love, intrigue, misunderstandings with a happy conclusion—the only question—who gets the girl?

The Chronicles of Ratha: Book 2 A Lion Among the Lambs—Erica Lawson It has been three years since Jordana Laren's path first crossed the Noorthi's - three years since she's had a drink, had sex and a life of her own. Her only excitement has been spent keeping up with her two year-old daughter, Rice, who is definitely a chip off the old block. All has been peaceful until one of the colonists becomes sick. Bad news shifts to worse news when the disease spreads through their community. Unable to get proper medicine, Jordana is forced to rely on the Noorthi healers to come up with a cure. Soon the herbs run out, leaving her with no choice but to search for more on the Noorthi home planet. What is supposed to be a simple pick-up flight turns into a nightmare. Can Jordana believe in herself like her Noorthi sisters do? Only then can she fulfill her destiny as The Chosen One. Follow the colorful cast of characters in this action-packed adventure sequel as they traverse the galaxy. Of course, nothing ever goes smoothly when Jordana is involved.

Cowgirl Up—Ali Spooner_ When the new ranch hand, Coal Bryan, arrives at the MC2, the last thing she's looking for is love. Her co-workers are surprised when Coal turns out to be female. Coal, used to the reaction, quickly earns the respect of the crew with her work ethic and skill with horses. Coal uses the strenuous work and friendship of the ranch hands to try and forget her broken past. Melissa Conway, owner of MC2, offers Coal a place to live in her home. They both are shocked to find they are linked in a way neither of them imagined. Mary Leah, Melissa's sister, arrives at the ranch to recover from a recent tragedy. The attraction between Mary Leah and Coal is instant and mutual. Can the three women survive their personal dilemmas? The love and friendship they develop certainly helps but will it be enough to bring them together. Ride along with the MC2, for boot scootin', butt kickin', dirt eatin', rodeo adventures, with a love story thrown into the mix.

If I Were a Boy—Erin O'Reilly Katie McGuire appears to have it all. A devoted husband, a job she loved, and a comfortable lifestyle. Helen Swenson is a successful financial director of a prominent investment firm, with an unfaithful husband, and few friends. Their husbands' annual trip to Padre Island National Seashore to reunite with their air force pilot squad becomes a pivotal point for the two women. Their lives take on a completely new meaning when an undeniable magnetism between them draws them together. Passion and secrecy becomes the norm, as they have no choice but to succumb to their attraction. Can the vacation love affair continue? When they leave for their respective homes, will they regret what happened? Life is not that easy to change and the people around them are the hardest to convince. There is no more powerful motivation than love. Except hate and there are plenty of people who want to see their relationship destroyed. Will Katie and Helen be able to make a life together work or succumb to doubts and the pressures of family? This story will fill you with the thrill of passion and the tenderness of love.

The Chronicles of Ratha: Book 1 Children of the Noorthi—Erica Lawson Jordana Laren is a hard-drinking, hard-fighting womanizer, who works as a freighter pilot in her spare time. Her latest customer drugs her, steals her ship, and abandons her on a desert hellhole called Rigeus, infamous penal planet for the worst women criminals. Her chances of survival aren't looking good. She has no food, water, or weapons, and the nearest bar is a million miles away. Just when she's ready to write her last will and testament, Jordana is rescued by a group of barely-clad women. Has she found nirvana? Her own personal harem seems like a possibility, until the intercession of their enemy, the Velkren. Their leader, Vel, remembers Jordana well, and not fondly. But why is Vel on this planet, surrounded by murderers, thieves, and bad-tempered bitches? Jordana knows Vel isn't a prisoner, so why is her nemesis on Rigeus mining mud, of all things? Jordana knows only one thing. She has to get off the planet before Vel kills her. Unfortunately, the women who saved her reveal themselves to be holy. They are the Noorthi, and Jordana's dream of endless debauchery becomes a nightmare of eternal servitude. The Noorthi make her one of them, marking her with a wrist tattoo, and leaving her no choice but to protect them with her life. The last thing Jordana wants is to become involved in galactic politics or heroic actions. But the tattoo ochre in her body is suddenly giving her morals and scruples, not to mention a better vocabulary! And she really can't pass up a chance to outwit Vel, whose megalomaniac plans are endangering not only the Noorthi, but the civilized galaxy itself. But Jordana is torn. Does she stop Vel at all costs, or does she get out from under the thumb of the Noorthi while she can? Some things were never meant to be easy...

Nesting—Renee MacKenzie_ Macy Stokes, a divorced mother who is struggling with her sexual identity, jumps at a once-in-a-lifetime opportunity to help her friends. She doesn't foresee it will put her in jeopardy of losing her son, Jeremiah. Fresh out of high school, Cam Webber travels to Augusta, Georgia, to reconcile with her aunt. When she learns that's impossible, she determines to gain acceptance from her aunt's partner, Sharon. Meanwhile, Cam sets her sights on Macy, but Macy has other ideas. Kenny Brewer is a good old boy who loves his wife, Dorianne, even when he thinks she's gone totally off her rocker. Dorianne gets it in her head that a local woman is her long-lost half-sister. But soon, her obsession with that is eclipsed by medical problems that involve them all. Set in Augusta, Georgia, *Nesting* explores the age-old issues of guilt, regret, and redemption, and the part they play in driving people to create and protect family-at any cost.

E-Books, Print, Free e-books

Visit our website for more publications available online.

www.affinityebooks.com

Published by Affinity E-Book Press NZ LTD
Canterbury, New Zealand

Registered Company 2517228